W9-ACP-214

Scott's Ark

Scott's Ark

Percy Walters

HH
HARBOR
HOUSE
Augusta

SCOTT'S ARK
By Percy Walters
A Harbor House Book/2005

For information address:
        HARBOR HOUSE
        111 TENTH STREET
        AUGUSTA, GEORGIA 30901

Jacket design by Elizabeth Bell

Library of Congress Cataloging-in-Publication Data

Walters, Percy, 1928-
Scott's ark / by Percy Walters.
    p. cm.
ISBN 1-891799-07-X (alk. paper)
1. South Carolina--Fiction. I. Title.
PS3623.A3665S23 2005
813'.6--dc22

                                        2005009750

Printed in the United States of America

10 9 8 7 6 5 4 3 2 1

Dedicated to
Nancy and VIA
without whose love, support, and encouragement
Scott's Ark
could not have been written

Read not to contradict and confute;
Nor to believe and take for granted;
But to weigh and consider.

Francis Bacon
1561-1626

1

The Prophecy

SUNDAY, JULY 20, 1969, marked the most monumental advancement by mankind since October 12, 1492, when Christopher Columbus discovered America, proving the earth was round. However, at Baucom's General Merchandise and Feed Store, located on the banks of the Little Pee Dee River, at the junction of Highway 38 and State Road 917, it was a typical, sultry South Carolina day.

Members of the Baucom family had operated the store for seven generations. John Baucom was the current owner and operator. The store was a source for groceries any and all supplies necessary for the many aspects of farming.

It also served as a place for various community activities, including political stump meetings. People cast their votes at the store during local and national elections as well. During June, July, and August the store was opened on Sundays after church.

On a daily basis, shortly after noon, three local semi-retired farmers gathered at the store to pass the time. During the winter, Homer Medlin, Elbert Honeycutt and Clyde Edwards huddled around a large, wood-burning, potbellied stove in the middle of the store.

This particular warm Sunday afternoon, they relaxed outside, under a live oak tree behind the store. The massive branches of the old oak hung low over the black meandering water of the Little Pee Dee River.

While family members did most of the actual work on their farms, the three lifelong friends whiled away many hours discussing anything: the weather, the condition of their crops, local politics, and even national and international political situations.

Lately though, they seemed to spend more and more time telling each other about their physical ailments. If one of them had a complaint about his health, the other two usually had the same problem. However, each man's ailment was aggravated or made worse by another vexing condition. They took turns lamenting, "Yes, but you two don't hurt like I hurt."

Homer and Elbert had lived all of their lives on their respective farms, which they had inherited from their parents. Except for the four years he attended Clemson University and the four years he spent in the United States Navy, Clyde had also lived on the farm he inherited.

During their boyhood, after they had helped their parents get the crops laid-by, they spent countless hours playing on the hard packed sand behind the store or jumping from the overhanging branches of the live oak into the slow flowing waters of the Little Pee Dee River. This was their way to cool off, even though they had to keep on their overalls.

Their favorite swimming hole was up the river about two miles. Because no houses were close to this spot, and the woods were thick on both sides of the river, the boys could strip off all of their clothes and swim and play stark naked.

Now the three spent most of their time sitting under the live oak reminiscing about bygone days, discussing anything that came to mind. They were perfectly content just to be with each other.

Sunday, July 20, 1969, was no different. Each man had his own special seat under the oak. Elbert always sat on a seat he had removed from the back of a 1957 Studebaker Champion, usually reclining as though he were a Roman nobleman in Caesar's Court.

Homer had attached plastic-covered foam rubber cushions on the bottom and the back of his chair to ease his piles and arthritis.

As usual, Clyde was in the straight back chair he had made years before. Because he usually sat with it propped against the trunk of the tree, one of the back legs had broken. He had repaired it by splinting the broken leg with a two-by-two board and some hay baling wire from his farm.

Elbert's seat, which was closest to the river, allowed him to spit his tobacco juice into the water and not mess up the cleanly swept, hard-packed white sand. Occasionally he would accidentally miss, but today he missed intentionally as he spat at an ant struggling to pull a dead wasp across the ground. With deadly accuracy, he hit the ant with a large mouthful of tobacco juice.

"That's disgusting," Homer said. "How could you do that to that little fella? Besides, look at the mess you've made."

Homer had always been the neat one, the one who didn't like to play in the mud when they were children.

While he watched the ant try to recover, Elbert chuckled to himself. His aim was as good as ever. Before long the ant began once again to drag the heavy burden toward its den. Although Elbert admired the ant's determination to carry on under adverse circumstances, he was dismayed he had not been able to kill it.

Homer interrupted Elbert's thoughts. "I guess I'll have to spray again for that dadburn boll weevil. That downpour of rain last night probably washed off all my cotton. Just sprayed yesterday. That stuff has gone up so much in price, I'll be lucky to break even this year."

"You might not need to," Elbert said. "Maybe the rain wasn't as hard as you thought it was."

"How can I afford to take the chance?" Homer asked. "The agriculture agent said this was going to be one of the worst years for the boll weevil in 20 years. With that forecast, I can't afford not to go on and spend the money to spray again. I've got so much invested in the crop already I can't take a chance. What do you think, Clyde?"

Clyde had always been the quiet one in the group. However, when he did speak, Homer and Elbert had learned over the years to pay a lot of attention to what he had to say. After all, he was the one with a degree from Clemson University, which was held in high esteem in these parts.

Clyde was by far the best thinker of the three. If his hands had not been moving while whittling on a wooden match stem, a casual observer might have thought he was asleep. His chair, as usual, was leaning against the trunk of the tree so only the two back legs touched the ground. The bill of his John Deere baseball cap was pulled so low, it appeared impossible for him to see what he was doing.

The first thing Clyde usually did when he joined the others after lunch was to start trimming a wooden match to use as a toothpick. Homer and Elbert had teased him for years about this. They said Clyde was so picky about his toothpick either no one could manufacture one right for him, or he was too tight to buy one.

Actually, shaping his own toothpick from a wooden match was a ritual, and sometimes a stress breaker. Making the toothpick was a very calming, meditative custom. Clyde had always tried to practice a wisdom his father had taught him many years ago.

He had said, "It's one thing to let people think you're dumb and another to open your mouth and remove all doubt." Because Clyde had learned this lesson well, he rarely did much talking. When he did, his friends paid attention.

Clyde placed the carefully trimmed toothpick in his mouth, shifted it slightly to one side, and replied, "The first thing I would do is have the agriculture agent come out and examine the cotton fields. That won't cost you anything. Find out if there is evidence of more weevils first. Also, I believe the cotton foliage can be tested to see how much of the pesticide is still on the plants. There may be enough to protect your plants."

INSIDE THE STORE, John Baucom had just finished waiting on two of his regular customers, six-year-old boys who had purchased their afternoon supply of popsicles and bubble gum. After the two boys left the store, John Baucom hurried out back to where Homer, Elbert, and Clyde were sitting.

"I just saw on television that a man landed on the moon at 4:18 p.m.," John said excitedly. "It even showed him stepping from the spacecraft onto the moon."

"I doubt it's really happening," Elbert interrupted. "It's probably some make-believe stuff like that radio program years ago when Orson Wells said we was being invaded by creatures from outer space."

"Well, I saw it with my own eyes," John replied.

"From what I've read in the newspaper, I reckon it's really happening," Homer piped in.

"Even if it is real, I don't see no need spending all of my tax money to put a man on the moon. I thought there's always been a man in the moon anyway," Elbert grumbled then laughed at his own joke.

"You sound like you're footing the whole bill," Homer chided Elbert. "Maybe they'll bring you back some green cheese." He slapped his leg, laughing at his witticism.

"Well it ain't funny, not one bit. You can't imagine how much money has been wasted on that project," Elbert snapped. "And for what? Nothing. The whole program is ridiculous. What good could possibly come from putting a man on the moon?"

"A lot of good has already come out of the NASA space exploration program," Clyde said quietly, as if speaking to himself. Without raising the bill of his cap or even looking up, he continued, "All of us have benefited from the space program and in the future we'll reap benefits beyond our wildest imagination."

"Name one," Elbert challenged. "Name just one thing, if you can, worth all the money that's been wasted getting a man to the moon."

"NASA has done more than just put a man on the moon," Clyde replied. "You and I cannot imagine the research that's been done as a result of the space program.

"That new pickup you just bought has a lot of plastic on it, plastic that's stronger than the metal used in the past. Some of it, I am sure, was developed in labs doing research for the NASA program. All of the research going on is not just for NASA. It's being applied to many aspects of life on this planet, so we all benefit from NASA's getting a man on the moon."

Elbert frowned at the thought of his truck having plastic on it, but he said nothing.

Clyde removed the toothpick from his mouth, looked at it pensively, and continued, "Let me tell you what, in the end, may be the best thing to happen as a result of NASA's space exploration and especially this trip to the moon."

Realizing that Clyde was preparing to say something profound, John, Homer, and even Elbert became very quiet, almost motionless in anticipation.

"Since World War II, the Soviet Union and the United States have been threatening to blow each other to kingdom come," Clyde said in a deliberate tone. "Both boasted they have many times over the number of nuclear warheads necessary to destroy the entire planet.

"On top of that, both say they've stockpiled enough nerve gas and biological weapons to annihilate every living creature on the face of this earth. If the earth isn't blown apart then every living thing could be killed by the gas or bacteriological weapons.

"Just think about the recent Six Day War between Israel and Egypt, Jordan and Syria. Those people have not gotten along with each other since Biblical days, and I doubt they ever will.

"Look at what could have happened if the United States had sided more with Israel, for example, and Russia had really gone to the aid of the Arab nations. Just for a minute, think what could have happened with just the touch of a button. We would not be sitting here today. I continue to be concerned about the Israeli-Arab or Judo- Islam conflict."

"Well, it didn't happen and the Six Day War is over," Elbert said, as he shifted uneasily on his car seat.

"When I think about it though," Clyde continued, "We may have another crisis looming on the horizon as great as the threat of global war. It could turn out to be a more serious threat to mankind."

"What could that be?" John asked.

"Our greatest problem may be the way we live," Clyde said.

Before Clyde could continue, Elbert interrupted with a critical laugh. "I've heard you say a lot of crazy things in our time, but that's about the zaniest. What's wrong with the way we live?"

Elbert glared at Clyde. He felt Clyde was being critical of the way he and his family were living personally and he was offended.

"I'm not talking about just you, Elbert. I'm talking about me, Clyde Edwards. I'm talking about Homer Medlin. I'm talking about John Baucom. I'm talking about all of us. I'm talking about people in New York City, California, Europe, Russia, China — people all over the world."

"Now wait just a cotton-picking minute," Elbert demanded. "Clyde, you sound like one of those television evangelists. Are you gonna moralize the whole world? When are you going on TV to get the whole world to straighten up and fly right?" Elbert laughed at his own wisecrack. He shifted and looked at the other three for support in his opinion.

"I'm not talking about people's morals," Clyde replied quietly. "But maybe I should go on TV, or at least someone should, to get people to change their way of living."

"There he goes, boys," Elbert crowed. "Reverend Turner better be careful or Clyde's gonna get his job in the pulpit Sunday. Are you gonna give us some hell-fire and brimstone, Reverend Clyde?"

Elbert was laughing so hard he almost fell off the Studebaker seat. Clyde almost lost his composure, but he was accustomed to Elbert's lifelong criticism, so he said very quietly, "Again I'm not talking about morals. Yet morals may have something to do with it. I'm talking about the way we actually live. I'm talking about how the world may be getting overpopulated."

"Now he says we're doing it too much," Elbert teased.

"Doing what?" Homer asked innocently.

"Go back to sleep, Homer," Elbert said.

"I'm talking mostly about how people, all of us, are polluting and poisoning this earth we live on," Clyde said, ignoring them both. "Just look at the Little Pee Dee River. When have you seen anyone catch a bass lately?

"When we were ten years old, we could catch a four-, five-, or six-pound bass almost any day of the week. If not a large bass, we could catch a string of large bream big enough to feed our families. When have you seen more than one or two small sun perch pulled from the river? We see children fishing along the river all the time, but they hardly ever catch anything."

"Maybe they just aren't as good at fishing as we were," Elbert said proudly.

"Be serious one time, Elbert," Clyde ordered. "Remember about seven years ago when we had that fish kill in the river?"

"But that came from the stuff dumped into the river from the bleachery north of town. We didn't do it," John said.

"I know it came from the bleachery. But that was seven years ago," Clyde replied. "If that was the only cause of the river being almost dead, then why haven't the fish returned?

"Surely, after seven years, as large as the flow of the water is, the fish should have repopulated by now. To the best of my knowledge, there has not been another toxic spill at the bleachery. The water isn't nearly as clear as it was when we were boys. So what's the problem? The problem is us, gentlemen. All people."

"What do you mean, us?" Homer asked. "I haven't done anything."

"Homer, your largest tract of tobacco comes right up to the river," Clyde said. "Not long ago you were complaining about the cost of several hundred gallons of pesticide you were having to put on the field. You've put out so much poison, there is not one weed in the whole field.

"And you, Elbert, were just complaining about how much insecticide you have already put on your cotton. If the rain has washed it all off the plants, where was it washed? Right into the river. I believe your field fronts for about a mile on the river.

"Now don't get riled up. I'm just as guilty, maybe more so. I've sprayed my crops just as much as either of you. So I'm not griping about you. John, although you don't farm, how many times have you dumped some of your garbage from the store into the river instead of taking it to the town landfill.

"In years past, I've seen you dump old oil into the river. Remember year before last when your kerosene tanks ruptured and 500 gallons of kerosene seeped into the river? We could see it floating on the surface.

"I'm not criticizing you any more than I'm criticizing myself. I'm sure these things have always hurt the environment, but now we are getting much more aware of the damage because there are many, many more people.

"Being small farmers, we have no concept of the pollution spewed into the atmosphere from huge manufacturing plants. If the population explosion continues, in the future pollution will be a bigger problem than it is today. Another problem is garbage. We don't hear much about it now, but we will in the future. With continuing population growth, garbage will become a tremendous problem."

"That's ridiculous," Elbert commented. "How can garbage possibly be a problem? We burn ours out here on the farm. The town has a landfill."

"That's exactly what I'm talking about," Clyde replied. "Last week when I was coming back from town, I decided, for some reason or other, to drive around by Stack Road. When I came by the town dump, it looked like it was running over with trash."

"I saw in the paper about a week ago that the landfill is so full the city fathers are looking for some more land to buy," John said. "The article said a decision had to be made very soon about where to purchase a site for another landfill, because the federal government was beginning to put pressure on the town officials."

"Maybe that's why one of the town aldermen approached me last week about selling that section of land on the east side of my cotton fields," Homer said. "You know where I'm talking about. It's mostly one big gully. Maybe it would be ideal for a town dump, but I ain't selling it to the town for no landfill. I don't want all that trash near my place. Besides it would ruin the value of my other property. No sir, I ain't selling for no town dump."

"This is exactly what I've been talking about," said Clyde. "If a little town like ours has such a problem with garbage, think what it must be like in a place like New York City or Los Angeles or Chicago."

"Okay, so we have a problem with pollution and garbage," Elbert said. "And we have the possibility of being blown off the face of this earth by an atomic war, and the struggle between Jews and Arabs is still going on. To me, that's all the more reason to stop wasting so much money on this silly space mess. The government should be spending our money trying to solve these problems." He nodded at Homer and John, hoping for approval.

Clyde completed the final shaping of another toothpick, folded his knife, and put it back in his pocket. He paused before placing the toothpick in his mouth.

"I agree with you 100 percent. Not only should we try to solve the problems of total world annihilation or self-destruction, we must. I mean must. We must solve these problems if mankind is to survive on this planet.

"But let me explain where space exploration may play a role, a very important role." Clyde paused and took a deep breath before continuing thoughtfully, "Now you'll think I'm crazy when you hear what I'm going to say, but some thought the Old Testament prophets were crazy too, yet look what happened."

"Where's your crystal ball, fortune teller?" Elbert sniggered as he spat another mouthful of tobacco juice into the river. When he realized Homer and John were not laughing with him, he shifted on the car seat and sat upright. "I'm sorry."

Clyde nodded his acceptance of the apology and placed the toothpick in the side of his mouth. "On a cold, clear November night, when I go outside and look up into the starlit heavens God has made for us, I can't help believing somewhere up there among all of those thousands of stars is a planet on which people could live."

Clyde spoke as if he were not aware of the other men sitting around him. He did not even look at the others. He gazed dreamily into space and time as if he could see something the others could not. "If we don't blow up this planet with nuclear weapons first, we will surely drown in our own toxic pollution and garbage. This trip to the moon may be the Good Lord's way of letting man learn how to make a spacecraft in which he can get to another planet. That way a few people will be able to leave this planet before it is blown up or self-destructs. Then mankind can start all over again."

Clyde Edwards had no idea what a profound, prophetic statement he was making when he said, "This trip to the moon may be God's way of leading man to make a modern day Noah's Ark."

2

YEARS LATER

"SCOTT! HEY, SCOTT WALKER!" shouted the man in the brightly colored Hawaiian shirt. He pushed through the crowd in Atlanta's Hartsfield International Airport, trying to get the attention of the clean-cut man in the United States Marine Corps uniform.

The Marine major had just entered the concourse along with a mass of people deplaning Flight 735 from Houston, Texas. Hearing his name, he turned, but seeing no one he recognized, he continued his brisk pace toward the baggage terminal.

Again the man in the brightly flowered shirt called out, "Scott Walker. Wait up, old buddy!"

Major Scott Walker turned again and realized the man in the loud, bright shirt and large sunglasses was calling him. He had no idea who the stranger was, even though the man called to him as if they were best friends. The voice did sound vaguely familiar.

As the man neared, he removed his sunglasses and Scott broke into a grin. "John? Is that really you? My God, you're not the John Johnston I knew at N. C. State University." The men clasped each other's shoulders and shook hands warmly.

"What's happened to you? Where's your necktie?" Scott inquired. "When we were at State, I never saw you without a tie. You wore one all the time, even at Lambda Chi functions. We used to joke you probably wore one in the shower or while sitting on the john. We even bet you slept in one. It's no wonder I didn't recognize you at first. You look like you've put on some weight since college too."

As Scott rattled on, John tried to ease him over to one side of the concourse. Not only were they blocking the corridor, they were attracting a lot of attention. John did not want to be noticed or overheard.

Scott rubbed the short sleeve of John's flowered shirt between his thumb and forefinger. "No wonder you have on sunglasses. I'd want to hide too if I was wearing this flower arrangement," he teased. "I believe this is the first time I've seen you since graduation. How many years ago was that? No, don't answer. It will make both of us feel old. I didn't see you at the 10-year frat reunion. Someone, I recall, said you were with some branch of the government. Is it the FBI?"

"Let's step into the sandwich shop for a drink," John said in a low voice. Placing his arm around Scott's shoulder, he practically pushed him into the small shop.

After ordering a soft drink for each of them, John said, "I thought you NASA fly boys always flew your own jets. Since when do you fly commercial? Seriously, what are you doing in Atlanta?"

"I just flew in from a conference in Houston. Sarah and the kids are flying up from Orlando to meet me. We're going to drive up to her parent's place in Highlands for a few days. Now, no offense, but what are you doing dressed like that?"

Again John ignored Scott's question. "I don't think I've seen any of the frat brothers since the blast at

Lambda Chi the night before graduation. God, what a party that was! Have you kept up with anyone? Who all was at the reunion?"

Without giving Scott time to answer, John continued, "Keeping up with you has been no problem. Seems like you're in the newspaper or on TV news every few months. How many times have you been into space already? And the extended flight to the space station set for this summer, will it be your fourth or fifth trip?"

"How do you know when that flight is scheduled?" Scott demanded, looking sternly at John. The date for the upcoming flight had not been announced.

"I must have seen it in one of the newspapers," John said nonchalantly, realizing he had made a slip. In an attempt to evade further questions, he changed the subject, "Bring me up to date with Sarah and your children."

"They're all fine."

"What are their ages?" John asked rapidly.

"Ann is 13, Douglass is 11 and Robert is nine. What about you? Any family?"

"Surely you remember Frances," John said. "We dated some when she was at Meredith College."

"What do you mean, some?" Scott said with a grin. "You spent practically your entire senior year at Meredith."

John looked at the empty glass he was holding. "Frances and I were married shortly after graduation."

"I didn't get an invitation."

"It was a very small wedding," John said. "Only relatives and a few of Frances's closest friends were invited. She wanted it that way."

There was a long pause in the conversation. John continued to stare, unfocused, at the empty glass. Thinking John was reluctant to continue talking about his situation, Scott asked, "What are you doing now?"

"Two years after we were married, we had a daughter," John went on as if he hadn't heard Scott's question. "She was beautiful, absolutely beautiful, from the very moment she came into this world. I was in the delivery room when she was born."

As he spoke, John continued to stare blankly at the empty glass, as if he were looking back at the moment his daughter arrived. "We named her Mary Beth. We call her Beth."

"You said, 'She was beautiful.' What happened?"

Startled back to reality, John said, "Oh, she's still beautiful. Beth is nine years old now. Only I don't get to see her very often. Frances really did not want a child. For her the baby was an accident. I longed for a child from the moment we were married.

"I don't see Beth very often because Frances left me over a year ago — 16 months and six days ago. Although Frances didn't want a child, she took custody of Beth just to spite me." John glanced at his watch as if to confirm the time.

"I'm truly sorry," Scott said.

"It's okay," John said, forcing a smile. "What time is Sarah's flight due?"

Scott looked at his watch. "In about 45 minutes. Where are Frances and Beth now?"

"Well, let's see," John said bitterly, "It's almost summer so Frances is at her parents' estate in Palm Beach. She also spends a lot of time at their place in Bar Harbor. In between, she is in Europe frequently and spends some time at the house we shared in Georgetown."

"And Beth, where is she?"

"Boarding school. Frances stashed her away at a girl's school in Connecticut. I get her for one week during the summer. That is, if I'm not on an assignment.

"Of course, if Frances has some social engagement during the holidays when Beth is out of school, I get to keep Beth. Frances won't let anything interfere with her social life," John added sarcastically.

Brushing away all thoughts of the past, John assumed a pleasant expression and attempted to control the direction of their conversation. "Tell me what it feels like to be in space, weightless and all that. Does the earth really look as beautiful from up there as the pictures we see in the National Geographic? Are things as quiet and peaceful as what I've seen about the flights on TV? God, to be that quiet, peaceful and stress free for just one day would be Utopia." John sighed, meditating on the thought.

Though John had attempted to change the subject, Scott was determined to pursue the matter of the flight time. After all, he and John had been close friends for four years at State. The fraternity gave them an even closer tie.

"Cut the bullshit, John," Scott said in a commanding voice. "What the hell is going on with you?"

Startled, John's eyes briefly met Scott's inquiring gaze. "Nothing," he muttered in a soft, almost timid voice then looked off into the distance.

I wish I could tell you. I wish I had someone to listen to me. I wish I had someone to unload on, someone to help me solve this predicament. I'm almost in over my head, John thought.

For a moment, he opened his mouth to share his dilemmas with Scott. Then he closed it, turning to look at the people rushing back and forth along the concourse. It appeared he was looking for someone.

When his expression changed, Scott thought John had indeed seen someone he was expecting, but then he looked down at his watch. "Well, it's almost time for my flight, old buddy. Look, it's been swell running into you again after all of these years." As if peering into the future, he added, "It won't be this long before we meet again."

Rising from his chair, John added, "No, don't get up. I can find my way. I've learned a little bit since my freshman year at State when I couldn't find my way to class. See you soon."

He grasped Scott's hand in both of his and after a brief shake, picked up his carry-on luggage, rushed from the sandwich shop and melted into the crowd.

Scott sat several more moments, finishing his soda. John hadn't changed a bit. He was as secretive and mysterious as ever. No one, even in the fraternity, knew much about John. He had been an okay guy, but there was something very elusive about him. He never talked much about himself.

If he was working for the government or the FBI, he had gone into the right profession. Come to think of it, he never did say where he was working.

You could not prove it by his looks, but he was the same old John that Scott had known at State. He shrugged. If John didn't want to share anything about what he was doing, why should Scott waste his time wondering about him?

Looking at his watch, Scott could hardly believe he had been in the sandwich shop almost an hour. Sarah's plane was due in 15 minutes. He deposited his empty cup in the trash and went in search of a monitor for arriving flights.

He learned Sarah's plane would land on time at Gate 7, Concourse A. Scott had arrived at Gate 23 on Concourse C. He had a long walk ahead of him and decided not to pick up his luggage until after Sarah and the children arrived.

As he passed the boarding area for Gate 6, Concourse C, Scott caught a glimpse of a shirt just like the one John had been wearing. The man stepped through the door and down the ramp before Scott could see whether or not it was John. But it had to be John. There could not be another shirt that colorful in the whole Hartsfield Airport.

Scott paused to read the destination of the plane. The marquee over the check-in desk indicated the flight was going to Columbia, South Carolina with a final destination of Memphis, Tennessee.

Why would John be going to either of those cities? Shaking his head indifferently, Scott continued toward Concourse A.

When he arrived at Gate 7, he could see the plane had arrived. Before he could sit down he heard Robert, his younger son, yelling, "Daddy! Daddy!"

The nine year old ran into his father's open arms. Scott picked him up and gave him a manly hug. Ann and Douglass rushed across the waiting area to give their father a big hug too.

The children were still clinging to their father when Sarah emerged, lugging their carry-on luggage. Scott put Robert down and, with the three children still clinging to him, hugged Sara in a long, warm embrace.

"God, it's great to see you. I've missed you so much," he whispered.

"How about us?' Robert demanded.

"I missed all of you," Scott reassured the children, "Now let's get our luggage and head for the hills of Highlands."

"But I need to go to the bathroom," Robert said.

"I told you to go before the plane landed," his mother said.

"But the plane was rocking too much," Robert

whined. "Besides, I was afraid I might fall through the john seat."

"Scott," Sarah said, "you take him to the restroom while Ann, Douglass, and I get our luggage."

"Douglass, here is my baggage check," his father said. "I have only one small bag. It's blue canvas. Sarah, I hope you brought some clothes for me. I had only uniforms with me in Houston."

Sarah smiled. "I brought plenty of casual clothes for you."

"Thanks, mom," Scott said, patting her gently on her fanny, before turning to Robert. "Come on, Robert let's check the plumbing. We'll meet the rest of you at the car rental desk. We better hurry if we hope to make it to Highlands in time for your grandmother's supper."

3

AFTER HE LEFT SCOTT, John Johnston hurried through the terminal to where his plane was loading for the flight to Columbia, S. C. He was flying tourist class, as always.

When he left his office three days before, he was the John that Scott had known at N. C. State University. He had been dressed meticulously in a tailored navy blue suit, white shirt with a stiffly starched collar, subdued paisley print necktie, and freshly shined black wing-tipped shoes.

Add in his black leather brief case, and John had looked the epitome of a classy, yet ordinary, young politician or executive embarking on a business trip.

His office, however, was anything but ordinary. The office, or headquarters as John thought of it, was located in a stately, antebellum mansion a few miles from Leesburg, Virginia, one of many satellite towns surrounding Washington, D.C.

The manor was surrounded by rolling, lush green pastures with whitewashed wooden fences. A stone guest cottage sat to one side, surrounded by a small apple orchard and a grove of pecan trees.

Larger-than-life bronze statues of rearing Arabian stallions stood guard on each side of the formidable gate. The metal gate was supported by tall square pillars of Tennessee flat orchard stone. It was always locked and would open only when the palm of an authorized person was placed on the monitor beside the driveway.

On the front of each pillar was a heavily embossed bronze plaque, with the name, EQUUS ESTATE, stamped in large, polished letters.

It appeared to be the country estate of an extremely wealthy person devoted to breeding and rearing thoroughbred horses. Several Arabian mares grazed together in one of the pastures, while their recently born foals frolicked on wobbly legs at their sides.

The first time John came to the office four years ago, he thought it strange that the driveway to such an elaborate house would run so very close to the barn and horse stables. Later he learned the barn had been located strategically so anyone approaching the house could be scrutinized by the latest state-of-the-art electronic surveillance equipment.

This equipment was manned and kept active 24/7 to record all comings and goings. A permanent log was kept on file. Outwardly, the huge white barn, and two smaller stables where the stallions were housed, looked like the typical horse farm.

The doors to the large barn were always closed, to camouflage the contents of the building. The windows of the two smaller barns were usually open, so the stallions could observe the mares in the pasture. This added to the legitimacy of the estate being a horse farm.

Six tall, white Doric columns framed the entrance to the mansion. There were only two stone steps from the driveway to the porch, which extended the full width of the house.

Earth-toned Tennessee flagstone covered the deep porch which was furnished with wicker furniture. John thought the only thing missing was a pitcher of mint juleps or lemonade and glasses.

Massive, carved walnut doors dominated the entrance. The doors opened into a lavish circular foyer, in the center of which was a marble-topped, ornately carved, walnut table. A grandiose arrangement of freshly cut flowers was always on the table.

Directly over the flowers hung an elaborate lead crystal chandelier, which contained hidden cameras and motion detectors. A wide, curved wooden staircase rose gracefully from the rear of the foyer to the second floor where sleeping quarters were located.

A large living room, library and several cozy parlors were located on the left side of the entrance. The other side of the foyer led to a large banquet hall, capable of accommodating 28 people for dinner.

Beyond the dining room were the servant quarters and kitchen. Beyond the kitchen was a well-stocked pantry. At the back of the pantry, behind a movable wine rack, was a solid metal door.

Located immediately to the right of the door was an electronic imaging device, which controlled the opening and closing of the door. The door would open only when the palm of an authorized person was placed on the glass plate of the device.

The doorway led to an elevator and stairwell that went deep underground to another locked steel door, also controlled by a palm identifying electronic device. Through this door lay the operations center for LAD, the Listening Arm Division of the Central Intelligence Agency.

The office consisted of a small conference room and an adjoining room filled with the most sophisticated communications equipment available. There were six additional small offices for John and the five other agents, and one for Neil Anderson, the CEO of LAD.

Finally, there were restrooms and even a small kitchen, which, to the best of John's knowledge, had never been used.

Except for the sophisticated communication equipment in the conference room, and Anderson's very plush office, all of the rooms were sparsely furnished. John's small office contained a desk and two straight chairs. A computer and a bi-fold picture frame occupied the desk. The brass frame held a picture of Frances, his estranged wife, and one of Beth, his daughter and the love of his life.

The entire estate had been built at the height of the cold war in the 1960s when underground bomb shelters were the rage. The facility had been constructed hastily to serve as an underground bomb shelter for the first family. However, it was soon evident the facility was too close to Washington to be safe for the President, and the estate was abandoned.

Only in the last six years had the facility been renovated to serve LAD. Near the restrooms and kitchen was a storage room from which a concealed door led to an underground tunnel. The tunnel led to the basement beneath the guesthouse. In the passageway was a complete backup system for electrical power and utilities to allow the office to function under any circumstance.

It was physically impossible to gain entrance to the underground office from the basement of the guesthouse because of the way the tunnel doors had been constructed. The tunnel only offered an escape path from the office.

It was in these self-sufficient offices, deep underground, that John received his assignments and made his reports. His mission was to collect covert information from third world countries, especially Arabic and Islamic nations. In this business, John was skeptical of almost everyone. It was his nature, and one of the things that had helped him survive.

Other than his boss, Neil Anderson, John knew nothing about his fellow agents. He had no idea what their role or duty in LAD was. In their clandestine business, it was usually best not to know.

John was skilled at his job. It was uncanny how much intelligence he could gather from foreign agents. Neil Anderson had great respect for his ability; however, he often wondered if John exchanged too much information to get what he wanted. John was aware of the mistrust.

When John left his office on this assignment, he drove a nondescript rental car to Dulles International Airport where he boarded a flight to Minneapolis. There he stayed one day, pretending to make business calls on several corporations. Next he flew to Dallas where he again pretended to call on three corporations, looking and acting the part of a typical career salesman.

He knew he was taking a chance when he left his Dallas hotel and went to a nearby restaurant to call his wife, Frances, from a pay telephone. He never contacted her when he was on a mission, but he was desperate to win her back. He thought it would be safe to call her at her parents' home in Palm Beach, where she had gone after telling him she was leaving him for good.

After the fourth ring, Frances answered with a cheerful, "Hello."

A lump formed in John's throat. It had been a long time since he had heard her voice.

"Hello?" Frances said again before John could gain his composure and clear his throat.

"Hi. It's me," he said softly into the telephone.

"Well, what do you want?" Frances said curtly, immediately recognizing his voice.

"I... I need to talk with you."

After a long pause, Frances snapped, "Well, talk. I don't have all night."

"I mean we need to get together and talk. I love you, Frances. I need you so much. When can we get together?"

After a long pause and much to John's surprise, Frances replied, "Right now. Come on over."

"I, uh, I," John stuttered.

Before he could finish the sentence, Frances repeated, "Right now. Come over right now."

"I can't right now," he said apologetically, "You know I'm not in Palm Beach."

With all the sarcasm she could muster she asked, "What's the matter? Is the little spy on another mission at Club 51 with his bleached blonde hussy?"

"Please don't be that way, Frances. I told you she was a foreign agent. I love you."

"You expect me to believe that? Don't make me laugh. If you had loved me, you would have taken the position Daddy offered you with his corporation. But no, you had to stay with your little secretive government job.

"I got sick and tired of your being away for days at a time, not knowing where you were, not hearing anything from you, and especially not knowing whom you were entertaining in some New York bar."

"But I explained things to you before we were married. When we were engaged, you thought my work at the FBI was exciting and when I transferred to the CIA, you were thrilled. At least you told me you were."

Hoping not to get into a fight over the telephone, John then asked, "How is Beth?"

"She's at school."

"At school? Where?"

"A boarding school in Connecticut." She did not tell him which school intentionally. She wanted to taunt him.

"Boarding school? You promised when we separated you would keep her with you in Georgetown and let her go to a day school there. You promised you would not send her alone to a boarding school."

"Well, I changed my mind. She's coming to Palm Beach when school is out to stay with me this summer."

"What's the matter? Did she become a drag on your social life?" John quipped with bitterness. "Did she interfere with your parties?"

Just as quickly, he became apologetic, "I'm sorry. I didn't mean that. Please. I love you. We can work this out. I'll be back on the twenty-third. Can I meet you then?"

"Look, it's over. But I'll tell you what you can do when you get back on the twenty-third. You can drop by my attorney's office. I've filed for divorce. You can talk to him and sign the papers while you're there. Don't call me again, ever!" She slammed down the receiver.

John continued to hold the phone to his ear, refusing to accept what he had just heard. He stood there, stupefied by the emotions racing through him. He loved and needed Frances; yet he hated her for leaving him.

He loved her, but he hated her for sending their daughter to a boarding school. He loved Beth. He hated Frances' love of parties and the social life. Although he loved and desperately needed Frances, the mother of his daughter, most of all he loved Beth.

His mind began to spin and whirl until he had to brace himself against the telephone booth. When John realized the finality of what she had said to him, his eyes began to water. Shaking it off, he gained control of himself, and hung up the receiver.

Although they had been separated for a few months, only now did he fully realize the futility of trying to salvage their marriage. Still, he was compelled to keep trying. He loved Frances very much, and they had a daughter together.

As he left the restaurant, he consoled himself with the fact he had a beautiful daughter who still loved him and whom he loved her very much. He vowed to himself he would take care of Beth always, no matter what his relationship with Frances.

He had wanted for his daughter to grow up with both parents, but if that became impossible, he would always be there for his daughter.

When he left Dallas the next morning for Atlanta, John no longer looked like the typical business executive. Instead he was the personification of a middle class tourist, dressed in a brightly colored, tropical print shirt, casual slacks, deck shoes and a soft leather carry-on. He had shipped his business suits and shoes by UPS back to his apartment in DC.

Following his chance meeting with Scott Walker, John was on his way to Columbia, S.C., where he would meet an assistant. Most of the time he worked alone, but on this mission he had requested a female agent to travel with him to the Bahamas.

4

JOHN'S PLANE was almost on time when it landed in Columbia. After he collected his luggage, he hurried to the coffee shop to meet his assistant. As he entered the shop, a beautiful blonde sitting alone at a table in the far corner rose and rushed toward him, enveloping him in a hug.

"I thought your plane would never get here," she said, kissing him lightly on the cheek. "I'm so excited to be going to the Bahamas; I can hardly stand it."

As she spoke, she led him back to the corner table.

"It's good to see you again, Sharon," said John. "Thanks for agreeing to assist me on this mission."

It had been a long time since the two had worked together. They had first met while training for the FBI. At that time neither of them was married, although both were romantically involved with someone else.

They had become friends, and their relationship remained one of profound, sincere caring based on mutual respect for each other's abilities and dedication to their profession.

After completing their indoctrination and training period with the FBI, Sharon Mitchell had returned to home state, California, and had married Brad Robinson, her college beau at Stanford University. Shortly after his assignment to Washington, John transferred to the CIA. He married Frances Van Pelt, whom he had dated for four years.

"I almost didn't recognize you," John said with a smile. "It must be the blonde hair."

"Your communiqué indicated we should look like a middle-class couple on vacation, or an executive and his mistress going away for a weekend tryst. Either way, I thought a blonde would have more fun. So which am I, wife or mistress?"

She pursed her lips a la Marilyn Monroe, and rubbed a long, shapely leg enticingly against his thigh. A man sitting across the room watched Sharon's actions and thought how he would love to be in John's shoes.

John grinned. "Either way, I'm a lucky man."

The tour to the Bahamas was a promotional three-day, two-night jaunt that was very popular because of its modest price. No one would be suspicious of their being anything other than a couple on vacation. They would blend in well on the inexpensive, crowded, off-season tour. Sharon was perfect cover for this mission.

"Maybe being a housewife would be better," John said, turning serious.

"Well then," Sharon replied demurely, "I'll be your prim and proper housewife, maybe even nag you a little."

She pulled her legs properly under her chair and folded her hands in her lap. "How's this?"

"You don't have to carry it to the point of nagging. Just the way you look will make any guy jealous of me."

"That's the nicest thing I've heard since I left Frisco," Sharon said, patting his hand. "Thanks."

"How's Brad?" John asked.

"He's fine. He's been really involved with his real

estate business," Sharon said. "It's booming. However, we took off for two weeks last month to go backpacking in the Cascades. Can you imagine me camping out in a tent?"

"Well, if I judged by the way you're dressed now, even with the wildest imagination, I couldn't picture you sitting by a campfire. No reflection on the way you look; you look great, especially for a mistress. I mean housewife."

"Thanks loads!" she said with a laugh. "But we had a wonderful time. I think I enjoyed it more than Brad did. The fishing was great. We even cooked and ate the fish on the site. By the way, how's Frances? I hope things are better between you now."

John looked away. "The situation has gotten worse."

Sensing he did not want to talk about it, Sharon changed the subject. "Here comes a waitress. Do we have time for lunch before our flight leaves? I haven't eaten. Have you?"

"We have plenty of time," He said, relieved she had not pressed the matter of Frances. "I'm hungry too."

After they ordered and the waitress was safely out of earshot, Sharon asked, "How are we flying to the Bahamas?"

"Bahama Air, a nonscheduled charter flight. It's a popular trip and I thought it would be an excellent cover for us."

Sharon wanted to know what it was a cover for, but she knew better than to ask. She was a professional always, even with such a close friend as John. She knew her job, and she did it, no questions asked.

John didn't tell her much for her own safety. The less she knew about what he was doing, the safer she would be.

After finishing lunch, they walked to the departure

gate. The waiting area was filled with excited tourists. A tour guide announced that all parties going to the Bahamas should come to the desk to check their tickets, and get their room assignments and key. This, they were told, would make things much simpler when they arrived at the Princess Hotel in the Bahamas.

The tourists immediately formed a line in front of the desk. John, never one to stand in line, steered Sharon to a row of seats against the rear wall of the waiting area.

"Mr. and Mrs. Hank Edmonds," the tour director called.

John leaned over to Sharon and whispered, "Oh, by the way, that's us."

Sharon was surprised to learn they were traveling under an alias and became keenly aware of the seriousness of this mission.

Immediately after boarding the plane, the flight attendants began to set the mood for three carefree days of partying in the Bahamas by serving the most popular drink on the islands: the famous Bahama Mama. Two attendants were also challenging people to participate in a five- and ten-dollar lottery.

"Hank, give me some money," said Sharon. "I feel lucky."

She had immediately slipped into character, assuring John all the more that he had made a wise choice in bringing her on this assignment. He handed her a five and a ten. She kissed each one of them goodbye and gave the money to the attendants.

"As we prepare to take off," said the senior flight attendant. "I have a roll of toilet tissue which I will place on the floor. When the plane starts down the runway to take off, we want to see how close to the rear of the plane the paper will unroll before it stops. If it makes it all the way to the rear of the plane, it will be a record and a good omen for an excellent trip."

As the plane lunged down the runway, the tissue began to unroll slowly down the aisle. When the plane began to lift off the ground, it unwound faster. It came to a stop against John's seat, but he quickly nudged it back to the center of the aisle. When the plane began to climb steeply, the roll sped all the way to the rear of the plane. A loud cheer went up, and Bahama Mamas were raised to toast a fun-filled trip.

JUST BEFORE THEY DEPLANED, John handed Sharon her forged driver's license. She looked at her photo and saw her name was Abigail Edmonds.

She nudged John with her elbow and said, "Gee, thanks for the name, but the photo shows a brunette."

Although John had been through customs all over the world hundreds of times, he was always a little uneasy under the stern scrutiny of customs agents, especially when he was using faked documents.

As the inspector examined their forged driver's license, Sharon, to distract the inspector, nudged John and said, "I can't wait to get to the slot machines. Since I won the ten-dollar lottery on the plane, I feel so lucky I know I'll hit the jackpot."

When the examiner looked from her license to her, Sharon patted her hair and smiled. "You like the new me?" The examiner motioned them through without comment.

Fortunately, the drive to the Princess Hotel was short, because they and their luggage were packed like sardines into an old dilapidated taxi. Grateful to already have their room assignment and key, they went directly to the room to relax and be themselves for a couple of hours.

Though they had worked together on several occasions, they had never been together in such an intimate situation. Both felt a little awkward once they were in the hotel room alone. John fumbled with his luggage, trying to appear busy, while Sharon tried to look casual unpacking hers.

It's no wonder Frances left me, John thought. *If she could see me now, I'd never get her back. Maybe I should have quit before I graduated from the FBI academy. Maybe I should never have transferred to LAD. Maybe I should have taken that job with her father. Hell, I've always been faithful to her. Not one time have I ever cheated on her, and I'm not going to now.*

He turned to face Sharon just as she turned toward him. For an instant they stood looking at each other from across the room.

"As they say in 'The Family,'" Sharon said, "'It's nothing personal. It's strictly business.'"

Both chuckled and the tension broke. "Frances has nothing to worry about."

John looked surprised. "How did you know I was thinking about Frances?"

"It's been all over your face since we walked in the room," she said then shrugged. "Besides, I was wondering what Brad would have to say if he could see us now."

"If I'm that easily read, I won't stand a chance at the poker table," John said, smiling sheepishly.

"Outside that door, I am the doting wife of Hank Edmonds," Sharon said. "But once we're in this room, I am Sharon, faithful wife of Brad Robinson; and you are John Johnston, faithful husband of Frances Johnston. This is not some movie or TV program, where a man and woman, no matter what their relationship, has to jump into bed naked just because they can."

"God, you're wonderful," John said, with honest respect. "I wish Frances could meet you. Maybe she would understand and would not be so jealous of my work and my being away from home so often. I really love her very much and don't know what I'll do if I don't get her back."

"If only she knew how lucky she is," Sharon said sympathetically.

"Thanks." Looking at the two queen-size beds, he asked, "Which one do you prefer?"

"You can take the one closest to the door. We'll have to make up one of the beds every morning so it will appear that we slept together."

John smiled. "That's why I brought you along. You think of everything."

"And I thought it was my blonde hair."

Relieved to have established the ground rules, they continued unpacking in comfortable silence. Once finished, John said, "Why don't you relax while I go down to the lobby and look around. When I get back, if you'd like, we'll dress for dinner and maybe go over to the casino."

"Sounds fine to me," Sharon said. "Take your time. I'm tired, and I'd like to bathe before dinner."

5

THE MAIN BUILDING of the hotel housed the registration lobby, restaurants, offices, and gift shops. Covered walkways connected the main building to three two-story buildings where the individual guest rooms were located.

The guest wings formed a large semi-circle around a beautifully landscaped area containing an outdoor restaurant, a performer's stage, and a huge, irregular shaped swimming pool.

Looking like a typical tourist, John strolled casually around the entire area. Although he appeared to be admiring the scenery, he was searching among the hotel guests for his contact. They had met on several occasions in Europe and knew each other by sight.

He ambled among the bathers lounging beside the pool in the middle of which was a large concrete boulder that looked like a cave, open on all sides. It formed an arch in the center of the pool where bathers could wade from the shallow end of the pool to the deeper end.

Several bathers stood in the water that cascaded from the arch. John's contact was not among them.

He entered the main hotel and walked to the activity

director's desk, picking up several brochures about hotel-sponsored activities. Then he sauntered into the gift shop.

Not spotting his contact, he went back to the portico and then to the outdoor restaurant where he selected a table in the far corner. From there he could see anyone coming from the main hotel and most of the guest rooms. He also had a good view of most of the bathers coming and going from the pool.

After ordering a Bahama Mama, he pretended to read the brochures as he continued to keep an eye out for his contact. He also contemplated the best place for them to meet safely. The tennis courts or golf course would not be suitable, but the pool area might be okay because it was so crowded.

Just then he found a two-hour glass bottom boat tour of the coral reef in one of the brochures. That might be a perfect place for their meeting. John raised his glass to sip the last of his Bahama Mama when he noticed the familiar figure coming through the door from the main building.

Raj was an ordinary looking person, average height and weight, and no distinguishing features with the possible exception of his hair. It was shiny black and combed from his forehead across the top to the back of his head. A generous amount of oily hair tonic held it in place. He also had a bushy moustache, which he did not bother to plaster down with oil.

Evidently he had just arrived because he was carrying a small suitcase as he walked by the restaurant where John was seated. Other than an almost imperceptible pause in his stride, Raj gave no indication he had recognized John. John continued to observe Raj until he was out of sight.

John started to leave the restaurant, but a calypso

band had come to the bandstand on the other side of the restaurant and began to play. Soon he was engrossed with the rhythmic beat of the steel drums. After several numbers, John was surprised to see Raj return to the restaurant.

Raj selected a table near the entrance to the restaurant, a good distance from where John was seated. It was a table John would have to pass by closely in order to leave the restaurant. Raj ordered a drink from the waitress and began to look at the brochures he had been given at the registration desk.

Having decided on the glass bottom boat tour for their meet, John circled the 10 a.m. time slot on the brochure and finished his drink. As he walked by Raj's table, John accidentally bumped one of the empty chairs and dropped the brochures beside Raj's chair.

"Excuse me," John politely apologized and picked up the brochures slowly, making sure the one about the boat tour was last and turned it in such a way Raj could see it clearly. Then he left the restaurant.

When John returned to the room, Sharon was seated at the dressing table applying makeup. She looked at his reflection in the mirror. "You met your contact."

"How did you know?" John asked, puzzled.

Sharon shrugged. "It's written all over your face."

John frowned. Either he was slipping or she was a hell of a lot better at this than he knew. He was going to have to be more careful, and get Frances off his mind so he could concentrate more on what he was doing.

As insignificant as her statement seemed, it shook John that his emotions showed outwardly. He attributed much of his success to having a good poker face. Jokingly, he often thought of himself as planet earth's answer to Spock, the Vulcan star of *Star Trek*, absolutely emotionless.

Sharon stood and said, "Let's go have a drink before dinner. You sure you want me to be your wife instead of your mistress? You could be my Sugar Daddy." She nudged him with her elbow trying to cheer him up.

"Be my obedient wife," he said with a sly smile. "On the way to get that drink, we need stop by the reservations desk and sign up for the glass bottom boat tour for 10:00 in the morning."

When they approached the reservations desk, the clerk cheerily asked, "Would you like the glass bottom boat tour or snorkeling on the reef?"

"No way are you getting me in the water with the sharks, Daddy," Sharon said. "We'll take the glass bottom boat. I'll probably get seasick. And remember, you said if I went with you on the boat, you'd give me equal time for shopping. I mean some real shopping and not just window shopping."

"We have space available on the 10 a.m. and 2 p.m. tours tomorrow."

"We'd like two tickets for the 10 a.m. tour," John said. "I'll pay cash." He handed the money to the clerk.

"A blue bus leaves from the front of the hotel every 30 minutes for the harbor," the clerk informed them. "If you catch the 9:30 shuttle, it's only a 10-minute ride to the harbor and you'll have plenty of time to walk the short distance from the bus stop to the pier. You'll see plenty of signs directing you to where the boat is docked."

"Let's make sure we have plenty of film before we go out in the morning," Sharon said.

"There's a shop beside the bus stop that sells film, if you need more," chirped the eager clerk.

"Thanks," John said, placing the tickets and change in his billfold.

Sharon took his arm as they left the lobby. "It's so

early, let's walk around the grounds before we go. Maybe we could stroll through the Bazaar. I hear they have some wonderful bargains. Then we could go to the Casino tomorrow night."

"Sounds good to me," John said.

THE NEXT MORNING, after a light breakfast in the hotel coffee shop, John and Sharon caught the blue bus to the harbor. Two other couples joined them, but there was no sign of Raj.

At the last moment, John said he had forgotten his camera and pled with the driver to wait so he could rush back to his room to get it. He was trying to buy some extra time for Raj to make the bus. However, when he returned Raj had still not arrived. They left without him.

At the harbor, John purchased more film at the shop near the bus stop, loaded the camera and started taking pictures. He was actually scanning the area to see if he could spot Raj.

"There's the sign pointing to the dock," Sharon said finally. "We better go. We don't want to miss the boat."

John took her arm, and they walked briskly toward the man-made harbor. All of the slips were occupied with boats ranging in size from a small skiff to a large ocean-going, luxury yacht.

The glass bottom boat sat in the first slip. It was about 28 feet long and could accommodate approximately 16 passengers around the glass bottom, through which tourists could view the wonders of the reef.

A young attendant, who would be their boat captain, navigator, tour guide and bartender, assisted John and Sharon down the ladder onto the boat. Already on board were two elderly Catholic nuns dressed in traditional black habits, a young couple they had seen on the flight from Columbia, and Raj.

He was seated beside the two nuns near the front of the boat, reading a pocket book edition of *Fodor's Guide to the USA*. He did not look up as John and Sharon sat down on the opposite side of the viewing area near the back of the boat.

The young couple was so engrossed with each other Sharon thought they had to be on their honeymoon. The elderly sisters, who were from a convent in Philadelphia, introduced themselves to the young couple. They were from South Carolina, and this was their first trip outside the United States.

When the nuns spoke to Raj, he closed his book, placed it in his pocket, and joined the ladies in conversation.

All of the tourists were chatting excitedly about the anticipated tour when the attendant announced, "May I have your attention, please. We will be leaving shortly. Reservations indicate there should be two more passengers. We will wait a few minutes more for them. In the meantime, I have Bahama Mamas for sale. Would anyone like one?"

He was in the process of serving drinks to the young couple when a man came to the stern of the boat and called for the attendant to come onto the dock.

After a whispered conversation, which John could not overhear, the young attendant leaned over the stern of the boat and said, "Ladies and gentlemen, because of an emergency, I have been called home. My replacement will be here shortly. Have a wonderful trip."

The attendant gathered his personal belongings, waved goodbye to the tourists, and ran hastily down the dock toward the bus stop.

The man who had spoken to the attendant remained on the dock until two more men came. Immediately both men boarded the boat. One of them announced cheerfully that because of the inconvenience, Bahama Mamas would be free of charge. He proceeded to make several drinks then began to prepare the boat for departure.

His burly partner did absolutely nothing to help. Instead he sat down, folded his arms across his chest and systematically scrutinized each passenger.

The arrival of the two men put John on alert. He glanced at Raj, but otherwise did acknowledge him. Nor did Raj make any attempt to speak to John. John and Sharon made a point of directing all conversation to the honeymooners, and Raj continued to be engrossed with the Catholic nuns from Pennsylvania.

The man who readied the boat evidently was a regular at the job. He assumed control of the boat and took them directly to several areas where they could view the coral reef. He was extremely familiar with the reef, describing thoroughly and accurately its various parts. Obviously he had conducted the tour thousands of times.

The second man was the one who concerned John. If one teenager had been scheduled to conduct the tour, why had he been replaced by two men? The second man remained silent and watchful. His stern demeanor was accented by his stocky, muscular physique. Several times, John noticed him studying Raj intently.

John took several pictures through the glass bottom of the boat. The brightly colored fish and underwater plant life swaying in the gentle currents were spectacular. At times the water was so shallow the bottom of the boat would almost scrape the reef. Then the depth would increase dramatically to over a thousand feet because of a sheer cliff in the ocean floor.

John handed his camera to the burly man and asked

him to take a picture of Sharon and himself. The man did so without saying a word and handed back the camera. He did not respond to John's word of thanks.

Raj acted like a typical traveler also. He asked several questions of the captain, and even addressed one to the burly man who was supposed to be their guide. The man made no reply, but merely shrugged his shoulders.

When the boat returned to the dock, the nuns from Pennsylvania were bragging they had not gotten seasick after all. One of them wondered if she would be able to get her land-legs back after rocking in the boat so long.

Raj assured her he would assist her off the boat and back to the van for the return trip to the hotel. He pulled his *Fodor's Guide to the USA* from his pocket and began asking the sisters about Pittsburgh. He told them he hoped to have time to go there while he was on vacation.

John and Sharon asked the honeymooners to join them at the beach to have a cocktail, but they declined. John thanked their captain for the nice tour and tipped him generously. He thanked them sincerely while his burly assistant looked on disdainfully.

WHEN JOHN AND SHARON reached the beach area, he rented an umbrella and chairs and ordered drinks. Careful to keep up appearances, he took several pictures and even asked the lifeguard to take a picture of Sharon and himself.

They placed their chairs a good distance from the other tourists so they could talk without being overheard.

"What a waste of time that was," John said with tired disgust.

"What could we do? With the sudden change of boat captains, it would have been foolish to make contact."

"How can you play the role of a dumb, giddy blond so well and yet be so sharp?" John asked shaking his head. "Did you pick out my contact?"

"I wouldn't have except for the burly guy staring at him. He was the man talking with the two sisters, wasn't he? Please tell me what I can do to help, because it looks like one of you has blown your cover."

"Yes, Raj is my contact," John said. "I can't believe someone is trailing him. Although we've worked together only a few times, I know he is one of the best, very skilled at covering his tracks. It's almost like he can become invisible whenever he wishes. Maybe it's just a coincidence, but I don't think so."

Seeing the worried concern on his face, Sharon laid her hand on his arm reassuringly. "I want to help anyway I can, but you have to be careful too. It could be you who is being followed."

They sat for a long time, not talking, only staring out beyond the restless surf. Finally John said, "I'm hungry. How about a sandwich at the restaurant beside the pool?"

"Sounds great to me," Sharon said, looking at her watch. "It should be about time for another shuttle back to the hotel."

RAJ RECLINED in a lounge chair under the portico on the far side of the pool. Although he seemed to be absorbed in a paperback book, he was keenly aware of John and Sharon's arrival at the restaurant.

Once they had eaten, he watched them walk to their room on the second floor. They were adjacent to the room where he had escorted the Catholic nuns after their boat tour this morning.

Evidently a new group of tourists had just arrived

because the walkway was suddenly crowded with people carrying luggage. Raj rose from his lounge chair and mingled with several people as they made their way to the second floor of John and Sharon's wing.

As they passed John's room, Raj gently tapped on the door. Sharon opened the door and he quickly stepped past her into the room. She closed it behind him just as quickly.

"I know I'm taking a chance," Raj said to John who was seated in front of the television, "but I'm being followed and this may be our only chance to talk. I have so much information for you."

He looked at Sharon doubtfully.

"Just let me change," she said, turning towards the bathroom. "I'll go down to the pool."

"That would be best," John said. "I don't want you too involved. We shouldn't be long."

"Fifteen minutes at the most," Raj assured her.

Once she left the room, Raj launched in, "I hope I have not compromised you, John. I suspected I was being tailed in Brussels. After the incident on the boat, I'm sure of it. I recognized the replacement guide from the airport in Brussels, though he was not on the flight with me to New York. I decided I better talk with you and then get off the island as soon as possible."

"Don't worry about compromising me," John said. "What's going on?"

Raj sighed heavily, "Where do I start? Before the downfall of the Soviet Union, some die-hard communist generals, instead of destroying their missiles according to an agreement with the USA, sold and smuggled six intercontinental ballistic missiles to Iraq.

"These missiles are capable of delivering atomic weapons to any target on this planet. Four missiles were sold to Iran. Two went to Libya. Two long-range

Russian atomic missiles were smuggled by the same generals to North Korea. These two weapons have the capability of reaching the west coast of the United States. I have been unable to trace what happened to the missiles the USSR tried to send to Cuba when Kennedy was your president.

"Hussein had the missiles sent to Iraq dismantled, and the atomic bombs buried in the deepest, abandoned oil wells in Iraq. That's why no weapons of mass destruction have been found, and they will not be found. It doesn't matter that Hussein has been captured. His loyal infrastructure has complete control of those weapons, each with more destructive power than the largest H-bomb ever produced by the United States."

Raj paused and leaned closer to John. "Those bombs can be exploded simultaneously. A geologist, whom I respect very much, told me the simultaneous detonation of those bombs at their great depth, close to the lithosphere, would cause catastrophic consequences for this planet.

"While your country is supplying Israel with sophisticated weapons such as tanks, jet fighters and missiles, Russia and China are selling small arms to Palestine and several other Islamic nations, especially in southeast Asia. Islam is burgeoning at an alarming rate in that area. China has been very quiet because its lucrative trading with the west has strengthened it economically, but their policies of complete governmental control are as deep-rooted as ever. The struggle between communism and capitalism is as serious as it ever was.

"Your present administration espouses all is well, and all the world loves the good old USA. All is not well, and much of the world hates America. The cold war is far from over. For those former Soviet generals, the cold war will never be over until communism is restored to the Soviet Union and it continues its struggle for world domination.

"Now the struggle between Islam and Judeo-Christianity is coming into the fore. Israel attacks Palestinians with sophisticated weapons obtained from the U.S., and the Palestinians retaliate with their best weapons — suicide bombers who obtain their weapons mostly on the black market.

"These bombers become martyrs of the highest order in the Islamic world. Their heroic sacrifice is recognized in the Islamic community as the epitome of patriotism. It has great influence on some Arab nations that in the past had professed friendship with the United States.

"For years, Saudi Arabia was a friend of the U.S. because America helped develop its oil production and purchased most of its oil. The United States also protected the Arabian nobility from a communist takeover.

"Now that the USSR is no longer a threat to the Arabian nobility, the cultural difference between Saudi Arabia and America is becoming an insurmountable obstacle. Both your government and the Arab diplomats in Washington will deny this vehemently. I cannot comprehend why the news in your country says so little about the actual perpetrators of the 9-11 attack on the U.S. being natives of Saudi Arabia.

"India and Pakistan still have irreconcilable differences about the disputed Kashmir region. Pakistan is still supporting Islamic militants according to my best sources in India, and both are capable of waging catastrophic attacks against each other.

"No one knows what is going on in North Korea. I cannot find out anything about the two intercontinental ballistic missiles the Soviet generals smuggled to that country. They're probably intact and used as models for

North Korea to add to its arsenal of atomic weapons."

Raj paused again, looking at John thoughtfully. "Please do not be offended, but why does the United States believe it is the only country entitled to develop and possess weapons of mass destruction?"

"I am not offended," John said, shaking his head. "I've asked myself the same question many times. Honestly, I do not know."

"The more America continues to support Israel militarily, the more unified the Islamic world appears to become. Palestinians, Arabs, and Muslims seem to be uniting against a common enemy: Israel, and anyone allied with Israel.

"A secret meeting of many Islamic and Arab nations is being planned for North Africa in the near future. When I get back to Europe and learn the date I will let you know. A confrontation of disastrous magnitude between the Islamic nations and Israel and the west is in the making.

"With the exception of North Korea, it probably will not be a frontal attack because those nations do not have the weapons of mass destruction to mount such an attack. Instead it will be an insidious attack by terrorists on the WMD stored in America.

"The attacks will be even more dramatic and destructive than those of 9-11. It will be an entirely different war; but all war is hell, nothing but sheer madness.

"Because much of what I have told you is contrary to your government's policies, I would be very careful to whom you report any of this. This is exactly what your government does not want to hear."

John nodded understandingly, went to his suitcase, pulled out an envelope and passed it to Raj. "The rest will be put into your account in Geneva."

Raj accepted the envelope with a nod. "May I stay until I hear some people to mingle with while leaving?"

"Stay as long as you like, and be careful," John said, "I'll put on my swimsuit and join my friend at the pool."

He extended his hand. "It's always good to work with you. Thanks."

John had been gone only a few minutes when Raj heard some familiar voices through the window. Peeking through the blinds, he confirmed it was the Catholic nuns from Pennsylvania. Quickly he stepped through the door.

"May I join you ladies for a drink before dinner?" Raj asked cheerfully.

"Of course," the sisters eagerly said in unison. They went on to suggest that maybe, after dinner, he could accompany them to the casino. They had never been to a casino and would love to have someone teach them how to play roulette.

AT THE POOL, John found Sharon lounging beside the water, engrossed in a paperback novel. He dipped a foot into the pool and kicked some water onto her legs.

"Now was that necessary?" Sharon asked as she closed the book.

"Couldn't resist," John said, smiling. "Why don't you cover me with sunscreen?"

John lay on his stomach on a lounge chair beside hers. As Sharon massaged the lotion onto his skin, John's thoughts turned to Frances. He imagined it was Frances's hands he was feeling on his back. How wonderful it would be if it were she sitting beside him.

But it wasn't Frances and she would not be happy if she could see him now. It was no wonder she had left him and was filing for divorce.

He thought of the assignment two years ago in New York City when he met a foreign agent at an elaborate nightclub. Unfortunately for John, the agent was a beautiful blonde and an inquisitive friend of Frances had seen them in a secluded booth.

Although it was strictly a business meeting, Frances's friend could hardly wait to call and tell her John was cheating on her.

That was the beginning of trouble between Frances and John. The irony of the entire situation was he had always been faithful to Frances. She was the only one he had ever loved and still loved with all of his heart.

Sharon brought him back to reality when she slapped him on his fanny and said, "That's all. You can do the rest."

She handed him the bottle of lotion and immediately dove into the pool, splashing him with the cool water. John jumped into the water hoping to get revenge by ducking her, but Sharon had already reached the other side of the pool where a game of volleyball was in progress. They joined in, playing on opposite teams.

"I'm exhausted," Sharon said, after her team won the match. "I'm quitting while I'm ahead."

"One more game," John insisted.

"Admit you're beaten," she gloated. "I'd hate to beat you two games. You would pout the rest of the trip. Come on, let's dress for dinner and go to the casino."

AFTER SHOWERING, Sharon came into the room dressed in her bathrobe and John went to get his shower. As she sat down at the dresser to apply her makeup, she was surprised by a knock on the door.

"Who is it?"

"Room service," came the quick reply.

"Room service?" Sharon repeated loud enough for John to hear. "I didn't order room service."

"I have an order for room 228."

"Just a moment." Sharon tied her bathrobe snugly around her waist and walked to the door. As she opened the door a crack, the attendant forced the serving cart against it so hard Sharon had to jump back to keep from being knocked down. He shoved the cart into the room and went about preparing it for dining. Sharon stood back, a little stunned, watching as his eyes skillfully scanned the room.

"Honey, where did you put my razor?" John called, stepping from the bathroom stark naked, shaving cream all over his face. "Oops, I didn't know someone was here."

He pretended to be embarrassed, attempted to cover himself, and jumped back into the bathroom. "Who is that?" he called through the door.

"It's room service. Did you order anything?"

"No. If you didn't, it must be a mistake."

The attendant looked at his order card. "It says here room 228, and this is 228." His eyes continued to search the room. "Maybe the kitchen made a mistake in the number, but I have a full course dinner for two."

"Well, we didn't order it," Sharon said firmly, ushering the man and his cart toward the door. "We have reservations at Le Chateau. So take the cart and make sure this is not on our bill when we check out."

After she closed the door behind him, she listened carefully until she could no longer hear his footsteps or the rattling of the dishes on the cart. She locked the door and leaned against it letting out a sigh of relief.

John came from the bathroom with a towel wrapped around his waist, his face still covered in shaving cream. "What was that about?" he asked.

Sharon looked at him intently and said, "I've no idea, but I've seen that man before."

"He's probably just some bus boy or attendant you've seen around the restaurant or pool."

Sharon looked at John with disgust and irritation. Did he still have no confidence in her after all this? Maybe she was playing the role of dumb blonde too well. Even John seemed to think she was one.

"After we got off the boat this morning, I saw him talking with one of the men who took us on the tour of the reef," she informed him. "I saw them together on the pier as we walked toward the beach."

"Are you sure?" John searched her eyes, considering the implications.

"Absolutely, without a doubt. And he really scanned our room while he pretended to set up the tray. Believe me; he's no busboy. He's a pro. Do you think they could know about you?"

"I don't see how. But in this business, one never knows. Maybe he saw Raj come here or leave. Raj told me he could have been followed from Europe. Maybe they're checking everyone on the boat tour this morning."

Sharon smiled, "Coming out of the bathroom naked should have convinced him we are legit. You deserve an Oscar for that performance. It was all I could do to keep from laughing at the way you jumped back into the bathroom."

AFTER DINNER at Le Chateau, John and Sharon strolled to the casino where John exchanged some bills for two rolls of quarters. He gave one to Sharon, and they sat beside each other at the slot machines playing the one armed bandits. Neither of them won anything, so they decided to move to the blackjack tables.

On their way, they passed the two sisters and Raj seated at a roulette table. The sisters were talking excitedly about a win they had just made and did not even notice John and Sharon as they walked by.

In less than an hour at the five-dollar blackjack table, John lost all of his chips. Sharon won $25. When John suggested leaving, Sharon pled that she was "on a roll" and begged to play one more hand. She bet all of her winnings on the next hand and won.

As they left the casino, both scanned the room. Neither Raj nor the two sisters from Pennsylvania were anywhere to be seen. Outside the casino, a large crowd was gathered at the corner of the double-lane boulevard that separated the casino from the hotel. An ambulance was just driving away.

As John and Sharon approached the group, they saw the sisters from Pennsylvania talking excitedly with a policeman. "We were waiting with our friend for the light to turn green when a man pushed him from behind and knocked him into the street. Before he could jump out of the way, a car with no lights on sped out of the darkness and ran over him. It never slowed down. He didn't have a chance."

"Did you see what the man who pushed your friend looked like?" the policeman asked in his British accent.

"No," she replied, "It happened so fast. He came from behind us, shoved our friend into the street then dashed away into the darkness."

"What did the car look like? Did you get the tag number?" the policeman asked.

"There was no time. The car came so fast and with no lights. The sound, when it hit our friend, was awful. All we could see was his motionless body lying there. I doubt if he knew what hit him. The emergency crew arrived quickly. They examined him and pronounced he was dead. That's when you arrived."

"Did your friend come to the island with you?"

"No," one sister replied, "We met him only this morning on a glass bottom boat tour of the reef. He was such a nice, friendly man. He joined us for cocktails this afternoon and then dinner before accompanying us to the casino. He taught us to play roulette and black jack. We won at both, thanks to his advice. Now he's dead. It all happened so fast. There was nothing either of us could do for him. It was awful. He was such a genteel person. I hope you find who did this awful thing. Our trip has been ruined."

John and Sharon remained in the shadows at the edge of the crowd. John did not want the sisters to see them. A cold shiver raced down his spine and caused the hairs on the nape of his neck to rise. He knew the sisters were talking about Raj and his death was no accident. He had been eliminated, but by whom?

Sharon clasped John's hand tightly, as she too realized the truth. As they casually worked their way around the crowd, they overheard the policeman inform the sisters he would accompany them to police headquarters. Neither of them spoke as they crossed the street and went directly to their room.

Once inside, Sharon turned to John. "I'm so sorry."

John turned the television on loud, just in case their room was bugged, and whispered, "I cannot believe Raj has been eliminated. We weren't friends. In our business, one does not make friends. But I liked him. Thank goodness we were able to talk this afternoon."

John sat down heavily on the edge of the bed and put his head in his hands. "God, it's good our tour is leaving in the morning. It will be great to get off this island and back in the States."

6

AFTER RENTING A MINIVAN, Scott helped Sarah and the children load the luggage, and they left for the Highlands. Traffic was heavy on I-75 through the business district of Atlanta, but after they exited onto I-85 and then onto I-985, traffic was not as congested.

They made good time on U.S. 23 and 441 until they reached Dillard, Georgia. Here they exited onto a two-lane state highway that became very narrow and curvy as they approached the foothills. Five miles of curves was all Robert could take before he became carsick. Fortunately, there was a roadside overlook where Scott could park the minivan safely and let Robert get out of the car to upchuck.

When they reached Highlands, they turned east on Highway 64 toward Cashiers. About two and one half miles east of Highlands, they turned left onto Flat Mountain Road.

"It looks like we're going through a tunnel because the trees are touching each over the road," said Douglass.

"Why is there a mirror in that tree, Daddy?" Robert asked. He was the most observant of the children.

Scott glanced at Sarah. "I don't remember that convex mirror being beside the road the last time we were up here. Robert, I guess it was put there for safety because the road has such a sharp curve in it. The mirror lets me see around the curve to see if another vehicle is coming."

Robert nodded, satisfied with the explanation. "I've seen them in the grocery store but never in a tree beside the highway."

It was late afternoon when they turned into the driveway of a gray wood cottage. The small, grassy front yard was freshly mowed and neatly trimmed. A low, stone fence made of local river-washed rock bordered the street side of the yard. Beside the driveway was a row of brightly colored dahlias. Large mountain laurel bushes were blooming at each of the front corners of the house.

Four stone columns, made of the same stone as the front wall, supported the roof covering the front porch. Freshly cut firewood was stacked against the stone columns on the ground level, slate porch.

Although it was the beginning of summer, Sarah's father always kept a supply of wood for the fireplace. They used it on unusually chilly evenings in the summer as well as in the winter to heat the entire house.

Behind the house was a small lake. Many years before Sarah's parents purchased the house, someone had built a concrete dam across the rippling mountain creek running through the back yard. The dam, with a little help from some beavers, had created the lake and Sarah's father kept it stocked with mountain trout.

Although the lake was small, a canoe was tied to the wooden dock. The children enjoyed rowing the canoe around the lake as well as fishing from it. They firmly believed the largest fish were in the middle of the lake, and each one wanted to catch the largest fish.

As the children opened the van door, their grandfather, Charles Douglass, came out of the house to greet them.

"Grandpa!" Ann, Douglass, and Robert shouted in unison as they rushed into his open arms.

"I was beginning to worry about you," Charles said to the children, and to Sarah and Scott as they got out of the car.

"Our plane was late leaving Orlando," Sarah explained, "and we were stacked up over Atlanta for almost an hour. Where's mother?"

"She's in the house preparing supper. I doubt if she heard you drive up."

Sarah embraced her father and winked at him as she said, "The children hope you haven't been feeding the fish. They want them to be good and hungry."

"Will you take us fishing now, Grandpa?" Robert and Douglass pleaded. "Please."

"Not now," Scott said. "You need to go inside and speak to your grandmother first. Then we need to unload the van."

"I'll bet she's making chocolate brownies," Douglass said excitedly and the three children dashed into the house.

Charles clasped Scott's hand warmly. "Kathleen and I are so happy you could get some time off to come up with Sarah and the children for a few days. I hope this will be a restful break for you. Maybe we can get in some serious fly fishing while you're here."

"Just sitting beside the lake and float fishing will be serious enough for me," Scott said smiling. He opened the rear door of the van and took out the heaviest suitcases. Charles came over to help him, but Scott waved him off. "Don't bother, the boys will come back and get them."

As Sarah, Scott and Charles entered the house,

Kathleen came in from the kitchen, hugging Sarah and Scott warmly.

"It's so good to see you," Kathleen said. "I can't believe how much the children have grown since I saw them last. Ann is no longer a little girl. She's a young lady now. It's amazing how she has changed in just a few months."

The three children, each with a handful of warm brownie, had followed Kathleen into the den. Ann, having heard what her Grandmother said, nodded her head emphatically and quietly whispered to Douglass and Robert, "And don't you two forget it either!"

"I hope you aren't too tired from your flight and drive," Kathleen went on. "You have time to get settled in your rooms upstairs and maybe even rest some before supper."

She turned to her granddaughter. "Ann, we've redecorated the room where you slept the last time. I hope you like it. Douglass, you and Robert take the room with the bunk beds. Sarah, you and Scott will be in your old room."

"I'm not tired and I don't need to rest," Robert stated with 9-year-old conviction. "I want to go fishing."

"You'll be tired after you bring up our luggage," Scott said. "And since your sister is now a young lady, I think if would be proper for you to bring her luggage to her room."

As the boys began to scowl, Scott said, "Even the large suitcases aren't too heavy for the muscles each of you claim to have. Lugging the suitcases will make those muscles bulge, so hop to it."

Douglass and Robert continued to scowl, especially at their sister, as they stuffed the last of their brownies into their mouths and stalked outside. Ann skipped up the stairs, humming to herself.

Sarah led Scott up the stairs to the largest bedroom, which was on the front of the house. It was the room she had stayed in when her parents first bought the house while she was in college.

She entered the room first and placed her purse on the dresser. Scott was right behind her. Pushing the door closed with his heel, he grabbed Sarah by the waist and pulled her onto the bed.

"Finally, I've got you where I want you," he whispered then kissed her passionately.

She returned his kiss momentarily and then tried to push him away. "Scott, the children. Ann is across the hall, and the boys will be next door."

"The children are busy," he said, trailing his fingers down her cheek. "I need you now."

He pulled her to him intent on kissing her again, but he looked down to see Robert standing at the foot of the bed. "Where do you want me to put your bag, Dad? Douglass is bringing yours, Mama."

"Thank you, Robert. Just leave it at the foot of the bed, and remind Douglass you and he are to bring up all the luggage, even Ann's."

Robert moaned as he turned and plodded from the room. It wasn't fair. His sister was bigger and older, plus she had brought more luggage than he and Douglass together. He marched across the hall into Ann's room.

"Get out," Ann said. "Grandma said this is my room."

"Douglass and I slept in here last time so we could look out the window and see the fish jumping in the lake," Robert whined. "Change rooms with us."

Huffing and puffing, Douglass came into the room and dropped Ann's luggage on the floor with a loud thud.

"Why don't you act like a lady and let us men have

this room so we can see the lake?" Douglass said sarcastically.

"Pick up my luggage and place it on the folding rack," Ann said airily. "You heard what Daddy said."

"Pick it up yourself," Douglass snapped defiantly.

"Mama," Ann called, "make the boys get out of my room."

Across the hall, Scott looked at Sarah hopelessly. "Will they ever stop fussing? I'll settle this right now."

"They're just doing what comes naturally," Sarah said, patting his arm.

"Being an only child, how do you know?"

"Look who's talking," Sarah said without thinking. "You're an only child also."

Immediately, she wished she had not said it. Scott was often sensitive about having been found abandoned on the steps of the hospital when he was not more than a week old.

He had been wrapped in a blanket with a Scottish tam on his head and placed in a basket made of woven bullrush stalks. The nurse who found him had named him Scott. The hospital was located at the intersection of Main and Walker Street, so Walker had become his last name.

Scott spent his youth among many different foster families. Three years was the longest he ever stayed in one place, and he was always the only child.

During his senior year in high school, he earned a full academic scholarship to N. C. State. He never learned his parents' identity, and though he did not try to hide his past, he never enjoyed talking about it.

Scott went into the hall and called to the boys, "Let's stop this fussing and get your things into the room your Grandmother said for you to use. Don't let me hear another word about rooms. That's final."

Robert and Douglass picked up their luggage and moved it across the hall into the room with the bunk beds. A moment later, Charles' deep bass voice called from downstairs, "Kathleen says supper is ready when you are."

Robert was the first downstairs Dashing into the dining room where his Grandfather was seated at the table, he announced, "Mama and Daddy will be here as soon as they finish kissing."

"I heard that," Sarah called as she descended the stairs. "Just wait until I get my hands on you."

"Tattletale. You're in trouble now," Ann teased as she passed through the dining room and into the kitchen to see if her Grandma needed any help

Sarah looked flushed and slightly embarrassed as she entered the dining room followed by Scott. She gave Robert a look, warning that he had better behave. He picked up on it at once. Quickly he rose and pulled out the chair for his grandmother to be seated. Kathleen was impressed and thanked him appreciatively.

Douglass was the last to enter the dining room. His father was holding the chair for his mother to be seated and he gave Douglass a look that said he had better hold the chair for his sister. He rushed over to do so, only mildly threatening to pull the chair out from her. Ann glared at him but thanked him politely.

Having overheard Robert's announcement about his parents kissing, Kathleen said, "Robert, your father has not seen your mom for a month. If your grandfather had been away from me for a month, he'd better kiss me good when he got back, especially if he wanted me to cook him a meal like this."

She kissed Charles lightly on the cheek and turned and hugged Robert. "Kissing is how we tell others we love them."

To the others at the table she said, "Now let's bow our heads and join hands while Charles says grace."

In the Charles Douglass home, saying grace was more than merely repeating rote. It was a sincere prayer of thankfulness for life's many blessings. "Father, we give you thanks for the safe arrival of Sarah and her family. We thank you for this beautiful day. We give you special thanks for the food we are about to eat and the hands that prepared the meal. Now bless this food to the nourishment of our bodies that we might be more dedicated to serving you. Amen"

"Grandma, this looks yummy good," said Robert rubbing his little hands together.

"It's my favorite meal," Douglass said. "Pass the mashed potatoes."

"Say please," Ann reminded him then added, "Whatever you're eating at the time is your favorite, you pig."

"Okay, cut it out," Scott said before things could escalate. "Besides, it's my favorite too — fried chicken, gravy, mashed potatoes, green beans, and biscuits. Nothing could be better."

"Thank you," Kathleen said with a big smile. "There's nothing I'd rather do than prepare food for my family, especially since all of you enjoy it so much."

"And I cannot think of any group who would enjoy it more than these chow hounds," Scott said, taking a bite of biscuit. "Mmm, this is delicious. Sarah, your biscuits are good, but these are unbelievable. Kathleen, give Sarah a few more hints about how you bake them."

"Yeah, and teach Mama how to make gravy like this, too," Douglass piped in.

"Now wait a minute, you two," Sarah said with mock anger. "Keep this up and both of you will eat TV dinners from now on."

"Your gravy is good too, Mom," Robert said diplomatically, "but there's something extra special about Grandma's gravy."

"Maybe it's the mountain air," Kathleen said, beaming with pride. "Save room for dessert. We have a strawberry pie and cookies."

AFTER THE INCREDIBLE MEAL, the children cleared the table while the four adults sat and talked. Sarah was so proud of the manners the children had displayed during supper, and she was especially happy when they volunteered to clear the dishes. Best of all, there was no fussing as they rinsed the dirty dishes and placed them in the dishwasher. She smiled to herself. Maybe there was hope for them yet.

Once the table was cleared, the children went outside to play. Sarah helped her mother finish cleaning up while Scott and her dad went out to the back porch. The two men sat in large, hand-made rocking chairs with woven rush seats. As Scott eased his tired frame into the chair, he exhaled a sigh of utter contentment.

They sat in complete silence for a few moments, savoring the coolness and stillness of the mountain air. Overhead the sky was clear. The only sound to be heard was the laughter and chatter of the boys as they chased lightning bugs.

Ann sat in the boat, which was resting part in the water and part on the near bank of the small lake, and dangled her feet in the water.

After some time, Charles said, "I hope things are going well at NASA."

"Fine," Scott replied. "Everything is right on schedule."

Charles did not push. He knew one of the purposes

of this trip was for Scott to get away from the stress of preparing for the next space flight. However, Scott liked talking to his father-in-law.

"Some people think because this will be my third trip into space, it will be routine for me," Scott went on, "but I am as excited as I was before my first flight."

Sarah and Kathleen finally came out of the kitchen and joined them on the porch.

"Surely it didn't take you two this long to finish in the kitchen," Charles said.

"No, it didn't," said Kathleen. "We've been having a long mother-daughter talk. Ann came into the kitchen and joined us. The three of us have had the best time just talking girly talk. Ann went upstairs to her room. I think she was sleepy. Douglass and Robert just came in for more brownies."

"Scott, your sons ate brownies as if they had not had supper," Sarah said. "They even took a handful with them when they went upstairs to bed. Mama, I'm embarrassed they took so many; but you can rest assured the brownies will be long gone before morning."

"It makes me feel very good to see them enjoy my cooking like that," Kathleen said. "Charles, aren't you ready for bed? It's past our bedtime."

"I guess so. Scott and I have been talking about his next flight."

"He was supposed to forget all about NASA on this trip. It's been a long day. I think I'm as tired as the children. Let's all go to bed."

"It has been a long time since I left Houston this morning," Scott said with a yawn. "With the time change, I've been up a long time. Going to bed is a good idea."

"Good night, Dad. Night, Mom," Sarah said, kissing them both. "That was a delicious dinner. Thanks for having us. Wake me in the morning so I can help you with breakfast."

"Good night," Charles said.

"We hope you sleep well," Kathleen added as they went to their room.

Scott climbed the stairs closely behind Sarah as they went toward their room. He slipped his hand under her dress and whispered, "Just wait until I get you in the room, I'll show you how much I missed you."

Sarah stifled a squeal and said, "Shh, you'll wake the children."

Once they were in the room, Scott pulled her to him firmly, but tenderly, and said, "God, how I missed you."

He kissed her long and hungrily.

Sarah returned his passionate kiss, but then she whispered, "But we can't. These walls are so thin. The children will hear us."

"I'll be quiet. See, the bed doesn't squeak. Well, not much anyway." He bounced up and down on the squeaky springs and mattress.

Quickly Sarah tried to hold Scott so he would stop bouncing on the bed.

"Mom and Dad's room is directly underneath us, and I'm not completely over my period. Although I need a loving as much as you do, I'm just not up to it. Besides you said downstairs you were very tired. We'll just have to wait 'til later. I'm sorry."

"That's okay," Scott said with a sigh, hugging her close. "I really am tired. Just let me hold you until we fall asleep."

He undressed to his boxer shorts, which he wore instead of pajamas, and quietly lay down on the bed watching as Sarah undressed and put on her nightgown. She was as beautiful and desirable as she had been on their honeymoon. As he admired her naked body, he wondered how she could still be this sexy after having three children. He loved her more than ever.

"I completely forgot to tell you I saw John Johnston at Hartsfield today," Scott said. "You remember him. He was in Lambda Chi at State. He's the guy who wore a necktie all the time. In fact, I didn't recognize him at first because he wasn't wearing a tie.

"He married after graduation and had a little girl, but now they're separated and she has custody of the child. I think it must have been a nasty situation. Other than that info, he was as secretive as ever.

"I remember hearing at a frat reunion years ago he was employed by some branch of the government. When I asked what he was doing, he said abruptly that it was time for his plane and walked away rapidly. I would swear I saw him board a plane bound for Columbia, S. C., but I can't imagine why he would be going to there."

Scott had fallen silent by the time Sarah slipped between the sheets and snuggled close to him. She was surprised, yet not, that he had fallen asleep. She knew he must be exhausted.

Gently she kissed him on the nape of his neck, wrapped her arm around his waist, and snuggled even closer to him. A sigh of utter fulfillment, security, happiness, and love eased from her body and she joined Scott in tranquil sleep.

SCOTT BECAME AWARE of someone shaking his shoulder.

"It's time to go," Robert said.

"Go?" Scott mumbled. "Go where?"

"Fishing. You promised we would go fishing first thing this morning."

"What time is it?" asked Scott, raising his head to look around. "It looks like it's still dark outside. Go back to bed."

"But you promised," Robert insisted. "Doug is already outside, but he won't put the worm on my hook. Please, Daddy, you promised."

Scott sighed. "Okay. But be quiet. You'll wake your mother."

"Too late," Sarah said. "But you did promise, Daddy."

As she dozed back into sleep, her last thought was how much she loved Scott for being so wonderful with their children. It gave her a feeling of warmth, love, and peace of mind.

Quietly Scott got out of bed, pulled on a tee shirt, shorts, and loafers and tiptoed out of the room behind Robert. He was careful not to let the back screen door slam shut because he did not want to wake the rest of the family.

His efforts were to no avail as he and Robert heard Douglass scream, "I've got one. Help! I've got a big one. Help, someone!"

It was barely light enough for them to see Douglass standing beside the lake with his fishing rod bent almost double.

"For Pete's sake, shut up," Scott admonished. "You'll wake everyone."

"Bring the net, Robert. I can't get him in. Hurry, dummy, or he'll get away."

Robert ran to the garage storage room and quickly came back with the fish net. Douglass was backing away from the side of the lake in an attempt to drag the fish onto the bank. He did this mostly by instinct because he had used a rod and reel very little. Most of his fishing had been done with a cane pole.

Douglass had backed so far from the pond's edge that the fish was almost on the bank. Robert ran to the water's edge and started to try to net the fish.

"Give it to Dad, you dummy."

But before he could say more, Robert had the fish in the net and was dragging it onto the bank, too excited to lift it out of the water. Douglass dropped the rod and reel and rushed to grab the net from Robert.

With pride beaming in his eyes and excitement in his voice, he turned to show the fish to his father. "Now that's the way a real fisherman catches fish."

"That's the way you have to have help getting it out of the water," Robert said. "If I hadn't helped, you would have lost him"

"Would not," Douglass said. "At least I don't have to get Daddy to bait my hook like some baby I know."

"Okay, then next time get your own net," Robert threw back.

"Cut the noise!" Scott said. "Both of you and now! I mean it."

"Is everything all right?" Charles called from his bedroom window.

Surprised, Scott, Douglass, and Robert turned toward the house. Lights came on in three bedroom windows almost simultaneously. Charles, Kathleen, Sarah, and Ann were staring out trying to see what all the shouting was about.

"I'm sorry they woke you."

"Grandpa, look what a big fish I caught." Douglass called, raising the net.

"I pulled it out of the water." Robert yelled out.

"Did not," Douglass shouted, starting towards the house with the net and the fish still on the line.

"Wait just a minute," said Scott. "Take the fish off the hook before you get the line all messed up. Besides, everyone in the house wants to go back to sleep."

Douglass laid the net on the ground and, using both hands, lifted the fish from the net. He looked at his dad and said, "Will you get it off the hook for me?"

Robert seized his opportunity to get back at his big brother. In a babyish voice, he teased, "Yanh, yanh, the baby can't get the fish off the hook."

"Make him shut up," Douglass said to their father. "Besides it's too big for me to hold in one hand."

"Yanh, yanh. The baby can't get the hook out."

Ann was still looking out the window of her bedroom and called to her father, "Dad, please make those turkeys shut up so a person can get some sleep around here."

"All of you better quiet down and now. I mean it," Scott said firmly as he took the fish from Douglass. "This feels like almost a two pound brown trout. It may weigh a little more than two pounds."

"It felt like it weighed a ton when I first hooked it. You can't imagine how hard it was to pull in."

"I pulled it out of the water," Robert reminded him.

"Did not."

"Don't start that again," Scott said, "or both of you will not fish any more. Go to the garage and get one of your grandfather's buckets to put this in. We need to keep it in water until we catch some more. This is a big fish, but not large enough to feed the entire family."

"Robert, go to the garage and get me a bucket," Douglass commanded.

"Dad said for you to get the bucket; and besides, it's your fish."

Douglass looked at his brother with disgust, shoved him almost to the ground, and ran to the garage to get a bucket. He returned quickly.

"Douglass, what were you using for bait?" his father

asked.

"A worm. May I take the boat out and fish from it?"

"Let's not use the boat," Scott said. "You caught this one from the bank and you can't do any better."

"Please put a worm on my hook, Daddy," Robert said.

"Don't say it," Scott warned as Douglass opened his mouth to tease his brother. "Just don't say a word, not one word."

Scott baited Robert's hook and let him cast it into the lake. Then he fixed a fly rod for himself and began casting a dry fly.

"Now I'll show both of you how to really catch fish," he boasted to his sons.

He was trying to cast the fly in the shallow, faster flowing water underneath some overhanging mountain laurel bushes on the opposite side of the lake. Much to his disgust, the fly became entangled in some branches hanging over the water. Both boys muffled a giggle, but instinctively knew this was a good time to remain quiet.

Finally Scott was able to pull the dry fly from the branches, and he continued casting around the far side of the lake.

Douglass tried to cast his bait in the same place where he had caught the trout. Scott hoped the two boys would not get their lines entangled.

He continued casting and working his way around the pond without any success for several minutes when Robert started yelling at the top of his lungs, "Help! Help! It's a whale!"

He was trying to reel the fish in, but just like Douglass, he was backing away from the bank more than he was turning the reel. Scott laid his fly rod down and rushed over to help his son.

"Don't back up from the water!" Scott called. "Just

hold the rod steady and turn the reel, not too fast though. You may break the line.

"Hold the rod up so the pole will stay slightly bent. That will keep the line taut so the fish can't throw the hook out. You're doing fine. That's it. Keep the rod bent. Keep on reeling. The way the rod is bending, it looks like you may have a whale after all. Easy now. He's getting close to the bank. If the fish sees you, he'll pull harder. Be very still."

"Help me, Daddy," Robert said excitedly. "Please help me".

"I'm helping." Scott was determined Robert would reel this fish in by himself, just like Douglass had done.

It would help build Robert's confidence in himself. He also did it so his sons would not be fussing over who was the better fisherman. As the fish was pulled very close to the bank, it began to thrash and leaped almost completely out of the water.

"Help! Help me, Daddy! It's getting away."

"Stay calm. Keep the rod upright so it will stay bent. You have him hooked well. He won't get away. Bring the net, Douglass."

Douglass had put down his rod and reel to come closer and watch. He picked up the net and tried to hand it to Scott who said, "Douglass, slowly move down the bank and put the net as deep as you can under the water."

As Douglass followed his instructions, Scott said, "That's it. Stand very still. Now ease the net deeper into the water. Robert, try to reel the fish in a little closer. Douglass, lift up when you think the fish is over the net. Jerk it up fast."

Robert's tongue was sticking out of his mouth as he concentrated and struggled. Scott hoped he wouldn't bite it off.

Finally the fish was guided over the net, Douglass jerked it out of the water with the flapping fish in it and brought it safely onto the bank.

"I caught it! I caught it!" Robert crowed. "How much does it weigh, Daddy? It's bigger than yours, Douglass."

Scott grasped the line and lifted the fish out of the net. As he removed the hook from its mouth, he held it in his hand as if to estimate its weight. "This is a large mouth bass. I guess it weighs about two pounds. It feels exactly as heavy as Douglass's trout."

"But it looks wider than Douglass's trout, and you said it has a bigger mouth."

"Mine is longer," Douglass said.

"Look, both of you caught trophy fish. They are about the same size, and both of you are better fishermen than I am. I haven't caught anything." Scott walked back to where he had left his fly rod.

The three resumed fishing in silence like true fishermen. Each was occupied with his own thoughts. The boys were relishing the excitement and pride of having caught a trophy fish. Scott was contemplating his excitement for his sons and his pride in them. Life couldn't get any better than this.

A little later, Charles came to the yard, but he did not bring any fishing equipment. He was perfectly content to watch his grandsons and son-in-law do the fishing.

"Grandpa, look at what Douglass and I caught. Daddy hasn't caught anything. He hasn't even had a nibble. Maybe he should fish with worms like we do."

"Mine is longer," Douglass said stubbornly.

"Both of them look like trophies. Maybe we should have them mounted," Charles said.

"We want to catch enough for supper for all of us," Robert said.

"It won't take many more this size to feed all of us. I'll clean all you catch, and your grandmother will cook them for you."

Charles must have brought them more luck because shortly after his arrival, Douglass and Robert each caught another fish. Proudly they showed them to their grandfather. They didn't even yell this time because Scott had convinced them that noise might scare the fish away.

Also trying to impress their grandfather, they removed the hooks from their fish and put them in the bucket with the others. Robert even baited his own hook and cast it back into the lake perfectly. Both boys wanted to look like old pros in front of their grandfather.

"That looks like two more nice bass. Another one or two like that, and we'll have enough to feed all of us."

He winked at the boys, and called to Scott who was still fly fishing at the far end of the pond, "By the way, Scott, how many have you caught? Looks like the boys are out-fishing you."

The boys giggled and called, teasing their father, "Yeah, Dad, you were gonna show us what? How many have you caught with that store-bought dry fly? Better switch to worms."

Scott pretended to ignore all three of them and continued casting the fly. Douglass hastily baited his hook and cast it as close to his favorite spot as possible.

Slowly and deliberately, Robert placed a worm on his hook, making sure his grandfather saw that he could bait the hook all by himself. Robert cast it back into the pond where he had caught the other fish.

By the time Kathleen called from the back porch to tell them breakfast was almost ready, Douglass had caught another bass and Robert had landed two pan-size bream. Scott had caught nothing He had not even had a strike. It was something the boys would not let him forget for a long time.

"Let's go to the house now. Your Grandmother will have breakfast ready by the time we get washed up."

Proudly Douglass and Robert picked up the bucket containing their catch. They pretended to stagger as if it were heavier than both of them together could carry.

"Let me help," said their grandfather.

"No thank you," Robert said. "Dad can help since he has nothing to carry back." He grinned at his dad. "Can you take our poles, please, since you don't have anything else to carry? It's all Douglass and I can do to carry the fish. They're so heavy."

Scott dutifully took their fishing rods. As Robert and Douglass approached the house, Robert called, "Mama. Mama. Come and look at what I caught. Daddy didn't catch anything. Come look."

"You caught all of these?" Sarah said, putting the appropriate excitement in her tone.

"I caught the longest one," Douglass announced.

"Did not," Robert said. "I caught the most, and I bet all mine weigh more than all yours."

"They don't either," huffed Douglass. "Grandpa, don't you have some scales to weigh fish?"

Before Charles could answer, Sarah said, "Your grandfather did have some scales, but I believe he lost them while fishing last year in the Chattooga River."

She turned to her father with a look that dared him to tell the boys differently. She did not want either Douglass or Robert to have proof one of them caught larger fish than the other.

Charles, although not willing to tell a lie, replied, "Well, I really don't know where my scales are."

Kathleen, knowing that was not the absolute truth, eyed him disapprovingly.

"Well, not exactly," Charles added sheepishly.

Trying to divert the boy's attention, Sarah turned to Scott. "Well, Mr. Fisherman, where are your fish?"

"Don't you rub it in. The boys have enough already." Then in an attempt to change the subject, he asked, "What's for breakfast, Kathleen? I'm starved. The boys got me up so early, my stomach feels like it's time for lunch."

"Ann and I have prepared your favorite — grits, eggs, country ham, biscuits, and my own fig preserves."

"Leave the fish here, boys," their grandfather said. "I'll put some ice on them. After breakfast, I'll clean them and freeze them for your grandmother to cook later."

Douglass and Robert put the bucket down and rushed into the house, pushing and shoving each other as they climbed the stairs.

"I caught the biggest," Douglass said.

"But I caught the most," Robert came back.

Downstairs, Scott shook his head. "Will they ever stop fussing and fighting?"

"Don't ask Charles," Kathleen said. "He's an only child and had only one child. But I had seven siblings, four brothers and three sisters. Agitating each other is perfectly normal and really is an expression of love between brothers and sisters."

Ann was pouring orange juice as the others came into the dining room. Without any prompting from his father, Robert rushed over to hold his sister's chair for her to be seated. Douglass did the same for his grandmother. Setting a good example for his sons, Scott held Sarah's chair as she sat down. Once Charles gave thanks, there was very little talking because everyone was hungry.

After they had eaten, Charles said, "If the children

would enjoy it, Kathleen and I would like to take them to Franklin to the ruby mine to look for gems. Some nice rubies have been discovered recently."

Kathleen had encouraged Charles to make the arrangements. She knew Sarah and Scott would welcome the chance to be alone after being apart for a month.

"We'd love to go!" Ann said. "Do you think I could find a big red one?"

"Me too," Robert chimed in. "I'd love to go."

"Well I don't know how big it will be, but we should be able to find some," Charles said. "We thought this would be exciting for you all and give your parents some time together."

"I'm all for that," Scott said, winking at Sarah.

Kathleen looked at Sarah and Scott and said, "There's one problem though. Your first cousin, Ruth, called last week. She and her husband, Bill, are here for the week from Richmond and insisted you join them for a round of golf.

"You remember what avid golfers both of them are. I told her she would have to wait and talk with both of you, but she was so determined she called the club and reserved a tee time for the four of you at 11:00 today.

"I told her I couldn't accept the invitation for you, but Ruth wouldn't take no for an answer. Anyway, she called early yesterday morning and said they would be by to pick you up at 10:45 sharp."

Kathleen looked at Scott very sympathetically.

"Don't worry about it, Kathleen," Scott said. "You did the best you could, and besides we have an out: I didn't bring my clubs."

Kathleen shook her head. "I told her you were going to be here such a short time you probably wouldn't bring clubs. Apparently she and Bill have two extra full sets for you to use. She was insistent on seeing you."

With a look of sufferance written all over his face, Scott resigned himself to his fate. He had not seen his wife in a month. He'd been with her for over 24 hours and hadn't been able to really touch her or make love to her. And now, just when Charles and Kathleen were thoughtful enough to entertain the children for the day, up pops an unavoidable golf date.

It looked like he wouldn't be able to make love to Sarah for umpty-eleven hours, if ever again. And to think he had looked forward to this. Oh, well, there was always tonight to look forward to.

Scott was jolted from his thoughts by the boisterous excitement of his children's bickering about going to the ruby mines.

"I'll bet I find the first one," Robert predicted.

"How can you?" Ann scoffed. "You don't even know what one looks like."

"I'll find the biggest one," Douglass piped in.

Sarah nudged Scott. "See what you missed while you were in Houston."

She rose and began picking up plates. "Come help the children and me get the breakfast dishes cleaned so they can leave for the ruby mine. Then you and I can get dressed for the golf. Ruth and Bill will be here shortly. I'm going to beat the socks off you."

"Your taking the children to the ruby mines for the day is the best suggestion I have heard in a long time," Scott said to Charles and Kathleen as he rose to help Sarah. "They could use a distraction the way they are chaffing each other. Many thanks."

Everyone was walking out of the house just as Ruth and Bill drove up in a Cadillac convertible. After all of the hugging and greeting and Ruth's marveling at how the children had grown, Charles, Kathleen, and the children left for Franklin. Ruth, Bill, Sarah, and a less than overjoyed Scott left for the country club.

After a miserable round of nine holes of golf — in Scott's opinion — Ruth and Bill suggested they skip the back nine and go directly to the nineteenth hole to really catch up on family news.

In the clubhouse bar, they took seat in a corner where they could talk quietly and not be disturbed by others or the TV. Scott participated, as best as he could, in the conversation, but he kept thinking he and Sarah could be alone now.

By the time Ruth and Sarah talked about all of the relatives, it was mid afternoon. Finally they left the club and drove to Sarah's parents' house. Scott was happy Sarah did not even suggest that Ruth and Bill's come in. As they drove off and Scott and Sarah went into the house, he thought maybe his luck was changing.

Sarah smiled at him, a sparkle in her eye. "Scott, I've got a surprise for you. First, go out and look in Dad's cellar at the back of the house. The key is in the kitchen. Look in the very back on the lowest shelf, and get one of daddy's bottles of homemade scuppernong wine."

Charles had dug a small cave-like cellar into the side of the hill in the back yard. It was about six feet wide, ten feet deep, and five feet in height. After framing the entrance with timbers, he had hung a small, but heavily insulated, door to keep out pests and also changes in temperature.

Here he stored many of the vegetables from his small garden. Mostly he used it to store his pride and joy: his homemade scuppernong wine.

Because of the depth of the cellar underground, the temperature remained an almost constant temperature of 55 degrees year round. Charles believed this temperature added almost as much to the bouquet and flavor of his wine as the scuppernongs themselves. He thought his wine rivaled any vintage ever to come from California or France.

It took Scott a long time to find the right key among the dozen keys on the ring. It didn't help that he was so excited about Sarah's planned surprise.

When he finally had the cellar door opened, he was amazed at the coolness of the interior. At the rear of the cellar, he saw a homemade wine rack with several bottles of wine on it. Each bottle was carefully stored on its side so the cork would stay wet.

Although Sarah had told him to get one on the bottom shelf, he read the label on several of the bottles. Each bottle was carefully labeled with a sticker Kathleen had designed for Charles. In addition to the date the wine was bottled, many of the labels contained a toast written about wine consumption.

Scott selected a bottle, dusted it, closed and locked the door and returned to the house.

By this time, Sarah had taken a shower and dressed and was in the kitchen busily making sandwiches of homegrown tomatoes and mayonnaise. She had also prepared Scott's other favorite sandwich, mayonnaise and olives stuffed with pimentos.

When Scott came into the house, he was surprised to find her in the kitchen making the sandwiches. His growing excitement was smashed.

Before his disappointment could show, Sarah said, "Rush upstairs and take a quick shower. I've prepared this picnic, and we've got to hurry before it gets to late. We need daylight for what I want to show you."

Scott shrugged and did as he was told.

When Sarah could hear he had finished his shower, she called upstairs, "Before you come downstairs, look in the hall closet and bring the plaid blanket on the top shelf. We will need it to spread on the ground where we are going for this picnic."

Picnic, smicknic, Scott thought to himself, *I wish you were up here naked in bed with me having a saknic.* But Sarah was so excited, he did not want to spoil her plans.

She finished packing the wicker basket that had been a wedding present for her parents. In addition to the sandwiches, she packed some grapes, apples and cookies. On top of the napkins, she placed the cork remover and the bottle of wine Scott had brought from the cellar.

She picked up the basket and called to Scott, "I'll meet you at the van. I have the wine and food. Hurry, or it will get too dark for you to see my surprise."

7

WHEN SCOTT CAME OUTSIDE, Sarah was in the
driver's seat. "I want to drive. Maybe I should blindfold
you so you can't find this spot again without me."

Scott sat in the passenger's seat without saying a
word. When they reached Highway 64, Sarah turned
the van east and drove about seven miles. Then she
turned onto Cowee Gap, a tar and gravel road, for about
mile.

Abruptly, the pavement ended and a very narrow,
gravelly dirt road snaked its way up the mountain. The
incline was so steep Sarah had to shift the automatic
transmission into low. Many years before, the road had
been used by a sawmill.

"Just where are we going?" Scott finally asked.

"Be patient," Sarah said, patting him on the arm.
"We'll be there in a few more minutes. Just a couple of
more curves to go, and you'll see one of my favorite
spots in the whole world. This is the final curve, and
we're here."

Suddenly they were out of the thick trees that
crowded both sides of the narrow road and in a small but
very lush meadow. Although a dense forest surrounded

the meadow, the vale had no trees except for one huge sugar maple standing almost in the center.

A narrow stream rippled through the green grass close to the base of the maple, winding its carefree way across the meadow and disappearing into the forest.

Sarah stopped the car, turned off the ignition and said, "What do you think?"

Scott looked around the meadow. He saw three other parked cars and three couples with children playing dodge ball in the meadow. He had hoped he and Sarah might be alone. Then he took note of the tall, dark green grass swaying gently in the summer breeze.

He leaned over and kissed Sarah lightly on the cheek and said, "It's beautiful."

There wasn't much enthusiasm in his voice, and Sarah noticed it, but she said nothing. She didn't want him to know she was aware of his chagrin because she still had an ace up her sleeve.

"Come on," Sarah said. "Bring the basket, and I'll bring the blanket. We'll spread our picnic beside the stream under the maple. No one is close to it."

They strolled through the waving grass to the maple tree where Sarah spread the blanket beside the crystal clear, bubbling stream. As she knelt on the blanket, she said, "The grass is so thick, it feels like being on a soft, fluffy pillow."

Scott placed the wicker basket on the corner of the blanket, sat down, and rolled over onto his back. Placing his hands behind his head, he said, "It's like lying on a cloud."

"Now just because you've been in space twice," Sarah said, "how would you know what it feels like to lie on a cloud?"

Gazing through the branches of the maple, Scott said, "I wonder how old it is and why there is only this one tree in the meadow."

"Well, folklore says that over 200 years ago, a young couple cleared the meadow of all trees except for this one maple, which they left standing to shade their cabin. At that time the tree was a mere sapling.

"They cleared an area of approximately 25 treeless acres and built a small, one-room log cabin for their home. The remaining logs were to be used to build a small barn for their cow. Unfortunately, the last tree he cut down fell on his wife, who was pregnant, and killed her and the baby she was carrying.

"The husband was so distraught he cursed all of the trees they had cut down, even the tree stumps. He blamed them for his wife and child's deaths. He placed their bodies in the one room cabin, piled all of the logs around it and set fire to it.

"Just before the cabin collapsed, he dashed into the cabin and it became their funeral pyre. And that is why no other trees grow in this meadow, only the maple sapling which the husband left as a temple to his wife and unborn child."

Opening the wicker basket, Sarah withdrew the bottle of wine and handed it to Scott. "Please pop the cork."

"Did that really happen, or are you pulling my leg?" Sarah shrugged. "That's what folklore says."

Carefully she removed two of her mother's Waterford wine glasses.

"Crystal for a picnic?"

"Daddy says his wine deserves only the best."

Scott removed the cork from the bottle and poured a very small amount of wine into the crystal goblet Sarah had handed to him.

He held the glass so he could examine the color carefully. Having approved of the vintage visually, he slowly swirled the wine in the glass and then smelled the bouquet. When this was satisfactory, he took a small sip and held it in his mouth several seconds before swishing and slowly swallowing it. Only then did he nod.

"Enough of this production," Sarah said "Pour me a glass."

"I think your daddy would approve of my ritual. Anyway, I think it's very good. I mean really good."

Scott poured both of them a glass and said, "Here's a toast to your father's wine. May he give us a bottle of this vintage to take home."

He touched his glass to Sarah's, and then they both took a sip of the wine. Again Scott held the crystal goblet aloft so he could study the color and clarity of the wine against the pale blue cloudless sky. "Really this is a very good wine. Its clarity is outstanding."

"Since when did you become such an expert on wine?" Sarah asked. "Just be sure you tell daddy how much you enjoyed it when we get back to the house. It will mean very much to him.

"Wine making and gardening are his pride and joy. Mother says it keeps him from being under her feet all day. Just tell him you enjoyed it. Nothing will make him happier than for you to ask him for a bottle to take home."

After they had finished the sandwiches and fruit, Scott said, "Now I could roll over and take a little nap right here. Even though the sun is about to set behind those trees, it still feels warm. I thought it would be much cooler in the mountains."

"Mother said it has been unusually warm during the day, but the nights seem to be as cool as ever. But you can't sleep now, lazy bones. There's something else I want to show you. Fold the blanket while I put all of the trash back in the picnic basket."

As they returned the basket and blanket to the van,

Scott noticed all of the cars and people had left. The shadows of the tall trees on the west side of the meadow reached almost all the way across the grassy meadow.

"Come on," Sarah said, taking him by the hand. They began to wind their way, following the brook toward the forest on the east side of the meadow. Soon Scott and Sarah disappeared into trees just as the brook had done.

The trees became so thick, and the mountain laurel and rhododendron so dense, Sarah had to turn Scott's hand loose as they worked their way deeper into the woods.

Scott stopped to admire the thick, dark green moss on a rock jutting out of the stream. He tried to move it, but it was anchored securely in the bed of the stream.

When he looked up, he was unable to see Sarah anywhere. He called to her, but she did not answer. It seemed the greenery had swallowed her. He squinted his eyes to try to see more clearly in the twilight, but he could not detect any sign of movement.

Again he called, louder this time, "Where are you?"

"I'm here. Over here," she replied, her voice sounded soft and muffled like she was far away.

"Over here, where?" Scott called back, "I can't see you, and you sound so far away. Where are you?"

He struggled through the entangled bushes, which had become so dense he could hardly get through them. He was startled when it appeared he was facing a solid rock wall.

He couldn't figure out how Sarah had disappeared so quickly. It was as if she had vanished. There was no way she could have scaled the vertical cliff in front of him. It was at least 12 feet high and straight up.

"Okay, so I'm lost," he called. Where are you?"

Laughing slightly, Sarah said, "Over here. Back up

from the wall about six feet, and look very carefully. You'll notice what looks like a very narrow path. You'll find the going much easier. It's probably a rabbit path."

"I think I can see the path now. But where in the dickens are you? It's almost dark. You still sound far away, like you are on the other side of the rock wall I almost ran into."

"Really, I am on the other side of the wall."

Scott pushed through the lush greenery. At first it looked as if he had run into the rock cliff again. However, as he pushed through the last thick rhododendron shrub, he saw a crack in the vertical wall just wide enough for a person to squeeze through.

Sarah smiled and extended both hands out to him and said, "Come in. This is what I really wanted to show you."

The fissure in the wall was at a diagonal so it was almost invisible when one looked straight at it. However, from an angle it was wide enough for a person to turn sideways and slide through the space. Scott did just that and emerged where Sarah was standing.

They were on a ledge about 10 feet deep and 12 feet wide. The bare rock wall behind the ledge rose vertically and curved slightly over the ledge, forming a small canopy over where they were standing.

The shelf was covered with the deepest, darkest green moss Scott had ever seen. It felt like the ground was covered in deep, plush carpet with a thick, foam rubber cushion beneath. It was as soft and spongy as an old-timey feather bed.

Sarah moved back from the opening so Scott could come farther onto the ledge and see what she was so excited about sharing to him. He moved to the front edge and gasped as he gazed at the panoramic landscape before him. There was no vegetation to block the view.

"My God, what a view," Scott murmured as he stared across the valley at the sheer cliffs of Whiteside Mountain and to the hazy range of mountains beyond.

The starkness of the bare granite of Whiteside contrasted with the dark blue of the next range of mountains beyond it. From the ledge, twilight appeared much lighter than it had when they were in the dense woods.

The dark blue of the nearer mountains faded into a lighter blue haze, which finally blended and faded into the sky above. In the far distance, it was difficult to distinguish between the mountains and the sky as dusk continued to fall.

Tenderly, Sarah observed each feature on Scott's face as he absorbed the majesty of the view before him. Finally, he turned to her and said, "It's beautiful here. And with this cliff behind us, it's like being in another world all by ourselves. It's so secluded. This is one of the prettiest views I have ever seen in the mountains. If only I could soar like an eagle down into that valley and then catch an updraft to glide over those distant peaks."

Turning to Sarah, he pulled her close and kissed her deeply. "No wonder you wanted to show this to me. It's awesome. How did you ever find this place?"

Sarah sat down on the plush moss. She pulled his hand so he sat down beside her. "When I was 16, my parents came to Highlands for the first time and rented a cottage for a week. We liked it so much, we came for a month the next summer. After that we came back each summer until Mom and Dad decided to buy the house they have retired to now.

"Daddy enjoyed driving on all the back roads and hiking all over these mountains. The little meadow where we had our picnic was one of his favorite places. We came there frequently.

"The third summer after they moved to Highlands,

Mother, Daddy and I came to the meadow for a picnic as we had several times before. At that time they had a dog, a Boston Terrier, named Mugsy. That day, we brought a small charcoal grill because Daddy wanted to cook hamburgers.

"He had a difficult time getting the fire started, and we were here longer and later than usual. By the time we finished eating and cleaned up our mess, it was getting dark. When Daddy called Mugsy, he did not come and we could not find him anywhere.

"Mother walked toward the car looking for him, and Daddy followed downstream searching for the dog. I came upstream this way; and after I had come into the woods, I thought I could hear his muffled bark.

"I went farther into the woods until I came upon what looked like the rabbit trail. I was certain I could hear Mugsy whining. I followed the sound as best I could, and I saw the crevice in the wall.

"Evidently Mugsy had been following a rabbit or chipmunk, and he went through the crevice. He could not climb back over the wall at the bottom of the fissure. As dark as it was, I could see the ledge clearly; and although it looked beautiful and inviting, I did not squeeze through the crevice.

"Mugsy was jumping with joy for having been found. I was glad to find him because I don't know what Mother and Daddy would have done had something happened to that dog. I pulled him over the wall and he dashed back toward the car as fast as he could. I took another look at the ledge and told myself I would come back when it was daylight.

"When I returned to the car, Mugsy was already in the car ready to go home. Don't ask me why, but I didn't tell my parents exactly where I found him. I just told them he was stuck between two rocks.

"It may sound silly, but I thought this would be my secret place. The next day, I drove out here by myself because I wanted to get a better look in broad daylight.

"I can't tell you how many times I have come here. You are the first person I've ever told about this place. I know this sounds silly to you, but sometimes, I pretend I am the only person who has ever been on this ledge."

They were silent, observing the view and absorbing the magnificence before them. Dusk continued to deepen.

"We've been to Highlands many times," Scott said. "Why have you never shown this to me before?"

"I don't know," she replied timidly. "Maybe I thought you would think it was silly."

"No way do I think it's silly," Scott assured her. "If I had found this place, I don't think I would have shared it with anyone either — well, maybe with you. But not just anybody."

"You're making fun of me, and you promised you wouldn't."

"No, I'm not. Really." In an effort to assure her he was not teasing, Scott said excitedly, "Look! There's Venus, the evening star, just beginning to twinkle. I wish I may, I wish I might, have the wish I wish tonight."

"And what is that?"

Scott lay back on the soft green moss and gazed into the heavens. After a long pause, he said softly as if talking only to himself, "Surely, out there somewhere is a planet where people can survive. There has to be one. I just know there is.

"It seems to get darker up here in the hills faster than it does in the flatlands of Florida. The sky is filling with stars. I don't think I have ever seen a clearer sky."

"Maybe because you're up so high you are closer to the stars," Sarah teased.

"Shh," Scott whispered, "Listen. Can you hear it?"

"Hear what?" Sarah asked as she looked around.

"There it is again. Shh.Quiet. Listen, and you can hear it. I hear it louder now."

"Hear what?" Sarah asked more curious than ever.

"My planet, my special star. I hear it calling me. Listen." He began to sing:

"Most people live on a lonely planet
Lost in the middle of a foggy sky
Most people long for another planet
One where they know they would like to be.
Special star has called me
Every night every day
In my heart, I hear it call me
Come away, Come away.
Special Star did whisper
On the winds of outer space
Here am I your special planet.
Come to me. Come to me."

"You incurable, romantic clown, you're paraphrasing *South Pacific*, but I love it," Sarah laughed, leaning over to kiss him lightly on the cheek.

"Look at that tiny, faint, flickering star just to the left of Pleiades," Scott said thoughtfully. "Circling around it, as faint as it is, may be a planet where people can live. Someone, someday, will be able to go there. I guess my wish is to be that someone."

Sarah interrupted, "Look, we came on this vacation to get you away from the upcoming mission. You, yourself, said you needed to get away from it all for a few days. So let's not have anymore talk about space."

Just then she saw a small clump of bluets blooming very close to the edge of the shelf. In the many times she had been to her secret hideaway, she had never seen any blooming flowers on it – only the soft green moss.

She moved closer to the edge and plucked one of the blossoms from the clump of bluets. She held the flower stem between her thumb and forefinger in order to spin the blossom around. She then placed the flower in her hair, on the right side to indicate she was taken.

The full moon, looking like an orange fireball, appeared in the gap formed by the twin peaks of Cowee Mountain. As the moon rose, its color changed from deep orange to bright silver, lighting the entire valley.

Sarah turned slightly and Scott could see her profile distinctly against the luminous moon. She pulled her knees up under her chin and locked her arms firmly around her lower legs. She did not look at him as she spoke, but gazed across the valley, "Promise me you won't laugh."

Scott had learned, long ago, that when she spoke in this serious tone she was going to share something very personal with him. It was another of the many facets of Sarah that fascinated him and made him love her. He was always learning something new, something special about her. It was part of the wonderful, ongoing excitement of living with Sarah Douglass Walker.

Again Sarah said, "Promise me."

"I promise," he said seriously.

"As you know, I went to summer school between my junior and senior year at Meredith. Daddy called me at school and said Mother was sick and he thought I should come home. I cut class and left on Thursday morning to drive here. By the time I arrived, Mother was feeling much better. It must have been a virus. She and I spent all day Friday together. I had brought my textbook, *History of Mythology*, with me because I had an exam the following week.

"Saturday morning, I told Mother I was coming to

the meadow to do some last minute cramming before the exam. She packed me a sandwich, apple, and thermos of tea. It was the middle of the afternoon by the time I parked the car and walked across the meadow to this spot. I was so engrossed in mythology that I lost all track of time. Can you see the notch between the twin peaks of the mountain in the distant range just to the left of Whiteside?"

"You mean Cowee Gap?"

Sarah hesitated for a moment. "No it's further in the distance."

"I see what you're talking about now."

"Suddenly I saw something that looked like it was trying to fly between the peaks. The moon was directly overhead, as bright as it is tonight or maybe brighter. At first, it was a mere speck of white, the whitest white I had ever seen. The speck became larger and began to take shape.

"As it came toward where I was sitting on this ledge, I could see it had wings, massive, white wings, which were beating majestically, but very powerfully and rhythmically. As it flew in front of Whiteside, I could distinguish that it was Pegasus.

"The moonbeams reflecting off the large wings and white body of the flying horse made the figure look as if it was made of silver. The muscular shoulders and legs were moving slowly as if the horse was merely strolling on air.

"It came closer with its ears pointed forward and its proud head arched high on a massively proud neck. The long, white mane flowed freely in the wind. I felt as if the steel blue eyes were staring completely through me, yet, I wasn't afraid.

"Then as Pegasus stepped onto the ledge, it was no longer a horse. It had taken the form of a man, tall, very erect and still just as white as Pegasus had been.

"With the moon reflecting on his broad, snow-white shoulders and narrow waist, the man looked as silvery as Pegasus had. Everything was so quiet. No sound had been made.

"The man, with his steel blue eyes intensely staring at me, took a step toward me and extended his gentle hand. I could hardly breathe; my heart was pounding so fast. Still I was not afraid.

"A feeling of warmth came over me like I had never felt before. It seemed as if my entire body was quivering and tingling all over. Before I could reach out to clasp the extended hand, I woke up. I had dreamed it all. The opened *History of Mythology* was still lying on my lap, the uneaten lunch still beside me.

"I was surprised no one was on the ledge. The dream had seemed so real."

Scott moved closer to Sarah so he could reach out his hand to her. As he did so, he said, "That was me."

"You promised you wouldn't make fun of me," she pouted.

"I'm not laughing. That was me," Scott reassured her, "Take my hand."

As she held his extended hand, Scott pulled her gently away from the edge of the shelf and said, "Would he have kissed you like this?"

He pressed his lips against her lips. She responded immediately, and he deepened the kiss.

"I love you," Scott whispered softly in her ear. "I've been dreaming of making love to you since I left for Houston. I've got to have you, now."

He pulled back slightly and looked into her eyes. "Would he have nibbled at you ear lobe like this?"

Scott tenderly took the lobe of her ear between his teeth.

"Would he have kissed you on your neck?" Scott asked as his hungry lips traveled down the side of her neck. By the time he reached her nape, he felt the hunger begin to rise within her.

She turned, pressed her parted lips to his and responded with as much feeling as she ever had, more even than on their honeymoon.

"Would he have cupped your breast like this?" Scott whispered as he placed his hand on her breast and began to fondle it tenderly.

Skillfully he unbuttoned her blouse and slid his hand inside where he could feel her breast more intimately. As he moved his hand over her breast and loosened her bra he could feel her nipple begin to firm until it was standing erect between his thumb and forefinger.

"Would the Pegasus-man have placed his hand on your knee like this?" Scott asked as he placed his hand on the inside of her knee and began stroking her thigh higher and higher.

"We shouldn't," she protested breathlessly, placing her hand over his. "Not here."

"Shh," he whispered, "I hear our special star calling, and we're alone on it. There's no one on our special star except you and me." Scott began to sing, "Here am I your special planet, come to me, come..."

Sarah surrendered, releasing the hand that restrained his on the inside of her thigh and guiding it even higher under her shorts.

"Make love to me. Love me," she begged as her lips met his and she responded with all her body.

"Would he have unbuttoned your shorts like this?" Scott asked as he deftly undid the buttons and slid his hand inside her shorts and underpants.

Skillfully, he removed both.

Eagerly Sarah unbuckled Scott's belt and unzipped

his shorts. When she ran her hand underneath his briefs and felt his excitement, she moaned with anticipation.

They undressed each other completely and, lying on their sides facing each other, they continued to caress each other tenderly yet hungrily. Rolling Sarah onto her back, Scott mounted her, feeling the moisture between her legs that eagerly awaited him.

She wrapped her arms around his broad chest and pulled him tightly against her until their erect nipples were touching. He entered her, shallowly at first, penetrating deeper with each thrust.

Sarah met each thrust with her hips. Locking her legs around his narrow waist, she pushed with her heels against his backside as if trying to engulf his entire body into hers.

As ecstasy approached, she sank her fingernails into his shoulders and bit into his arm and chest trying to muffle her scream. At the same moment, she felt all of the tautness of his muscles explode with one last deep thrust.

With a sigh of relief, his rigid body relaxed and Sarah felt the essence of her husband's masculinity flow into her body. He kissed her lightly on the lips then rolled onto his back, pulling her to nestle into his side.

They lay holding each other, gasping for air, saying nothing, feeling only the bliss of the moment. Staring into the starry heavens, each savored the rapturous delight, the feeling of satisfaction, release, completeness, and fulfillment. For a brief moment the two had become one, experiencing a joy beyond all description.

"Thank you. Thank you. Thank you," Scott said, once their breathing had returned to normal. "I needed you badly, and I love you more than ever."

He let out a sigh of contentment. "This loving was better than the first time on our honeymoon."

Sarah rolled onto her side and began to circle his nipple with one finger.

"For a moment," she hesitated then continued, "For a moment, I not only heard your special planet, I was up there floating beside it. It was the strangest, most wonderful feeling. Everything felt so fresh, clean and pure. The planet was silver, and at the same time, a beautiful, lush green, almost the color of the moss we are lying on. That was the best loving you have ever given me. For a moment, I thought I would pass out."

Scott rolled onto his side to face her and said, "Now listen lady. I know I'm good, but you don't have to exaggerate." Then he teased, "I'll leave a big tip."

"You're making fun of me," she pouted.

"No, I'm not," he assured her. "Let me just hold you for another moment before we have to leave our special planet."

He placed an arm under her neck and the other around her waist to hold her closer. Oblivious to the night chill, they continued to stare into the heavens and revel in the closeness and oneness of the moment.

Sarah thought about the many wonderful times they had had making love, but never had there been a time when she had a fantasy as vivid as the one tonight.

She felt she had actually been floating amongst the stars. They had been so close yet she was unable to touch one. She stretched out her arms again and again, but her fingers were unable to touch the star with all of its freshness and purity.

Many times in the future, Sarah would muse this night of ecstatic delight.

8

BEFORE SUNRISE Sunday morning, Robert slipped quietly into his parents' room, tiptoed to Scott's side of the bed, gently shook his father, and whispered, "It's time to go fishing, Dad. Get up and let's go while they're hungry, before Douglass wakes up."

"Go back to bed," Sarah said in a normal voice. "There will be no fishing today. It's Sunday, and we're going to church with your grandparents."

Sarah was the lightest sleeper in the family.

"Why can't I go fishing? This is my vacation too," Robert said stubbornly.

He jumped on the bed and crawled over his father to his mother's side so he could plead more effectively with her. He gave her a big hug, kissed her on her cheek, and said, "Pretty please with sugar on it. May we go fishing?"

"No!" was Sarah's quick and emphatic reply.

"Why can't we go fishing this morning?" Douglass asked as he too entered the room.

"Because we are going to church," Sarah said firmly.

"But it's my vacation too," Douglass whined. "Why do I have to go to church?"

Scott turned on the bedside lamp and scowled at his sons. "You heard your mother. No fishing! We're going to church, and that's that."

He always supported Sarah's disciplining the children. Never would he contradict her in front of them. Frequently their children, like most, tried to play one parent against the other in order to get their way. This never worked in the Walker household because each parent backed the other's decision.

"You heard your mother. Now scoot. And don't forget to smile," Scott ordered.

Disappointed, but not daring to show it, Robert crawled off the bed and started toward the door. When he reached the door where Douglass was still standing, Robert's first impulse was to hit Douglass, or at least say something to him to start a squabble.

Bantering with his brother or sister was one of Robert's favorite pastimes, but the tone of his father's voice had warned him this was not the time to be fussing, even with his brother. So he said to Douglass, "I think I hear Grandpa downstairs. Come on let's go see what he's doing."

Scott rolled over, put his arm under Sarah's neck and shoulders and pulled her toward him. "When can we go on another picnic?"

"Well, certainly not now with those two roaming around and Ann asleep in the adjoining room. Last night will have to do you for awhile," Sarah answered, sympathetically kissing him on the cheek. "I think I smell Daddy's coffee. Come on, let's go downstairs and have a cup with him before breakfast. He usually gets up very early on Sunday for his coffee and newspaper before breakfast."

Before Sarah could move, Scott rolled over on top of her and kissed her passionately. She responded immediately to his hunger, but then pushed him away saying, "We can't, not now. I think I hear Ann walking this way."

"But when?" Scott asked with exaggerated anxiousness.

"Take a cold shower, that will cool you off. Then let's go have that coffee."

She slipped from underneath him, put on her robe and bedroom slippers, and went downstairs. Disappointed, Scott went into the bathroom to shave and shower before joining Sarah and her father in the kitchen.

Kathleen was already preparing Scott's favorite breakfast of ham, grits, and eggs again. Sarah called Ann to come to breakfast. Robert and Douglass, who were throwing the baseball in the yard, heard the call. Immediately they put up the ball and dashed into the house for a hearty breakfast.

Getting the children to dress and be ready to leave for church on time was the usual chaos for Sarah and Scott. When the children were small, Scott frequently felt as if he lost more religion trying to get the children dressed and ready for church than he received after he got there.

Even though they no longer had to dress the children, it took as much effort as ever to get them to dress themselves and be on time.

"Ann won't come out of the bathroom," Robert yelled to his mother.

"Remember what I warned each of you," Sarah called back firmly.

"I'll never understand how Ann can spend so much time in the bathroom dressing," Scott said.

"And until you are a teenage girl, you never will," Sarah quipped.

Ann finally came out of the bathroom, but before Robert could go in, Douglass shoved him aside and went into the bathroom and locked the door.

Robert hammered on the door. "I was next."

"No you weren't," Douglass teased through the door, "On Sunday when we are on vacation, we go from the oldest to the youngest. So I'm next."

"But you stink it up too much," Robert shouted loudly, hoping one of his parents would hear his complaint and come to his aid.

"Again, see what you missed while you were in Houston," Sarah said. "It's your turn to settle this before Mother and Daddy hear them."

Even though Sarah had been an only child and had no brothers or sisters to fuss with, she had a motherly understanding of her children's sibling rivalry, and she had adjusted to their squabbling.

Robert looked up at his father forlornly. "I can't go in there now 'cause Douglass stinks it up too much."

"Maybe he's not using the john," Scott said sympathetically.

"He is," Robert said, nodding furiously. "I heard him grunting. I can even smell it through the door."

"You can't smell through the door," Douglass retorted. "And besides I don't stink it up as much as you do. You're the real stinker in the family."

"Cut it, not another word, either of you," Scott said. "Douglass, turn on the exhaust fan, now! When your mother and I come down, both of you better be downstairs fully dressed and waiting for inspection before going to church. Don't forget, smile like you're happy."

Having heard the stern, military-like order, both boys knew it was time to straighten up and fly right. Scott strutted back to their bedroom where Sarah was applying her makeup.

With a smirk of pride on his face, Scott brushed his shoulder as if to say making the children behave was no problem. He walked over to where Sarah was sitting at the dresser, and while kissing her on the cheek, he teased, "See how easy it is."

Sarah restrained the urge to belt him. "Stay with them 24 hours a day for one week, just one week, and then see how easy you think it is."

"I couldn't do it," Scott said sincerely, "I love our children, and they are very good. But I don't know how you do it 24/7. I love you for it though." He turned her to face him and kissed her with tender meaning.

Kathleen and Charles were already in the yard with the children waiting for Scott and Sarah. All seven of them piled into the van, and Scott drove to the First Presbyterian Church on Main Street in downtown Highlands.

Because they were late, Kathleen knew the parking lot behind the church would probably be full, so she directed Scott to park in front of the church. Parking was allowed in the center of Main Street because it was so wide. Scott found a space immediately.

They rushed up the steep steps to the open doors of the church where they were welcomed by a greeter in the vestibule. The service was beginning and Kathleen noticed the pew where she and Charles usually sat was occupied. They were probably flatland tourists. Because of the large number of tourists, the sanctuary was always more crowded on Sundays during the summer.

The congregation stood for the invocation as the usher led Kathleen, the children and Charles down the right aisle to the seats on the fourth row from the rear of the sanctuary. Sarah and Scott followed, taking seats on the pew immediately behind the others.

At the end of the invocation, the congregation

remained standing for the congregational singing of the morning hymn, which was listed in the church bulletin as "God of Earth and Outer Space." Scott, when he read the title of the hymn, proudly shrugged his shoulders and nudged Sarah as if to indicate it must be fate that had selected that particular hymn for today.

Sarah smiled at him and whispered, "Mother probably requested it to be sung for you. She is so proud of you."

As the congregation began singing, Scott gazed through the tall window immediately beside the pew where he was seated. Multicolored stained glass of irregular shapes surrounded a yellow star and formed an arch at the top of the window. The lower, main part of the window consisted of rectangular panes of antique English leaded glass surrounded by smaller rectangular red panes. The irregularities of the antique translucent panes distorted everything visible through the window, giving objects a mystical sentience.

Sarah nudged Scott and urged him to sing.

"God of earth and outer space,
God of love and God of grace,
Bless the astronauts who fly
As they soar beyond the sky.
God who flung the stars in space,
God who set the sun ablaze,
Fling the space-craft thro' the air,
Let man know your presence there.
God of atmosphere and air,
God of life and planets bare,
Use man's courage and his skill
As he seeks your holy will.
God of depth and God of height,
God of darkness, God of light,
As man walks in outer space,

Teach him how to walk in grace.
God of man's exploring mind,
God of wisdom, God of time,
Launch us from complacency
To a world in need of thee.
God of power, God of might,
God of rockets firing bright.
Hearts ignite and thrust within,
Love for Christ to share with men.
God of earth and outer space,
God who guides the human race,
Guide the lives of seeking youth
In their search for heav-'nly truth.
God who reigns be-low, above,
God of universal love, Love that gave Nativity,
Love that gave us Calvary. Amen"

After the singing ended, Scott sat down with the rest of the congregation and continued to gaze at the words of the hymn he had just sung. He became self-conscious and felt like the entire congregation might be staring at him. At the same time, he was pleased someone cared enough about his being here to sing that particular hymn.

He told himself he must remember to thank Kathleen, if she was the one responsible. He continued to ponder the words:

"Bless the astronauts who fly
As they soar beyond the sky."

The words gave Scott a warm secure feeling. The phrase "beyond the sky" caused him to gaze once again through the window. A tall tree outside the sanctuary was so distorted Scott couldn't tell what type of tree it was, only that it was green.

He gazed above the swaying branches into space where small puffy clouds drifted lazily across the sky. He hoped the lift-off from Kennedy Space Station would be on a clear day, and the sky would not be as hazy as it appeared now through the church windows.

His daydream had him lifting off from the Space Station at that very moment. He imagined he was in command of the spacecraft as its rockets struggled and strained to free it from the grip of the earth's gravity.

He was completely oblivious to what was happening in the sanctuary as he tried to navigate the craft and help lift it above the clouds. He was totally unaware of Reverend Ray McClain announcing he would be reading from the Old Testament.

Scott imagined the feel of the tremendous power of the modified boosters, their increased thrust rocketing the craft through the clouds into the clearness of outer space.

From the pulpit, Reverend McClain announced, "I will be reading selected verses from the sixth, seventh, and eighth chapters of the book of Genesis:
'And God said unto Noah...'"

Every muscle in Scott's body jerked to attention at the words. He felt like he had been struck in the face by a bolt of lightning. His body quivered and became taut, rigid, as if called to attention by the Commandant of the Marine Corps himself.

Snapped out of his daydream, Scott turned his full attention to focus on the minister. His eyes were riveted on the minister's mouth as he continued to speak the passages from the Old Testament.

Sarah felt Scott's body jerk and turned to look at him. She was shocked at how ashen his face appeared.

She nudged him and whispered, "What's wrong?

Are you okay?"

He did not respond. He was not aware of her nudging him. He did not hear her questions. He was transfixed by the words coming from Reverend McClain. The preacher continued:

"The end of all flesh is come before me
For the earth is filled with violence
Through them...I will destroy them
With the earth.
Make thee an ark.
Everything that is in the earth shall die.
But with thee will I establish my covenant.
And take thou unto thee of all food that is eaten.
And it shall be food for thee."

Reverend McClain was a skilled speaker. He had a talent for making everyone in the congregation believe he was speaking solely to them. Always, he was careful to address both sides of the sanctuary. However, this morning it appeared he was directing all of his words to one person on the right side of the sanctuary.

The Reverend's wife, Pauline, noticed this. She always sat in the third pew from the front on the left side of the sanctuary. From where she was sitting, it appeared her husband was reading the scriptures to someone on the right side of the sanctuary.

She shifted ever so slightly on the pew in order to see if she could determine to whom her husband was directing the scripture reading. It appeared to her the Reverend was directing his remarks in the direction of the Douglass and Walker families.

She would have to remind him it was one thing to pay attention to a special guest, but another to ignore the rest of the congregation. She repositioned herself. Yes, she would be sure to remind the Reverend of this immediately following the service.

Reverend McClain continued:

"And the Lord said to Noah
Come thou and all thy house into the ark;
For thee have I seen righteous before me
In this generation,
And Noah did according unto all that the Lord
Commanded him.
And every living substance was destroyed
Which was upon the face of the ground
Both man, and cattle, and the creeping things,
And the fowl of the heaven:
And they were destroyed from the earth:
And Noah only remained alive
And they that were with him in the ark.
And God remembered Noah."

He closed the reading with, "May God bless the reading of His Holy Word."

Scott remained spellbound. "Come thou and all thy house into the ark," kept reverberating through his mind. Perspiration popped out on his forehead.

Again Sarah nudged him and inquired if he was feeling okay. After a moment, Scott shrugged his shoulders to indicate he was okay. He removed the handkerchief from his hip pocket and wiped the perspiration from his brow.

He tried to focus on the anthem the choir was singing, but he was unable to stop the words from echoing over and over again until they were etched indelibly on his conscious and subconscious mind.

Even when Reverend McClain began his sermon, Scott did not hear one word he was saying. Although he was staring at, through, and even beyond the minister, Scott kept hearing only the words of scripture:

"The end of all flesh is come before me... Come thou and thy house into the ark... Come into the ark... Come... The ark, the ark... Come, come, come... The end of all, the end of all..."

He was totally unaware of what was going on until Sarah gave him a hard prod in the ribs. Then he realized she was beginning to rise for the benediction. The choir sang the Choral Amen.

Scott breathed a sigh of relief, not that the worship service was over, but that the words of the scripture about Noah and the ark were no longer racing through his mind.

Before they stepped into the aisle to leave, Sarah asked, "Are you sick? What happened?"

"Honestly, I don't know," Scott replied hesitantly.

Reverend McClain was in the vestibule greeting each member of the congregation as they left the church. Pauline, his wife, was at his side.

The Douglass and Walker families were the last to leave the sanctuary. The minister had some cheerful words for the Walker children and a sincere, warm handshake for Charles and Kathleen. He greeted Sarah with a big hug. Then he turned to Scott and grasped his hand.

Reverend McClain did not shake Scott's hand, but continued to hold it firmly. Their eyes focused intently on each other until the minister said, "It's nice to have you worship with us this morning. I know Kathleen and Charles are enjoying your visit. I hope you heard and understood the scripture reading clearly."

"Yes, I understood it completely," Scott replied softly.

The minister released his hand and Scott followed his family down the steps to the sidewalk in front of the sanctuary.

Several tourists who had attended the service recognized Scott from the many times his name and picture had been in the newspapers and on TV in relation to space flights. Members of the church who had not been able to speak to the Walkers in the sanctuary were also on the sidewalk to greet them.

Kathleen was very pleased to show off her grandchildren, Sarah, and Scott to her friends at the church.

From the front door of the church Reverend McClain waved to the Walkers and Charles and Kathleen as they finally got into their van. As he turned to go back into the vestibule, he mumbled quietly, "For God has seen thee righteous in this generation."

"Who's righteous?" Pauline asked.

"Scott Walker," he said automatically.

"How can you say that?" Pauline asked in surprise. "You don't know him that well."

"You're right," he replied meekly. "I don't know him that well. The words just came out. Something must have inspired me to say that. I don't know why."

"By the way, what did you mean when you told Scott Walker you hoped he heard and understood your scripture reading?" Pauline asked insouciantly.

The Reverend frowned. "I don't recall saying anything like that."

"You must have because Scott said he understood completely," Pauline rebutted.

The Reverend's frown held. "All I recall saying was that it was nice having him and his family worship with us, and that I know Charles and Kathleen are enjoying Sarah, Scott, and the grandchildren being here."

Pauline knew she had heard them speak to each other about the scripture reading. Why did her husband deny it? She was puzzled and also worried about her husband.

"Let's go into the study for a few minutes before

you take me to lunch."

Pauline sat while her husband removed his robe. "Last week you were working on a sermon for this Sunday about salvation, to be accompanied by a scripture reading from the New Testament. When and why did you change your mind?"

"I don't know," her husband said honestly. "I can't give you any reason. I do know when it happened though. Last week when Charles and Kathleen Douglass came by the church, I was in my office working on the sermon for today. I overheard them talking with Paul, the minister of music. Kathleen said something about Scott's upcoming flight into space, and Paul said he knew a most appropriate hymn to sing if it was satisfactory with me.

"Before I knew what I was doing, I erased all of the notes I had made about salvation and the accompanying scripture passages. I began writing the scriptures I read today from Genesis. I have no idea what compelled me to select those passages."

Reverend McClain smiled and looked seriously at his wife. "Could I possibly have been motivated by God? At the time I didn't know why, but I know now. I was compelled to read that scripture passage to Scott Walker. Now that it's done, I feel a great sense of relief."

Pauline looked at her husband and said, " Ray McClain, I love you. I am very proud of you, and yes, God could have inspired you to read those passages and every word you preached in your sermon. You are that kind of minister."

She rose from her chair, walked to her husband and kissed him on his forehead. They held each other closely.

"So, where are you taking me for lunch today?"

AS SCOTT DROVE from the parking spot, Sarah asked, "What did Reverend McClain mean when he said he hoped you heard and understood the scripture reading clearly?"

"When did he say that?"

"He said it to you while he was holding your hand. You must have heard him because you said you understood it completely."

"I don't recall anything like that, and I have no idea what happened to me during the service. But everything's okay now."

Because the children and her parents were in the van, Sarah did not press the matter further. Like Pauline, she was very puzzled about what happened, and she would continue to ponder it.

As they drove away from the church, Kathleen announced Charles was taking all of them to lunch at the Veranda, a restaurant beside Lake Toxaway. Her Christmas present from Charles each year was Sunday lunch at a restaurant of her choice for a year. Not having to cook on Sunday was, in her mind, one of the best presents any husband could give to his wife.

Sarah told Scott to remember that next Christmas and every Christmas thereafter.

MONDAY MORNING, Sarah, Scott and the children said their goodbyes to Charles and Kathleen and drove to Atlanta to catch a flight back to Florida and home.

9

AFTER RETURNING from Highlands, Scott was extremely busy at the Kennedy Space Center trying to catch up after his vacation.

Today was no different. It had been a typical, but long, physically and mentally exhausting day. When he arrived home, Ann, Douglass, and Robert were playing soccer in the yard. Although Scott was tired and stressed after an extraordinarily long day at the center, he took off his jacket and joined his children in the game. He was dedicated to, and enjoyed, spending time with his children.

Ann was the most coordinated and athletically gifted of the three. She relished competition, especially physical contact, yet, five minutes later she could be the most delicate, ladylike girl. Her transformation from one character to the other was almost like Jekyl and Hyde.

In the house, Sarah paused from her supper preparation and, with pride, watched her family through the kitchen window. A feeling of the warmth and security of family and love came over her.

She went to the door and called them to come to supper. All four came into the kitchen, still arguing about who had won. The children had inherited their father's competitiveness.

Sarah reminded them they had time to wash and cool down before the meal was ready. The children went to their rooms. Douglass and Robert shared a bedroom and bath. Ann had her own bath and bedroom.

When they returned to the kitchen, Scott was seated at the head of the table, his usual place. Ann sat on his right. Douglass and Robert sat on his left, and Sarah was seated at the opposite end of the table. Robert held the chair for his mother to be seated when she brought the last bowl of food to the table.

The spread was a family favorite: meat loaf, mashed potatoes and gravy, green beans and biscuits with Grandma Kathleen's homemade apple butter. A huge bowl of freshly cut fruit would be dessert.

Robert took a sip of iced tea and, smacking his lips, said, "Mama, you make the best tea in the whole world. It's so good, mmm. What a cool way to celebrate a win."

"Robert, we gave them a lesson today. Didn't we, partner?" Scott said.

"There will be no gloating at the table," Sarah reprimanded her husband. "First, we join hands to thank God for the blessings of this day. Scott, you lead."

Scott prayed, "Our heavenly father we praise you and give you thanks for this beautiful day, our wonderful health, this food and the hands that have prepared it. We pray you will bless this food to the nourishment of our bodies that we may better serve you. Amen."

Before Robert turned his mother's hand loose, he added, "And p.s. God, please teach Ann not to cheat at games."

Ann quickly added, "God, help baby Robert to stop being a poor loser."

Then Sarah added, "And God, please, please, may they stop fussing and fighting. Amen. Now let's eat."

Eating together at mealtime was a hard and fast rule in the Walker home. Prayer before a meal was not just a ritual. It was a necessity, prayed from the heart with meaning.

Sarah also insisted the children get up early enough to dress and sit down together to enjoy breakfast before dashing off their separate ways. She would not tolerate any of the children scooping up a doughnut from the table and rushing off to school.

Breakfast was also a time to share what each was planning for the day, just like supper was time for each person to share the events of the day. Frequently, Douglass, Robert, or Ann would have some of their friends for supper.

Sarah and Scott always welcomed their children's friends. The friends of the children enjoyed coming to the Walker home for supper because, Mrs. Walker, as they called her, was the best cook in the neighborhood.

Subconsciously the children's friends envied the rules established in the Walker home. The Walker children knew what they could do and what they were not allowed to do. Each Walker child was well aware of what was expected of him or her and what their role and responsibility in and to the family was.

Although they complained about them at times, the children's responsibilities were properly assigned. By fulfilling that responsibility, each child received a feeling of being an essential part of the family. It established a sense of pride in each child, and a tremendous sense of security.

After supper, Scott and Sarah excused themselves, left the table and went to the screened gazebo in the backyard. Sarah saw to it she and Scott had time just for each other. This child-free time gave them a chance to stay connected.

It was the children's responsibility to clear the table, put away the leftover food and clean the kitchen completely. After that they would go to their rooms to study and do homework, if there was any.

No television was allowed on school nights except for the early news. Scott encouraged them to watch the news because he wanted them to know what was going on in the world. After studying, each child would bathe and be in bed before 9:30 p.m.

A gentle breeze was sighing through the screen of the gazebo as Scott and Sarah sat on the glider. They rocked gently back and forth.

After a long silence, Sarah said, "I just couldn't resist adding to Robert's post script during the blessing. The fussing has been going on since they learned to talk. Their constant bickering and picking at each other drives me crazy, and I get so tired of it. Sometimes, I think they literally hate each other. Thank goodness they're in school. That lets me get away from the fussing for a few hours."

"God must have given you something special in order for you to stay with our children all day," Scott said. "I don't know how you do it. I couldn't. But hang in there, as the old saying goes, 'This too shall pass.'

"Their fussing and fighting is just normal sibling rivalry. Last week when I picked them up after school, an older student was picking on Robert. Actually he was astride Robert on the ground pummeling him in the face.

"Before I could get out of the car, Douglass and Ann stepped in and pulled the bully off. Ann literally gave him a bloody nose. I overheard her telling the guy to never let her see or hear about his touching her brother again.

"Our children bicker constantly, but heaven help the person who picks on one of them. I was so proud of Douglass and Ann, and I even heard Robert thank them."

By the time Scott and Sarah came back into the house, the children had completed their chores, studied, bathed, and were fast asleep in bed.

Sarah and Scott bathed and soon Sarah was asleep in Scott's arms. Although he was mentally stressed and physically exhausted by a long day at the launch site, he found sleep a long time coming.

A SINGLE DROP of rain splattered on a single green blade of grass beside Scott's head. He was lying on his back where he had picnicked with Sarah in Highlands.

He turned to watch the fractured drop of water slide down the shaft of the blade and disappear into a clump of grass. A larger drop of rain fell on a single blade of grass on his other side and he turned to watch it roll down and melt into the cluster of blades.

Another drop fell on his right then on his left.

The raindrops became larger and larger and fell faster and faster. Drops of rain were falling all over his body now, but he did not feel wet.

Soon the rain was coming down in torrents. The ground became saturated, and there was no place for the water to go. Scott felt like he was actually lying in water. The thought entered his mind the water would soon cover his body and he would drown.

Still lying on his back, he felt the water rise to the level of his ears. He strained to get up, but could not. He could not lift his hands, arms or legs from the grass. He was totally immobilized and helpless.

He felt as if each blade of grass had sprouted tentacles, which pierced deeply into his back and wrapped around his arms and legs. The tentacles constrained Scott completely, preventing any movement.

The deluge continued, and the water felt cool to his body. Scott attempted to see through squinted eyes as the heavy rain fell on his face. The cool water began to feel warm and he saw flashes of jagged lightning zigzag across an ominous sky, creating an eerie yellowness. Thunder exploded overhead.

Panic gripped his body. An extra large drop of rain fell close to his right side. Instead of splattering and forming a circle of ripples, the raindrop instantly burst into a yellow, candle-like flame.

Scott wanted to extinguish the flame with his hand, but the blades of grass kept a vice-like grip on his hands and arms as he struggled to free himself. He could not extinguish the flame.

A large drop of rain fell on his left side, also bursting into yellow flame. Again, he tried desperately to free himself, but was unable to move. The falling raindrops turned into sinister, yellow spheres that burst into flames the moment they touched the earth.

Scott was petrified when the first yellow ball fell on his chest and burst into a small flame, but he felt no pain or burning sensation. His body was soon covered with small flames.

A bright speck appeared in the sky directly over Scott's head. The speck enlarged and moved closer and closer. At first, it looked like an elliptical disc. It became as brilliant as the midday sun, but it did not blind him.

He looked directly at the disc without having to squint or shade his eyes. The disc became larger and larger until it hovered directly over Scott's body. A hazy mist surrounded the circle, and human lips appeared in

the haze. The lips moved, and a voice called out saying:
"And God said unto Noah
The end of all flesh is come before me
For the earth is filled with violence through them...
I will destroy them with the earth.
Make thee an ark.
Everything that is in the earth shall die.
But with thee will I establish my covenant.
And take thou unto thee of all food that is eaten.
And it shall be food for thee.
And the Lord said to Noah
Come thou and all thy house into the ark.
For thee have I seen righteous before
Me in this generation.
And Noah did according unto all that the Lord com-
manded him.
And every living substance was destroyed
Which was upon the face of the ground
Both man, and cattle, and the creeping things,
And the foul of the heaven
And they were destroyed from the earth
And Noah only remained alive
And they that were with him in the Ark.
And God remembered Noah".

The brilliant disc flew away and came to rest like a Star of David, glistening atop the space shuttle, Constitution, standing on the launch pad at the Kennedy Space Center.

In the misty haze lips moved and called, "Come! Come Scott into your ark. The end of all flesh is come before me. Everything that is in the earth shall die. But with thee I will establish my covenant. Come thou and all thy house into the ark."

Reassuringly, the voice called louder, hypnotically

from the Star of David atop the space shuttle, "Come! Come Scott into your ark! Come thou and all thy house into your ark!"

All at once, Scott freed himself from the stranglehold of the grass and ran through the flames toward the space shuttle. Bombs exploded in fiery mushroom clouds all around him.

He searched frantically for Sarah and their children in the flaming chaos. The smoke from the exploding bombs stifled him. He attempted to call to his family, but he could not utter a sound. He was speechless.

Bombs continued to fall and explode. The earth trembled. As he dashed toward the capsule, the earth parted. Buildings and people fell into the scorching crevasse. In a frenzy, Scott fell to his knees and flailed his arms toward the heavens in despair.

Awakened by Scott thrashing in the bed covers, Sarah shook him forcefully. "What's wrong?"

Still half-asleep and dazed, Scott grabbed her protectively and demanded, "Where are the children? I can't find the children!"

"You must be dreaming. The children are in bed," Sarah said reassuringly as she cradled his head to her breast and gently massaged his sweating temples.

"God, it was awful," Scott mumbled "It was more like a nightmare than a dream."

He shook as if he had chills and fever.

"Your pajamas are soaked. Do you have a fever?"

"I don't think so. I dreamed I was running. I couldn't find you or the children."

"We're all safe." Sarah said soothingly. "Tell me about it."

Pensively, Scott began, "It was so strange. Everything was so urgent and ominous. Now this may sound really crazy to you, but those lips, there was something very reassuring about those lips."

"Lips?" Sarah asked, her feminine curiosity roused. "What lips? Whose lips? Start at the beginning and tell me every little detail. I mean every little detail."

Scott began with his lying on the grass in the meadow at Highlands. He described the rain, being tied to the ground by the blades of grass and the rain turning to fire that did not burn him.

He told her about the mist surrounding the brilliant disc and how the lips spoke to him. He told her of the earth shaking and splitting open, and the buildings and people falling into the crack.

He told her how the disc moved atop the space shuttle like the Star of David and how the voice called to him to come. He described his panic when bombs exploded and he was unable to find her or their children.

"You poor thing," Sarah said sympathetically as she squeezed him tighter in her arms. "It's no wonder you're sweating so."

She held him reassuringly for several more moments, and then she said, "I wish you had not told me this before we had breakfast. Now it could come true."

"Don't be ridiculous. You and your superstitions," Scott teased.

He got out of bed, took a shower, and put on some dry pajamas. When he returned, he said, "Turn over so I can hold you and let's go back to sleep. I have a difficult schedule tomorrow."

He held her snugly and kissed her lightly on the nape of her neck. They lay very quiet and still, absorbed with deep meditations about the dream.

Suddenly Scott bolted upright in bed. "Those lips! Those were the lips of Reverend McClain."

It took awhile for Sarah and Scott to fall asleep again and then the telephone rang. Usually Sarah answered the telephone when it rang in the night, but because Scott was the light sleeper tonight, he answered it with a grumpy hello.

There was a long silence. Thinking it might be a crank call, wrong number, or even a telemarketer at this ridiculous hour, Scott practically bellowed, "Hello!"

"Scott, it's me," the voice at the other end said apologetically. "It's John, John Johnston. I am sorry to call at this hour. I forgot you are 10 hours behind me. Will you be around the Kennedy Space Center next week? I need to see you as soon as I can get there."

"Yes," Scott answered reflexively.

"Good. I'll see you in a couple of days. Again I'm sorry about the late hour."

Before Scott could say anything, John hung up.

"Who was that?" Sarah mumbled sleepily.

"He said John Johnston, but I couldn't tell for sure. It was a bad connection, and he said he was 10 hours ahead of us. He must be on the other side of the world."

10

AFTER JOHN AND SHARON'S FLIGHT landed in Columbia, S. C., they said their goodbyes and Sharon caught a flight to San Francisco. Still shaken by Raj's assassination, John continued to try to come to a conclusion about who was responsible.

Was Raj assassinated by a foreign power? Could the heinous act have been perpetrated by another division of the CIA? John shuddered at the thought but admitted it was possible.

What he needed was a long, hot shower and a restful night's sleep. Tomorrow he would report to Neil Anderson at LAD.

Before he left Columbia for Reagan National Airport, he checked his voice mail at LAD and his apartment. There were no messages at the office, however a coded message was recorded on the answering service at his apartment.

The urgent message suggested time was of the essence, and John should be in Seoul, South Korea sooner than ASAP.

He immediately made reservations on the next flight to Vancouver, BC. He would have time to go to his apartment and shower. Sleep? No. Neil Anderson? He would have to wait for John's report until he returned from Korea.

John's plane arrived in Vancouver in time for him to purchase a ticket to Seoul. He never purchased round trip tickets. He purchased tickets to each stop on the way. This made it more difficult for anyone to follow him or track his movements. However, on his return trips, he usually flew as direct to his final destination as possible.

After landing in Seoul, John telephoned his contact. A female voice answered the phone in polite Korean. When John asked, in English, to speak with Sam, the voice on the other end of the phone quivered, regained its composure, and in a distinct British accent inquired, "Is this Bubba?"

"Yes."

Bubba was the alias John had used in communicating with Sam. There was a long pause, and John could hear an attempt to muffle a cry.

The person continued, "I am Sam's wife."

She broke down and began to cry. Finally she composed herself and continued softly, "Sam is dead. He was killed two days ago by a bomb during a meeting with an infiltrator from the North. No one has claimed responsibility, and the authorities are not investigating the incident. Sam had left me a message to open in case he did not return.

"I opened it yesterday and the message said when Bubba calls, tell him not to come here. Also tell him it may not be safe for him to go home because the North is sending his Uncle Sam a big message soon. That is all the note says."

She began to sob uncontrollably.

"I am very sorry about your loss," John said, his

mind spinning. "I would like to see you to express my condolences personally, but from what the note says, it is best I not come there, for your safety as well as mine. I thank you for this information, and I am very sorry."

He hung up the telephone.

John's mind spun as he tried to sort out all of the meanings in Sam's message. Someone was sending a big message to Uncle Sam? What kind of message? Don't come here? Don't go home? Why?

Slowly, John's mind began to clear. Regardless of the warning, his first impulse was to leave South Korea as soon as possible. He had to go home immediately. There was nothing else in Korea for him, and he had to make a report to his boss.

Most importantly, he had to talk with Scott Walker. John decided to call Scott even though it was after midnight in Florida.

He boarded the next plane to Chicago's O'Hare. From there he flew to Dulles International and went to his apartment for a much needed rest and to clean up before reporting to Neil Anderson at LAD. John had no idea what he would tell Anderson about the meeting with Raj in the Bahamas, but he decided he would not mention this trip to South Korea.

11

THE MONITOR APPROVED John's palm and the gates to Equus Estates opened promptly so he could pass through. The drive through the pastures and orchards was as impressive as ever as the young colts frolicked around their mothers.

He parked in his usual spot in front of the mansion. When he entered the mansion, the floral arrangements in the foyer were a mixture of a dozen different varieties of brightly colored flowers.

In the pantry, his palm print opened the door to the elevator that led to the basement. Each security checkpoint all the way to Anderson's office worked perfectly. Everything looked normal, yet John was extremely nervous. The hairs on the back of his neck began to rise.

When John entered his boss's office, Anderson was seated behind his elaborate, walnut desk shuffling papers. A balding 66 year old with narrow, beady eyes, Neil Anderson had been with the CIA in various capacities since his graduation from Columbia University. He was a very impersonal, nothing-but-the-facts individual who was devoted fanatically to his profession.

Without acknowledging or greeting John, Anderson

emphatically said, "I have just received a new directive from The Hill emphasizing there are to be no reports or leaks of information that could compromise or negate the policies the present administration is advocating and sanctioning. I hope you comprehend fully that directive, and you will abide it."

The stern warning sent shivers up John's spine, but he tried to not let it show. Anderson continued to arrange papers and finally sealed them in a manila folder. Without even looking at John, Anderson succinctly asked, "Well?"

Anderson's cooler than usual reception irritated and, at the same time, frightened John. He really wanted to reply, "Well what?"

Because he was as dedicated to his job as Anderson, John refrained from saying anything.

Anderson continued, "How was your assignation with your confederate from San Francisco?"

Anderson's insinuation the Bahamas trip had been an excuse for a tryst really angered John. He could feel the blood rushing to his head and cheeks and prayed Anderson did not notice. He recalled Anderson's snide remarks when John requested Sharon accompany him to the Bahamas.

The first time they met, John thought Anderson was suspicious of everyone, especially him. Since that time, nothing had happened to change John's mind. Maybe Anderson was envious of the success John had in his work. In any case, Anderson's personality made him perfect for the clandestine, covert activity of the Listening Arm Division of the CIA.

"God, she's a looker," Anderson said, obviously referring to Sharon. John's first impulse was to reach across the desk and smash his boss in the mouth.

Instead he coughed lightly and said, "My contact did

not show."

As soon as the words were out of his mouth, John wondered what he was doing. Had he gone crazy? What was wrong with him? It was idiotic to lie to a superior. Superior. That was the problem. Anderson thought — no Anderson knew he was superior, superior to John anyway.

Stay calm, old boy, John said to himself, *Stay calm.* He tried to slow his racing heartbeat. He had never lied to any boss in the past, never turned in false expenses, or padded his account in any way. Everything about his work had been above reproach, so why now? Why such a blatant lie?

John's questions were answered when Anderson replied, "Did you really have a meeting arranged in the first place? I hope she was worth it."

John shifted in his chair slightly to help conceal his urge to knock Anderson's teeth down his throat. Because he wanted to keep his job, he would not give in to that urge. He sincerely believed the work he did contributed to the national security of the United States.

"'My contact did not show.' Is that your report?" Anderson asked.

"Yes," John said with finality, staring directly into his boss's suspicious, accusing eyes. "My contact did not show."

Anderson finally turned away from the glare in John's gaze and reached for another manila folder, indicating the meeting was over.

"Any messages for me?" John asked as he rose from his chair.

Anderson replaced the file he was holding, opened the file drawer, pulled out a thin folder and handed it to John.

"If that's all," John said, taking the file, "I will be in

my office filing my report."

"That shouldn't take long," quipped Anderson, adding, "By the way, your wife called just this morning to say she and Beth would be at her parents' compound in Ft. Lauderdale."

John took the folder and closed the door gently as he left the room, so as not to reveal his anger to Anderson. He walked hurriedly down the narrow corridor toward his cubbyhole office.

Someday he would confront Anderson to find out what the problem between them really was. He had no idea what made his immediate boss so suspicious of him, but then again, Anderson was suspicious of everyone in the organization.

Come to think of it, everyone connected with LAD was that way, well almost everyone. It seemed no one trusted anyone, and backstabbing was the norm. At times like this, John wondered why he stayed. He hoped it was not because he was as non-trusting as Anderson or a gifted back-stabber like so many at LAD.

The thought made him shudder because he believed he stayed in the organization to gather information that could, in some small way, be helpful in preserving the American way of life. To many, it might sound pretentiously patriotic, but that was his reason for staying with the organization.

When John reached office # 7, he opened the door to the small, sparsely furnished room. With its small metal desk and the chair with a green vinyl cushion, the office looked exactly as it had before he went to The Bahamas.

Attached to the desk was a credenza with his computer and printer. There were no pictures on the walls, no plaques, no government seals, no nothing.

John's room was much different from Neil Anderson's plush office with its walnut furnishings and sumptuous executive leather swivel chair. The one personal thing in John's office was the bi-fold Baldwin Brass picture frame containing wallet size photos of Frances and Beth.

He picked up the frame and stared at each picture for several moments. Beth was even more beautiful than the last time he had looked at her photo.

He focused on Frances's portrait. Why did she have to leave him? What had he done to cause her to no longer love him? With a deep breath of resolution, he decided he was not giving her up. They had to work this out, they would work it out, whatever the problem was.

He placed the photos back on the desk. He didn't dare call Frances from here because all calls are recorded. He would call her tonight. His week to be with his daughter was coming up soon.

His vision focused again on Beth's picture and he mumbled softly to her image, "Don't worry, I will always be there for you, and I will always protect you."

John turned to the computer, completing and printing his report on the Bahamas trip in a matter of minutes. It confirmed the lie he had told to Anderson.

He realized he must contact Sharon to let her know what he told Anderson. It would be just like Anderson to call Sharon to see if she would confirm John's report.

Sharon would not have to make a report to the FBI. As far as that organization was concerned, she had been on personal leave. If Anderson should see, by chance, a report of Raj's death in Nassau, that would confirm why John did not make contact. Probably Anderson would not find out when Raj died.

Reasoning all of this, he was relieved he had not accidentally dropped Raj's name to Anderson. Still, that did little to relieve John's conscience about having lied to his boss.

12

AFTER FILING his report, John flew to Orlando, rented a car and drove directly to the house Scott and Sarah had rented for the summer.

They had chosen Winter Park because it was a short commute to the John F. Kennedy Space Center, but it was also far enough away that Scott could relax and escape from the stress of the upcoming flight when he came home at the end of the day.

John drove around Winter Park to familiarize himself with the streets, especially the highway leading to the space center. It was late afternoon when he located Scott's house. The address was 1001 Memory Lane.

He parked the car around the corner from the house. From here he had a good view of anyone approaching Scott's house from any direction. He enjoyed watching a girl and two boys playing baseball on the front lawn.

He had been there about 15 minutes when he noticed a minivan pull into the driveway. He watched as Scott got out of his car. The girl was the first to rush over and give Scott a big hug. Both boys followed. Scott removed his jacket and began to play ball with them.

The game was getting exciting and competitive when Sarah came to the porch and called them to come to supper. Scott was at bat and struck out, giving him an excuse to be the first one to the porch where he kissed and hugged his wife.

John watched as the children picked up the markers they had placed on the lawn for bases and the rest of their equipment and entered the house. He sat there a long time absorbing the beautiful scenario of family life he had just observed. He thought about the wonderful, happy memories being made at 1001 Memory Lane. It was an appropriate address.

John truly envied Scott's life. He believed he, Frances, and Beth had come close to experiencing that same wondrous life. John had married Frances, his college sweetheart, whom he loved with every fiber of his being, and they had a beautiful, healthy daughter. He had had it all, that is, until Frances shocked him by announcing she was leaving him.

The three of them were at home eating supper one night when Frances looked directly into his eyes and coldly announced, "I no longer love you. I'm leaving."

Beth was too young to comprehend what her mother meant by saying she was leaving, but the child fully understood Frances saying she did not love him. Tears ran down Beth's cheeks, and John wiped them away with his napkin. Frances left the table while he tried to console their daughter.

Immediately after Beth was born, Frances told him Beth would be his one and only child by her. At the time, John thought her remarks were prompted by the pain of childbirth. He now believed Frances never wanted to have children, period.

He was thankful he had been able to persuade her to have Beth instead of having an abortion. Recalling

Frances's statement that Beth would be his one and only child by her, he realized she might have been considering leaving him even then.

Slowly it began to sink in. Maybe she never had truly loved him. These thoughts troubled John's mind until he realized it was almost dark. Surely Scott and his family would have finished eating supper by now.

John went to the front door and rang the doorbell. Robert opened the door.

"You must be Robert," John said with a smile.

"Yes. I am, but do I know you?" Robert replied with a puzzled look on his face.

"No. You don't. I am a friend of your daddy. Your dad and I went to college together. We were even in the same fraternity, Lambda Chi. I also know your mother."

"In that case, come in. At first I thought you were some kind of salesman. Daddy, Mama, someone is here to see y'all," Robert called as he led John to the living room. "Have a seat. They'll be here in a minute."

Shortly Scott and Sarah entered, followed by Ann and Douglass. Scott was startled when John rose to greet them. He did not look like the same John Johnston he had seen in Atlanta. He was dressed in a navy blue suit, with a white shirt and neatly knotted conservative tie. This was the way Scott had always seen John when they attended State.

Because of the way John had acted in Atlanta, Scott gave him a cool reception. Sarah, however, gave John a warm welcome. After introducing the children, Sarah reminded them they needed to finish cleaning the kitchen, bathe, and complete their homework.

The children were in a year-round school. After shaking his hand and telling John they enjoyed meeting him, the children excused themselves and went to do as they had been told.

Sarah had noticed Scott's cool greeting so she sat on the sofa beside John, and said, "Scott told me about seeing you in Atlanta. I want to hear all about Frances and your daughter, Beth."

Beaming with pride, John said, "Beth is a beautiful nine year old, the image of her mother. There isn't much to tell about Frances. She has filed for divorce, but I still love her very much and hope we can get back together.

"The last time she and I talked, she said there was no possibility of that happening. I guess I will just have to accept losing her, but I will never give up my daughter, never. Right now Frances has custody. I have visiting rights one week a year, but I am appealing that decision."

"I'm very sorry," Sarah said with genuine sympathy.

Before she could continue, John interrupted, "Scott, I want to sincerely apologize to you for the way I acted at Hartsfield. I know I've always been stupidly secretive. I was even more so that day because I was on a mission. That's why I was dressed the way I was."

John chuckled slightly and continued, "I was trying to travel incognito. I remember your exact words when you told me to cut the bullshit. Excuse me, Sarah. Scott, would it be best if I talked with you alone?"

"As far as I am concerned, it's fine for Sarah to be in on the conversation."

"To put it as candidly as possible," John continued, "the bottom line is, I am a spy."

Scott and Sarah were obviously startled and John was a little reluctant to continue. He knew he could rely on Scott's confidentiality, but he questioned Sarah's not divulging the facts he was going to share with them. John looked at Sarah intently, pleading with her silently not to relate to anyone what he was about to tell them.

"Of course I have a much more respectable title: National Security Agent with the CIA," John went on,

"But really, I'm just a spy."

He did not mention the LAD section of the CIA. As far as the government was concerned, LAD did not exist. It was an unacknowledged branch of the CIA.

John continued, "Scott, I wanted to share some of this information with you in Atlanta. I didn't know why, but I wanted to. Too many ears were listening. In my work, one can never be too careful. You see, I'm suspicious of everyone, just like I was when you and I were at State. I guess that's why I've lived this long and been as successful as I have in this business."

John took a deep breath and plunged in, "Recently, I've learned much of the tension in the world today goes back to the cold war struggle between the USA and USSR With the collapse of the Soviet Union and the disarmament treaties between the two countries, the USA was deluded into thinking the cold war was over. For many of the die-hard, former Soviet military communists, the cold war never ended, and it never will.

"The disarmament treaty between the U.S. and USSR was a farce. Countless Soviet missiles were not destroyed as they were supposed to be. Instead, they were smuggled out by communist officers, sold and shipped to Iran, Iraq, Libya, China and North Korea.

"Two of the missiles almost made it to Cuba. It is not known where they are now. Also, the United States did not dismantle all of their nuclear-armed intercontinental ballistic missiles as the treaty called for.

"At least six missiles were camouflaged and left completely armed intact in underground silos in mid western states. The four missiles in Iraq were dismantled and the nuclear bombs were buried in extremely deep, abandoned oil wells. They are still armed and can be detonated remotely.

"It all goes back to a struggle between capitalism

and communism. To many, that struggle is still going on. There is also a struggle between ideologies: different cultures, different religions, and different economies. The struggle between Israelis and Palestinians is just the tip of the iceberg. A conflict between Islam and Christianity is lurking in the background. A devastating conflict is coming and soon. No place on this planet will be safe.

"I was on my way to the Bahamas when I saw you in Atlanta. I met with an agent in Nassau. That's where I learned some of this. The agent warned me to be careful to whom I reported this information. You see, this is contrary to what our government is saying. That's why I haven't even told my immediate boss any of this. Reporting this would get me into a lot of trouble.

"The entire government seems to be deluding itself into believing all is well between the U.S. and the rest of the world. All is not well, but our government does not want to hear anything otherwise.

"The government advocates the rest of the world loves good, old America. The administration will not tolerate anything contrary to their thinking. Whoever would propose anything otherwise would be eliminated quietly. That's why I lied to my boss.

"For the first time ever, I filed a false report. I reported I did not meet my contact in Nassau. I was afraid to voice what I learned to my superiors because I actually fear for my well being. My contact in the Bahamas was assassinated there, and I no longer feel safe at the office or anywhere."

John sighed. "For some reason, I feel relieved I've shared this with you. I had to tell someone, and I guess you're it. You're probably pondering why I'm telling you. Really, I'm wondering about that too. I just don't know.

"Sometimes I feel like a voice crying out in the wilderness. I'm afraid to say anything at work, and I do not feel safe, especially with my immediate boss. When I saw you in Atlanta and knew you would be going into space soon, something told me you could help me with my dilemma. I haven't figured out how."

Suddenly John's facial expression changed to a look of excitement. "I know why I had to tell you! No place on this planet will be safe for Beth except your space craft."

John paused, startled when he realized what he had said. Scattered pieces of his dilemma began to fall into place. Protection of Beth was his ultimate priority.

Scott and Sarah sat in stunned silence trying to get a grasp on what John had told them.

"Frightening, isn't it?" John said softly.

"If you're saying what I'm hearing, it's more than frightening," Scott said. "It's an inconceivable horror. How certain are you this is going to happen, and when?"

"From what I have learned so far, there's no doubt in my mind a worldwide conflict is in the making. In the past, wars have been specifically drawn battle lines between nations. This will be a struggle between nations, cultures, religions, ideologies, and economies — the have and the have not.

"Unlike any other war before, this will be global devastation by terrorists from all over the planet. When it will happen, I don't know, but I believe it will be very soon."

John paused, frowning. "Now that I've figured out how you, by being the commander of the next space flight, fit into the scheme of things, I am relieved Now I have to figure out a way to get Beth on that ship with you."

Looking at his watch, he stood abruptly, "It's getting

late. I should go now."

"You're more than welcome to stay the night here," Sarah offered.

John shook his head. "Thanks, but I have to catch a plane back to D.C. tonight. Tell your children goodbye for me."

Scott and Sarah accompanied John to the front door. Scott shook his hand firmly. Sarah gave him a hug and said, "I hope things can be resolved between you and Frances. If we can help in any way, please let us know."

"Thanks," John said as he walked to his rental car. He glanced at his watch again and saw he would have to hurry if he was going to catch the direct shuttle from Orlando to Reagan National.

Sarah and Scott remained on the porch, their arms around each other. They watched silently until the taillights of John's car disappeared in the distance.

"Just hold me," Sarah whispered, "After that, I really need to be held."

"He must be going crazy, if he hasn't cracked up already," Scott said as he wrapped both arms around Sarah and held her securely. "Although he may be absolutely right about different ideologies, that part about Soviet generals having smuggled nuclear weapons to middle eastern nations and North Korea is hardly plausible.

"I have a hard time believing it, but then again, anything is possible. The U.S. may not have dismantled their nuclear missiles as they promised to do."

"Although it is farfetched, I can believe it," Sarah said. "Some people never forget or give up. As for me, I would like to forget John even came here tonight."

"Not me," Scott said.

"Why?"

"I'm wondering if there could be a correlation

between what John said about the space capsule being safe for Beth and the nightmares I'm having about the shuttle. Maybe something supernatural is going on."

Sarah shivered. "Let's go in. Either it's getting cold or what you're saying is giving me the chills. Oh, Scott what are we going to do?"

13

THREE WEEKS had passed since Scott returned to Kennedy Space Center from Highlands. On this morning, he checked in earlier than usual. Opening his e-mail, he found an order for him to meet Harry McDonald, his boss, at the Johnson Space Center in Houston ASAP.

Scott requisitioned an F-15 from the center so he could fly to Houston. He called Sarah from his office to tell her he would be leaving immediately and would call her from Houston after his meeting with McDonald. He had never received an order in the form of an e-mail from his boss. The message had a feeling of urgency.

After he was airborne, he telephoned McDonald's office and told the secretary he was on his way and would arrive about 1 p.m., Houston time. He added he would call when he arrived at the airport to set up a definite meeting time and place.

Scott landed in Houston exactly on schedule. Promptly, he telephoned McDonald's private number. Much to Scott's surprise, McDonald's private secretary, Abigail Spencer, answered.

After Scott identified himself, Abigail said, "Scott, Mr. McDonald said to give you his thanks for coming to play golf with him this afternoon. He said there's no need for you to come by the office. He'll meet you at Forest Hills Country Club at 2 p.m., his reserved tee off time."

"That's all?" Scott asked anxiously.

"That's all Mr. McDonald told me to tell you," Abigail replied. "I hope you have a good round of golf, but be sure to let the boss win. It will be much easier for everyone. When you return home, please give my regards to Sarah and your children."

Scott thanked Abigail for the message, folded his cell phone, and placed it in his vest pocket.

On the drive to Forest Hills Country Club, Scott thought something had to be wrong. Harry's e-mail was so brief and urgent. Why hadn't he just telephoned or left a message on Scott's recorder? All this rush and Harry McDonald wanted just to play golf? He couldn't believe it.

He didn't even like the sport, especially when he lost. Harry had him fly all the way to Houston for a round of golf? Something was up. Something was wrong. One thing was certain, he would find out what was going on soon enough.

Scott went directly to the pro shop when he arrived at the country club. He was told Harry McDonald was waiting for him outside where the golf carts were parked.

Sure enough, Harry was seated on a golf cart, waiting to go to the first tee. Dressed in golf knickers and two-tone black and white wing-tipped golf shoes, he looked as if he were going to lead the tee off for the Masters in Augusta.

"Get in," Harry barked. "Hopefully we can get in 18 before dark."

"What are you trying to do, psyche me out?" Scott

asked, smiling. "You're dressed up like some 1940s PGA champion, and I don't even have golf shoes."

"Just get in the cart. You won't need golf shoes. We're not going to play that seriously today. I have an extra set of clubs in the cart for you."

"By not letting me wear spikes, you're making sure I lose," Scott said.

Harry was dressed like a professional but he wasn't going to play seriously. Who did he think he was kidding? Well, Scott would humor him anyway. He sat down on the golf cart, and Harry drove to the first tee.

"You're the guest. Hit away," Harry said. "Give me something to shoot at."

After taking a couple of practice swings, Scott placed his ball on the tee and did as he was told. He drove the ball about 150 yards straight down the middle of the fairway.

"How's that?" Scott asked with a proud smirk.

"Not bad," Harry acknowledged, "but it really wasn't very long. A quarter says I'll outdistance you by at least 25 yards."

"You're on."

Harry's drive was much more than 25 yards farther than Scott's, but it sliced through the woods out of bounds.

"I win," Harry said. "The bet didn't say it had to be straight, just longer. Pay up."

"Since it's out of bounds, don't you want to hit another?" Scott asked, handing over the quarter.

"No," Harry said. "Let's just ride out to your ball, and both of us can play from there."

"Don't you want to look for the ball?" Scott persisted.

"No," Harry said again. "I doubt if we could find it. I have several more."

As they drove down the fairway toward Scott's ball,

Harry asked bluntly, "What happened while you were on vacation?"

Scott was startled. This must be what the mystery was all about. After a long pause, he said, "Nothing. Why do you ask?"

"Is everything okay between you and Sarah?"

"Everything is fine at home. Why do you ask?"

"Your work; you seem distracted from the project. You've even become difficult to work with."

"Who's complaining about my work?" Scott asked defensively.

"No one especially. It's something I've noticed. Sometimes you're ill-tempered, and you're not paying attention to details. That can be disastrous on any space venture. You have not been yourself since you returned from Highlands. It's as if Scott Walker is in a daze."

When Harry referred to you by your full name, you knew it was serious.

Harry continued, "I know something must have happened. That's why I called you to come here, so we could talk away from the office. Playing golf was the best way we could discuss this with no one else around to eavesdrop or wonder what we're meeting about.

"No one is scheduled to tee off behind us, so we can take our time, play golf if we want to or just spend the time discussing the situation. No one will be the wiser."

There was a long pause. Scott got out of the cart, addressed his ball and drove it short of the apron in front of the first green.

"Nice shot," Harry said, though golf was the furthest things from either of their minds. Scott got back in the cart and drove up to the edge of the first green. Harry did not play a ball.

"Some members of the committee have suggested replacing you for this upcoming shuttle to the

International Space Station," said Harry.

That really jolted Scott. His grip tightened on the steering wheel of the golf cart until his knuckles blanched white. Harry McDonald had always been a father figure for Scott, and he could always rely on Harry to be trustworthy. Sure he was direct and to the point, even brusque with a lot of people, but Harry was always candid.

Before getting out of the cart, Scott said, "Let's not play out this hole." He picked up his golf ball and sat back down in the cart.

"Fine with me," Harry said. "I didn't want to play golf anyway. Talking about this situation is much more important."

"Everything is fine between Sarah and me. The children are fine," Scott said, staring at the golf ball as he rolled it back and forth in his hand.

Finally, he looked directly into Harry's eyes and confessed, "Something did happen while we were in Highlands."

Scott began with every minute detail about his experience during the worship service at the First Presbyterian Church. He was relieved to finally tell someone other than Sarah about the incident.

Harry sat motionless, absorbing every word Scott spoke. Scott then told how he had almost forgotten what happened at church until a week after they returned to their home in Winter Park and he had the dream. He described the apprehension, frustrations, the rain, the fire, the explosions and outright terror that had turned the dream into a catastrophic nightmare.

"The thing that bothers me most is the dream has repeated itself seven times since we returned from Highlands," Scott said. "Each dream starts exactly the same as the one before, but each time it's clearer and ends more disastrously than the first.

"If you could envision Reverend McClain's lips speaking to me from atop the space shuttle, you would understand why I have been so shook-up. Sarah awakens me each time because I am thrashing about in the bed and yelling. I've wondered many times what would have happened if Sarah did not wake me.

"I guess I have been hard to work with. Sarah says I've been irritable, even with our children; however, the dream continues over and over, night after night. If only it would stop. I've shared it with Sarah each time. Maybe my telling you will help the dreams to stop.

"I know this probably sounds very childish to you, but rest assured I will become more aware of how I am acting. You will see a complete turn around in my work ethics. Please, I beg you, do not let me be relieved from commanding this upcoming flight to the ISS."

Having confessed the entire occurrence to his boss, Scott started the golf cart, bypassed the second tee and drove slowly down the winding cart path toward the second green. Neither spoke.

Because no other golfers were in front of or behind them, Harry motioned for Scott to cut through the rough to the seventh tee. Harry got out of the golf cart and went through the motions of washing a golf ball in the ball scrubber near the tee.

Harry continued to pull the brush scrubber up and down in the water although it was a new ball. Finally he removed the ball from the container and dried it with a towel hanging on the post. He took a sip of water from the nearby water fountain and sat back on the golf cart.

Turning, he looked directly at Scott. He stared so long and so intently Scott became uneasy, squirmed on his seat, and said, "What?"

Harry did not even blink. Scott felt his boss was

staring right through him. He thought maybe he had made a terrible mistake by confessing, but he had to tell someone other than Sarah.

Involuntarily, Harry's head began to move slightly side to side as if his conscious mind was trying to deny the validity of what he had heard Scott say. His body language was telling Scott none of this could be true, it wasn't happening. All the time, Harry's eyes were riveted on Scott's face.

"What?" Scott pleaded again.

After what seemed like an eternity, Harry shifted slightly on the seat of the golf cart, turned away from Scott, and gazed into the clear blue sky at the horizon.

When he spoke, it was like he was talking as much to himself as to Scott. "You asked 'what?' I'll tell you what. When I put together what you have told me with what I have experienced recently — well it's not humanly possible, not possible at all, no way."

Harry got out of the golf cart and walked back to the water fountain. He took several swallows of water, turned, and motioned for Scott to come sit under the shed with him.

"I wish you would share with me what you are thinking," Scott said uneasily.

"I'm frightened, truly scared for the first time in my life," Harry said. "Had you not told me what happened in Highlands, I would never tell you or anyone what I am going to share with you now. Even my wife has not heard this, though I have told her I have been having a very realistic dream over and over."

"I sense you know now why I was reluctant to tell you about Highlands and my dreams," said Scott.

Harry nodded. "Yes, I do understand. I feel exactly the same trepidation sharing this with you, but now I must. Our 12-year-old granddaughter, Jennifer, has come to spend the summer with Martha and me here in Houston. She is our one and only grandchild. Martha and I have enjoyed her so much.

"We have been taking her to our place at Galveston Beach. We go horseback riding almost every weekend. She is a wonderful girl. Martha and I have really bonded with Jennifer.

"Scott, you probably will find this hard to believe. I have been having the same dream, over and over again. Like so many dreams, who, where, what, and when frequently are blurred, but this one always has the same setting.

"Jennifer and I are trying to get to the space shuttle, which is standing ready to be launched. Suddenly flames rise from the ground. Bombs are exploding around the shuttle. A wall of water, taller than a skyscraper, is racing from the ocean toward the shuttle.

"Clearly, I see you, Sarah, and your three children inside the shuttle. The door to the shuttle is closed, and I am knocking frantically to get you to open the door so Jennifer can get on board. I see you coming to open the door, but before you can, I wake up.

"Now you see why I am troubled. I have never been anything but realistic. I have lost count of how many times I have had this same dream. Like your dreams, it becomes clearer each time.

"Always, I have believed in nothing but scientific facts, but now I'm not so sure. When I put your experience and mine together, I think I could believe in something supernatural."

"I know exactly what you mean and how you feel," Scott said. "If you think you are perplexed now, wait until you hear the rest of my story.

"Since you and I talked last, a college friend came to see me in Winter Park. His name is John Johnston.

Actually, we bumped into each other in the airport in Atlanta where I met my family before going to Highlands. That was the first contact we've had since we were fraternity brothers at N. C. State.

"In Atlanta, I thought he acted weird. He was very evasive and secretive. However, when he came to our house recently, he really opened up.

"He is a National Security Agent and he said the cold war is still going on between the U.S. and some die-hard ex-Soviet Generals who smuggled nuclear missiles from the USSR to Iran, Iraq, Libya, China, and North Korea.

"He said the struggle between Israel and Palestine is not territorial or political, but is a theological struggle. I have no idea where he learned all this, but he believes there will soon be an overwhelming devastation worldwide.

"He had no idea why he was unloading all of this on me, but he said he had to tell someone. Then his expression changed and he knew why he had to tell me. The upcoming shuttle flight to the ISS was the answer.

"With all the destruction and terrorism coming, the space shuttle will be the only safe place for Beth, his daughter. John said he had to get Beth on the shuttle. Although his wife has custody of Beth, John has vowed to take care of his daughter no matter what happens.

"When the connection between the Space Shuttle and Beth's safety became apparent to John, he said abruptly he had to go but he would see us again soon. Now my dreams are more puzzling to me than ever before. Do you think this, in any way, could relate to my dreams, or yours about the shuttle and Jennifer?"

"Right now it adds to my mystification," Harry said with a heavy sigh. "I will have to ponder it at length. You know how practical and realistic I've always been.

I will sort through this."

The two men sat under the shed for a long time. Neither spoke or looked at the other. Finally Harry said, "Maybe we should go back to the club house. It's almost dark."

"I agree," Scott said, rising to his feet. "I want to call Sarah and let her know I'll fly home tonight.

"Martha and I have been considering renting an apartment on the ocean close to Kennedy Space Center. I want hands-on control of this flight," Harry said "Jennifer will stay with us there this summer. After all this, I know we will definitely move to Florida soon, probably next week. I want to be present for the lift-off instead of supervising it from Houston."

After they returned the golf cart to the clubhouse, they shook hands and clasped each other's shoulders warmly.

"Thanks for coming," Harry said. "I have a lot of thinking and planning to do. Have a smooth flight back to Cape Kennedy. We'll figure this out somehow. Don't worry about being replaced on the flight. I want someone on that shuttle who will open the door and let Jennifer in."

14

WHILE CHECKING E-MAIL in his office, breathing suddenly became difficult for John. For the first time he could remember, his tie felt tight around his neck and perspiration popped out on his forehead. He became acutely aware of the fact he was deep underground. The small office seemed even smaller, and claustrophobia tightened the noose around his neck.

At first, John thought he was having a heart attack and he panicked. He loosened his necktie. That helped.

Get a grip on yourself, John, he thought. *You're not having a heart attack. All you need is to get out of this office.*

He diagnosed his condition correctly because he was having an anxiety attack. If he could get above ground, he would be okay.

He shut down the computer and left the office without speaking to anyone. When he walked by Neil Anderson's office, he saw his boss sitting at his desk, but he did not pause to speak to him. Anderson was busy, and John was in a hurry to get above ground.

When he walked into the fresh air in front of the mansion, he took a long deep breath and felt better immediately. He recognized work was getting to him and he was extremely stressed. The fact he had lied to his boss continued to haunt him. He decided he had to get away, away from everything connected even remotely with his occupation.

His first impulse was to call Frances for help, but he knew better. He could not even visit his daughter, Beth, to find solace. The divorce decree allowed John to be with his daughter only one week a year. Thank goodness his week was coming up soon.

Maybe driving would relieve some of his stress. He had no idea where he wanted to go, but he wanted to keep moving, even if aimlessly. Before obtaining a rental car, he called his boss and left a message that he would not be available for seven days.

John gave Anderson no reason for being away or where he was going, mostly because he had no idea where he was going.

He just drove south from DC. He stayed away from the interstate highways where traffic was too fast and too congested. He was in no hurry, and he drove on less traveled highways, U.S. 1 and 301, until he was well into South Carolina.

He decided he would drive to Pawleys Island and stay for a few days. John had read a brochure describing Pawleys Island as being "aristocratically shabby" and very quiet.

He had never been there, but a quiet, laid-back place was what he desperately needed. It was south of bustling Myrtle Beach, which would be too lively and crowded for him. Pawleys Island sounded like the ideal place to get away from it all.

He turned off highway U.S. 301 onto State Highway 38 and had driven several miles before it dawned on him that he did not know the way to Pawleys Island. He did not have a road map, and although he was an international traveler, John felt lost. He came to an intersection with no highway markings.

In one corner of the intersection sat a dilapidated country store and gas station. Most of the paint had peeled from the wooden structure. The billboard over the front of the aged building was so weathered John could not determine the name of the store. It looked like it began with a B.

The building was in such disarray he thought the store must be closed or abandoned, but as he turned into the lot, he saw three men sitting under a large oak tree behind the store. The massive limbs of the live oak hung low over a slow moving black river.

He parked his car and walked around to the rear of the store. As he approached the men, all three stopped talking and scrutinized the stranger carefully.

"Excuse me. I don't mean to break up anything, but I'm lost. I need to get directions to Pawleys Island. I didn't see anyone in the store. Is it open? I need gas and would like to get something to drink."

"It's open and you're not lost. You're at Baucom's General Merchandise and Feed Store, or what's left of it. I own the store, but I'm closing it for good next Friday," the youngest looking man said, "My name is Henry Baucom. I'll gas your car. How much do you want?"""

"Put in $20.00 worth, please."

"Just go in the store and get what you want to drink," Henry said. "Go on in the back door. The cooler will be on your right, half way to the front of the store. All drinks are fifty cents."

John found the soft drink cooler, made his selection, left the money beside the register, and went back outside. Henry had finished pumping the gas and returned to his chair beside the river. "I left $20.50 beside the register."

"Thanks. Now pull up that old wicker rocking chair and set a spell with us. This here is Jeffry Honeycutt and the other one is Bill Edwards," Henry said, gesturing to the two older men with thinning, gray hair. Both wore well-worn denim overalls.

John sat down gingerly in the wicker rocker. It looked very old and fragile, and he was afraid it would collapse under his weight. Once he was safely settled, he took a sip of his drink.

"You ain't breaking nothing up," Jeffry Honeycutt said, chuckling. "Bill Edwards was lecturing me and Henry about the state of affairs in America."

"Poke fun if you want to," Bill said, "but things are in bad shape in this country."

"He's been fussing about the immigration of so many Hispanics," said Jeffry.

"I'm not fussing about their coming to this country. Most of them seem to be hard working, family-oriented people," Bill explained. "My concern is that our government is not requiring the immigrants to learn to speak English and to conduct all their business in our native language.

"Retail stores have to put up signs in Spanish, and I can't read 'em. The government has to pay translators to work at the Social Services, county health departments, and hospitals. Forms have to be printed in Spanish for these people. That's expensive, and it makes things I buy cost me more.

"If those immigrants want to speak their native language at home, that's their choice, but when in Rome, do as the Romans do. In the United States of America, Romans speak English. I don't recall the government doing anything for the Italian, German, Chinese, Greek or any other foreign immigrants when they came to America in the past. Those immigrants had to learn English. If they didn't, they went home.

"How can immigrants blend into the community and become a loyal part of it if they are unable to communicate in English?"

"It's a cinch I ain't gonna learn Spanish," Jeffry piped in.

Bill Edwards continued, "They'll never feel like they're Americans. When the U.S. invaded Iraq, the majority of Americans rallied around the flag and backed the American government.

"Not speaking or understanding English, why would these people want to support the government's action? There are so many immigrants now they soon may divide the country. Just look at what's happening in California.

"Another problem is the tremendous number of immigrants in this country illegally. It is unbelievable how much they get from the government even though they're breaking the law.

"What's the difference between illegal and being a crook? Apparently our government is saying it's okay to break the immigration law. To me, that sends the message it's okay to break any of our laws. Many pay no taxes, and yet they are eligible for free hospital, medical, and dental care and many other services.

"Being here illegally, they'll have no allegiance to the United States. I cannot understand why the officials in Washington are unable to see what a huge problem this is. It will get much worse as time goes by unless the government changes some of its policies. It's time the government stopped being politically correct and called a spade a spade.

"Let's face it, there has been a race problem in this

country for a long time. Whites and blacks look different and come from different cultures. But, because they can speak the same language, they are able to work through these differences.

"A lot of progress has been made in the last century, and more progress will continue to be made in the future because blacks and whites can and will continue to talk with each other.

"Both races, having been here hundreds of years, feel like they are Americans. Both feel a loyalty to the United States. As long as the Hispanic immigrants refuse to function in English, I see no way they can become loyal American patriots and blend into the American community."

"Speaking of Afro-Americans," Jeffry interrupted, "I heard on the TV not long ago that a number of them are wanting the government to give them something called reparations because their ancestors were slaves.

"I ain't too educated, but I don't know of any society, culture or group of people that wasn't enslaved at some point in history. Don't get me wrong — slavery was wrong and is wrong, awfully wrong.

"Do you reckon the Egyptians would consider paying reparations to the Jews today because, in Biblical days, the Israelis were enslaved in Egypt?

"My ancestors were too poor to have slaves. But how in the name of common sense can the government give something to a slave's descendant to compensate the slave who has been dead for years? I think it's just a case of somebody wanting to get a handout from the government."

"I remember something my daddy said about a speech John F. Kennedy made when he was president: 'Ask not what your country can do for you, but ask what you can do for your country.' We need thinking like that in this country today," Henry Baucom said.

John listened to the three men without making any comment. He did not nod his head in affirmation or disagreement. He was amazed at their logic and simple solutions to problems besetting America.

"While we're complaining, let me get something off my chest," said Bill. "I saw on the television last week a program on CBS news about education in India. Would you believe they have surpassed the U.S. in many branches of technology?"

"Says who?" asked Jeffry indignantly. "I don't believe it."

"Well, it's true according to this report," Bill said. "A university, called the India Institute of Technology in Bombay, is producing the smartest chemical, electrical and computer engineers in the world.

"To gain admission, a student has to pass an extremely difficult test. There is no such thing as buying one's way in, or being admitted because of someone you know. Indian children begin to prepare for this entrance test when they are in the first grade of school.

"The son of one prominent university official could not pass the test, and his father was not able to get him admitted. Instead the son came to an Ivy League college in the U.S.

"Less than two percent of the applicants are admitted to IIT, which has the most rigorous curriculum in the world. Meritocracy is the only factor considered for admission. That's why India has become the leader in technology.

"Colleges in the U.S. have to accept applicants on factors other than academic merit. In some cases, the brightest students are unable to gain admission. The admission policies of American universities have some good qualities, but I wonder if some of these policies are contributing to the U.S. falling behind."

"I don't think that's as serious a problem as all of these law suits we read about in the paper almost every day," Jeffry said. "Some of them are so ridiculous. But the awards some of the juries give ain't no laughing matter, especially the ones dealing with tobacco.

"In 1965, the Surgeon General put a warning on all packs of cigarettes: Smoking is hazardous to your health. Now, how could any smoker blame the tobacco company for ailments he might suffer because of smoking? No one made the smoker suck on that weed or chew it. The person smoked or chewed because he wanted to.

"If the tobacco user suffers any ill effects from smoking or chewing, he should pay for it himself, not the tobacco company. Now I hear the lawyers are going after the fast food industry because some glutton claimed fast food made him a fatso. No one wants to take any responsibility for his actions. Most everybody wants someone else, or the government, to be responsible, or they want a free handout. The legal system in this country is in chaos."

Henry Baucom chimed in again, "Speaking of lawyers, I remember Ralph, one of the store's best customers, saying one of America's biggest problems is the fact we have too many lawyers in Columbia and Washington making our laws.

"Ralph died several years ago, but he said we need more representatives from all walks of life. The lawyers, or 'liars' as he called them, make the laws to profit their profession.

"For example, if I buy a piece of land from you and we agree on the price, we have to get a lawyer to draw up and finalize the papers. That's the law. Lawyers in Columbia and Washington have made the law so complicated, you and I cannot execute the transaction ourselves.

"I can't give the money for the property directly to you. The lawyers don't trust you enough to pay them. I have to send the money to the lawyer who takes his cut and then sends the rest to you. But I guess it's our fault we have them."

"Don't blame it on me," Jeffry said defensively. "What have I done?"

"I don't mean you particularly. I mean people in general," Henry said. "We haven't always been honest in our dealings with each other, so we have to get lawyers to settle our disputes.

"If people had always been honest, there would never have been a need for lawyers to start with. Lawyers don't seem to be interested in justice. They just want to win their case. In a case where there is no doubt about the guilt of a criminal, a slick lawyer will look for some technicality to get the criminal freed from the charges.

"Now I read in the newspaper that a few people in the federal government want to put a lid on the monetary amount some of these lawsuits award. Hell will freeze over before that happens.

"Lawyers are running the government. Maybe, as Shakespeare supposedly said, lawyers should be hung. We are led to believe the President of the United States, the House of Representatives and the Senators run this country. They do not. America is controlled by judges. Many judges are appointed simply to pay off a political debt, and the lawyers are their watchdogs."

"Speaking of government, I want you to think about this," Bill said. "After the U.S. defeated and literally destroyed Germany in World War II, the government said we needed to rebuild Germany. After we defeated

Japan, the government said we had to rebuild Japan. I'm not an economist, but today Germany and Japan are probably better off financially or economically than the United States.

"After that fiasco in Vietnam, no telling how much aid was sent to that country. Now the U.S. has torn up Iraq. The government wants billions to rebuild what the government just destroyed. Tear something down and then pay, or have the working citizens of the U. S. pay, to rebuild it. It doesn't make sense to me.

"Many Americans believe the Federal Government is paying to rebuild Iraq. We ordinary working taxpayers are paying for it. Some never realize the Federal Government cannot pay for anything until it takes money, in the form of taxes, from its working citizens.

"Will our government ever learn you can't buy friendship by giving to people or countries? I can't win your friendship by giving to you. The minute I give something to you, that tells you I think I have more than you have, or I am better than you. It may give me the big head, but it makes you feel inferior. And no one wants to be made to feel inferior."

"I hope that don't mean you're gonna stop giving me a Christmas present. But we exchange those, don't we?" Jeffry slapped his thigh and laughed.

Although the three men were discussing serious problems, John realized how relaxed he had become while listening to them pass the time of day. Life was lived at a much slower pace here on the banks of the Little Pee Dee River.

People like these three were the backbone of America. Many people would consider these men to be ignorant rednecks, but John silently agreed with many of their remarks. He thought they had more common sense than many of the governmental officials in

Washington. John took another sip of his drink and asked, "Are the three of you from around here?"

Jeffry nodded. "Yep. Lived here all our life. Henry took over running the store when his father died in 1972. The Baucoms have owned this store now for eight generations."

"Jeffry, just who are you talking to?" asked Bill.

Jeffry was stunned. He looked seriously at John and said, "Look here, stranger, I didn't get yo' name, or where you're from. For all I know, you might be from the IRS or some undercover government agent or spy."

"My name is John Johnston, and I'm from North Carolina." Chills ran up John's spine when Jeffry suggested he could be a spy. If he only knew how correct his assessment was.

Because John was a 'Carolina boy,' he was accepted by the three men. Jeffry, especially, was relieved to learn John was not some foreigner from New York or Jersey. John relaxed again when they did not ask about his occupation.

"As I was saying before Bill so rudely interrupted me," Jeffry went on, "it is sad Henry is having to close his store next week. This used to be one of the most active stores in the county. Businesses just dried up after Wal-Mart opened in town.

"Wal-Mart is one of the worst things to ever happen to a small town down south. Those giant stores drive out all of the Mom-and-Pop businesses. Small stores can't compete.

"The middle class working people are disappearing in this country, and that's the group of people who helped to make America the greatest country on earth. Now we're becoming a nation of a few extremely wealthy people and many extremely poor, like many other countries in the world.

"Bill, tell John that poem you preach to me and Henry all the time. You know the line you said summed up what is happening in America today."

Bill Edwards nodded. "My daddy taught me this. He quoted it frequently. It's a line from *The Deserted Village* written in 1770 by Oliver Goldsmith: 'Ill fares the land, to hastening ills a prey, where wealth accumulates, and men decay.'

"For America, there may be more truth in those words today than ever before. Corruption in this country seems more prevalent than ever. Honesty and integrity are disappearing fast."

Jeffry Honeycutt, always the one to come up with something funny said, "Well, I sho' ain't decaying, cause I ain't accumulated no money."

Then seriously he added, "Wonder why our government wants all those billions of dollars to rebuild Iraq. With all the oil that's supposed to be in Iraq's oil wells, maybe Iraqis should pay for it themselves. Speaking of oil, do you ever wonder what fills up the space where the oil is pumped from? I do. It's a puzzlement."

"Insurance is a big puzzlement to me," said Henry. "That's a huge, wealthy business. Those companies practically own this country. As long as I am paying them premiums, everything is fine. Let me file a claim against them, and it becomes a problem.

"Insurance is the longest four-letter word I know. The insurance company even tells me what doctor I can go to and how often, and what the doctor can do when I get there.

"But now that I am closing the store, insurance will not be the problem it was. The problem now is trying to find a job. That will be hard at my age. A lot of manufacturing plants are closing in this area, and a lot of people are out of work.

"The same companies firing workers and closing here are manufacturing the same product overseas because of cheaper labor. The companies get richer and the working American gets poorer. The U.S. government could stop this trend by slapping a stiff tariff on those companies who import foreign products. Then these products would cost the same as if they had been made by American workers.

"That will never happen because the owners of the factories contribute more to the politicians than the average worker can. It's a vicious cycle like Bill said, the rich get richer and the working class get poorer."

"Think about the wealth being created for those companies that manufacture tanks, bombers, jet fighters, submarines, and other weapons of mass destruction for our government," Bill said. "If the U.S. is already the most powerful nation on this planet, from whom or what do we need to be defended? The only answer I can come up with is we need to be defended from ourselves.

"Think about the cost of developing, testing, manufacturing and storing weapons of mass destruction. The figure must be astronomical. Who pays for this? You guessed it, the working American, us.

"I don't fully understand what the Gross National Product is, but I'll bet spending for defense or national security is a big portion of it. On the other hand, if all defense spending stopped today, what would happen to the economy? It would probably collapse. It's a vicious circle. Even I don't know the answer.

"However, speaking of national security, I wonder how many times a governmental official stamps a document CLASSIFIED to keep Americans from knowing something they are entitled to know. It's a means whereby the government can cover up something. Personally, I think it happens frequently."

"Calm down Bill. Give it a rest," Jeffry said. "You've preached enough. Me and Bill are farmers, John. I took over my daddy's farm when he died in 1975, and I've been running it ever since.

"Bill's daddy, Clyde Edwards, was the first in his family to go to college. He went to Clemson University, and got a degree in agriculture. Mr. Clyde was a smart man, quiet, but smart. My daddy used to say that when Clyde Edwards said something you could rely on its being the truth and being something important.

"Bill, my daddy thought your daddy had an uncanny foresight like he could see far into the future. It's a shame you didn't inherit some of your daddy's smarts." Jeffry chuckled and patted his lifelong friend on the shoulder. "Just kidding, old buddy. You're okay in my book."

The shadows of the live oak reflecting on the water lengthened as the sun continued to move to the west.

"John, I believe you said you were lost," Henry said. "There's a free map on the back of the front door. Come on and I'll show you some back roads, good roads though, that will take you right to Pawleys Island. It's a pretty drive through some beautiful farmland.

"Gentlemen. It was a pleasure meeting you," John said as he rose to follow Henry. "I've enjoyed listening to the three of you. I needed this quiet time. You seem to have logical solutions to some complex problems facing this country. I've learned a lot. This is a beautiful and peaceful place. It's no wonder you spend so much time here. I would stay here as much as I could. I hope you men know how lucky you are to have such a restful place."

John followed Henry into the store where Henry marked the secondary roads John could follow to Pawleys Island.

"Is there any cost for the map?"

Henry shook his head. "No, it's free with the gas."

"I appreciate it very much, and I can't tell you how relaxing this has been for me," John said. "It's incredible how I have unwound. It's almost supernatural.

"Listen, I hope you find a satisfactory job with long pay and short hours. Good luck." They shook hands, and John left the store.

After John cranked his car, he pulled beside the store where he could see the two men still sitting beside the river. He watched Henry returned to his chair underneath the live oak.

John envied them. They made problems seem easily solvable. He paused for a moment, absorbing the idyllic scene, a replica of a bygone era in the South. Then he waved goodbye and drove toward Pawleys Island.

As he drove, he realized, for some unearthly reason, the couple of hours spent at Baucom's General Merchandise and Feed Store listening to those three men had revived him completely.

He no longer needed to go to Pawleys Island. Now he was eager to get back to solving his own problems. He needed to see Scott Walker again and meet with Scott's boss at NASA. As soon as possible, John got on Interstate 95 and headed south toward the Kennedy Space Center.

15

"HARRY, THIS IS JOHN JOHNSTON, the person I've been telling you about," said Scott. "John, this is Harry McDonald, the CEO of NASA."

The two men shook hands cordially while scrutinizing each other thoroughly.

"Harry, it's a pleasure to meet you," John said.

"Scott has told me so much about you, John. I was looking forward to this meeting."

John turned to face Scott, his expression asking if he could trust this guy and talk freely with him. Scott nodded his head affirmatively.

"John, you can be as candid with Harry as you are with me. Everything you say will be held in utmost confidentiality."

John looked relieved and turned to gaze into Harry's steady eyes as if to confirm what Scott had said.

"I hardly know where to begin," he said. "I have so much information to share with you."

"Begin wherever you wish," Scott said. "I have shared with Harry everything you told Sarah and me when you came to our house in Winter Park."

"When I was at your house, I don't believe I told

you much about Saudi Arabia. American oil companies helped the Saudis develop their oil many years ago. When USSR's communism was at its peak and trying for global domination, Saudi Arabia sided with the west because America was the best purchaser of Arabian oil and the Saudi nobility were afraid the Soviets would take over their country.

"Now that the USSR has collapsed and communism is no longer a threat to the rulers of Saudi Arabia, the Saudi king and nobility are more concerned with American customs overthrowing their way of life.

"The cultural and religious ideological differences between the United States and Saudi Arabia are driving an insurmountable chasm between the two nations. The rulers of both nations will deny this vehemently.

"However, all but one of the perpetrators of the 9-11 disaster were natives of Saudi Arabia."

Harry looked confused. "What has that got to do with the upcoming shuttle flight to the ISS?"

"Evidently, Scott did not make it clear enough for you to see what is happening on this planet," John said. "Secretly, Saudi Arabia is aligning itself with the rest of the Arab world, which is more united than ever before. A conflict between Islam and Judeo-Christianity and a conflict between communism and capitalism is about to come to realization.

"A fact you rarely see in the news is that some Christians are advocating that Islam is espousing people to join them or be killed. At the same time, some Christians preach if people don't join them and believe as Christians believe, they will spend eternity in Hell.

"I'm not saying one is good and the other is evil. That's not for me to say because both profess to worship the same God. I see no way these differences can ever be reconciled.

"The conflict between Islam and Judeo-Christianity is about to become an all-out war. With the religions preaching supposedly in 'God's Holy Name,' it must be enough to make God regret having created man and this planet.

"In the 1700s, nations fought by marching their armies shoulder to shoulder in straight lines to face each other and fire their muskets at point blank range. Then, in World War I, battles were fought in trenches. World War II was fought from foxholes and with bombs dropped from planes. If such is possible, it was a 'civilized' war. Certain targets were 'off limits' to bombing and fighting. It was considered a 'just' or 'clean' war.

"Later, wars became police actions trying to control who would be allowed to have weapons of mass destruction. In each of these conflicts, it was easy to tell who was the enemy and where he was.

"That's not the case with the impending conflict. A conflict, unlike any other war that's been seen on this planet, is ongoing right now. In other words, gentlemen, I believe Armageddon is a reality, and it is here now.

"In past wars, the battle lines were drawn explicitly. There was no doubt about who was foe and who was friend. This is the dawn of a conflict called Terrorism. There will be no battle lines. No place on this planet will be safe from Terrorism. There will be no uniforms to indicate who is friend or foe.

"It will not be a struggle of nation against nation. It will be a struggle of one culture and ideology versus another. It will be a war between economies, the have and the have not. It is a conflict of unbelievable annihilation.

"Harry, you asked me what does this have to do with the shuttle. When I visited Scott and Sarah in Winter Park, a vision came to me about why I was sharing what

I had learned with them. The safety of my daughter, Beth, is foremost in my mind.

"No place on this planet will be a haven from the annihilation that is coming. The only safe place will be the space shuttle in flight."

Scott and Harry stared intently into each other's eyes searching for answers. Neither moved. Neither blinked.

John became uneasy watching them. He shifted in his chair nervously. "What?"

Scott and Harry remained absolutely motionless. John was not sure they were even breathing.

"What?" John said again, his voice pleading.

After what seemed like an eternity, Scott turned to face John and quietly said, "What Harry and I have to say to you may sound more farfetched. After we tell you about our recent experiences, you will understand why all you have told us did not sound preposterous to us."

Scott then told John everything that happened in church while he was in Highlands, emphasizing the scriptural passages about Noah. Then he described all of the dreams that had been haunting him for weeks.

"Harry," Scott said when he was finished, "I think you should share your dreams with John."

Harry nodded. In great detail and a reassuring voice, he told John about his dream of trying to get his grand-daughter, Jennifer, aboard the shuttle, Constitution.

John was mesmerized by their narratives. He sat mouth agape, unable to move.

Finally, after a long period of silence, Scott asked, "Well?"

"A headline on the news last week read, 'Three Mile Island Melts Down Again.' That was no meltdown," John said. "In spite of what was released to the press, it was a nuclear explosion set by terrorists.

"My office knows it, but will not admit it publicly. The explosion of the Atomic Energy Plant in Hartsville, S.C. was also caused by terrorists. The government announced the explosion was caused by negligence. Negligence, my foot, it was deliberately set.

"You know, the United States looked for weapons of mass destruction in Iraq and could not find any. As I told you, those bombs were buried deep in abandoned oil wells and are still under the control of some Iraqis. Heaven help us all if or when those bombs are exploded simultaneously.

"What worries me most is that most of the weapons of mass destruction are located right here, in the United States. We have more such weapons than the rest of the world put together.

"That's a shocker, isn't it? These weapons were never inactivated according to the agreements with the USSR. Additionally, the United States continues to build, test, and stockpile these weapons.

"Weapons of poisonous gases, weapons of biological warfare, and nuclear energy plants are all sitting duck targets right here in America. All could become easy victims of terrorists.

"Why does the U.S. government believe we are the only nation entitled to have weapons of mass destruction? I cannot understand why we continue to develop, build, and store more of these horrendous weapons every day. It is maniacal, if not suicidal.

"The United States, Russia, France, and China have enough nuclear-armed submarines to destroy all life on this planet.

"The recently established Department of Homeland Security will have a difficult time trying to accomplish what it was established to do — protect the USA from attack by terrorists. Why? In this country, the research, development, testing, and storage of weapons of mass destruction have been such secretive, hush-hush, classified affairs that very few governmental officials know of their existence, not to mention where the weapons are located.

"If terrorists do not already know where the weapons are stashed, they will find them. The Department of Homeland Security has a formidable, if not impossible, assignment.

"Scott, you asked me what I think. When I combine your and Harry's vision, I wonder is God telling us the shuttle could become a modern day Noah's Ark.

"Scott, do not your dreams say for you to 'come into your ark and bring all of your family?' I hope you will consider Beth part of your family. Harry, wouldn't you like for Scott to open the door and let Jennifer get in the shuttle?"

Harry nodded affirmatively as he and Scott gazed at John in amazement. He made everything seem so simple. He was giving voice to the messages God had been sending to Scott and Harry. John was a voice "crying in the wilderness."

"I think it is time the three of us get busy to bring this call to fulfillment," John said.

"Arrangements can be made for Scott and his family, including Beth and Jennifer to be on the shuttle," Harry said. "Scott will need a co-pilot. That can be arranged. But," Harry paused for a long moment, "what if Armageddon doesn't happen?"

"Well, Scott and his crew will have had a nice jaunt into space and back," John said. "Ann, Douglass, Robert, Beth, and Jennifer will be the first youth in space. From all of the information I have gathered, I see no way for any place on this planet to be safe for humans or any kind of living creatures."

"The purpose of the flight to the ISS is to take enough supplies for an extended stay in space and to test some new equipment to help solve some of the problems of an extended stay in weightlessness," Harry said.

"The only change will be in personnel. Let's get busy then. We have a lot of work to do. Let's roll!"

16

SARAH AND SCOTT invited Harry and Martha McDonald and John Johnston to come for a cookout on Saturday night. When the guests arrived, Sarah welcomed them and introduced each of the guests.

"Where are your children?" John asked.

"Their grandparents have taken them to Disney World," Sarah said, "but they will return late tonight."

John nodded. "Don't get me wrong — I love your children — but I'm glad they're not here. We all need to talk seriously. As providence would have it, next week is the one week a year I am allowed to be with Beth. With your permission, I would like to bring her here tomorrow to meet you and your children.

"I'll call Frances tonight to see if I can pick Beth up a day early. If Beth can get to know you and Scott, and especially Ann, Douglass, and Robert, even for a few days before lift-off, it would help to reassure her tremendously."

"She will be welcomed wholeheartedly," said Sarah. "I think it's an excellent idea."

"Surely, Harry, you are not going to follow through with this preposterous plan," Martha McDonald said.

"Woman, all systems are go!" Harry proclaimed. "John, I think getting the young people together is an excellent idea. Sarah, I would like to bring Jennifer soon, if that's okay with you. Tonight she's staying with one of our neighbors while we're here.

"She is so easy going I don't think she'll have any trouble adjusting to the sudden change. We've told her nothing about what's going on, but we will before we bring her to your house."

"We look forward to getting to know her," Sarah said. "I believe Jennifer is about the same age as Douglass, and Beth is approximately the same age as Robert. The five young people should enjoy each other tremendously."

"I will do my best to pick Beth up in the morning and bring her to your house late tomorrow afternoon, if that's okay," John said.

"That will be fine," said Sarah. "Martha, you bring Jennifer tomorrow, or let Harry bring her. The sooner we all get to know each other the better things will be."

"Sarah," Martha said with concern, "surely you do not go along with this absurd idea?"

"I believe in my husband," Sarah said quietly but firmly, "but I also know something providential is happening."

"But Harry, how can you possibly pull this off?" Martha asked.

"Wife, don't worry. I will pull it off. The flight is scheduled for lift-off Friday. Everything is on schedule. Monday, I will have some space suits modified to fit the children. It will be done off base, and no one will know about it.

"At the last minute, the crew scheduled for this flight will be detained. Scott and his co-pilot, Gary Powell, will board then Sarah and the four children will be ushered aboard quickly.

"Before they are aboard, Scott and Gary will have all of the lift-off procedures coordinated with the control tower. Lift-off will be immediately after Sarah and the children are on board.

"I will handle all of the details, and assume full responsibility. As Harry Truman said, 'The buck stops here.' I am beginning to believe there will be very little, if any, time left for objections or repercussions."

"Let's stop now and enjoy the cookout," Scott said. "It's time to eat."

Soon after they finished eating, Martha excused Harry and herself, because they needed to pick up Jennifer before it was too late. They thanked Sarah and Scott for having them.

As soon as Martha and Harry left, John telephoned Frances at her parents' estate in Palm Beach. The butler answered and confirmed she was home.

"May I speak with her, please?" John asked.

"Who is calling?"

"Just tell her it's an old friend." John knew Frances would not come to the telephone if she knew he was the one calling.

"Hello?" Frances said.

"It's me."

As soon as she recognized John's voice, Frances snarled, "Well, what do you want?"

"Next week is my one week to be with Beth. I'm in Florida, and wondered if I could pick her up in the morning."

"You know damn well the judge ruled one week, and that doesn't begin until day after tomorrow." Frances spoke with all the bitterness she could muster.

John's first impulse was to shout, but he restrained his emotions and pleaded, "I know my week doesn't begin until Monday, but this is only one day early. Please let me pick Beth up in the morning since I am already in Florida. I will not be with her longer than seven days. I promise."

Frances did not answer for a moment then sighed, "In that case, you may pick her up tomorrow if you swear not to keep her longer than seven days.

"The law says you may not be with her more than seven days each year. Beth will be ready by 8 a.m., not a minute before. Do not disturb me when you come."

As Frances slammed the telephone on the receiver, John felt only relief.

17

SUNDAY MORNING, promptly at 8 a.m., John pulled the elaborate ringer beside the hand-hewn double front doors of the van Pelt estate on the oceanfront of Palm Beach.

The butler opened the door and formally said, "Yes?"

Beth was descending the wide spiral staircase when she saw her father through the opened door. She dropped her overnight bag and ran toward him.

"Daddy! Daddy!" she screamed and leaped into her father's outstretched arms.

John hugged her tightly a long time, and kissed her warmly on her cheek. It had been a whole year since he had held her.

Several times during the year, he would go where he could see Beth from a distance. Frequently, he had been near her school and watched when the chauffeur picked her up.

Beth had taken horseback riding lessons in Connecticut, and he had watched her ride there. She handled her horse with confidence and rode beautifully. John was proud of his daughter. Even though he was not allowed to get close enough to speak to her, seeing her from a distance was better than not seeing her at all.

He could at least keep up with how fast she was growing. Neither Frances nor Beth was ever aware of his presence throughout the year.

John finally released his hug and let her down. He stood back at arm's length and said, "My, just look at how you've grown. I love you so much. We've got a lot of catching up and a lot of exciting things to do."

He hugged her to him again.

The butler, with an air of aloofness, looked at them disdainfully. John asked him to bring Beth's luggage. Before he could hand the bag over, John demanded, "Have Frances come down here right now!"

"But Ms. van Pelt is still asleep and not to be disturbed."

"I don't care what she said. You get her down here now."

John glared at the butler until he meekly turned to go up the stairs, but Frances had been awakened by Beth's screams.

From the top of the stairs, she called, "What is it?"

"It's Mr. Johnston, Ms. van Pelt. He said to get you down here now."

It suddenly registered with John that the butler had called Frances 'Ms. van Pelt.' Apparently she had reverted to her maiden name when the divorce was finalized. He glared at his ex-wife with a confusing mixture of love and hatred then checked himself. He didn't want his daughter to see the hatred he felt at that moment.

Frances sauntered down the stairs to the first landing. "Remember, you said you would have her back a day early. Seven days is all she can stay with you. So, what else do you want?"

"I thought you might want to give your daughter a goodbye hug, in case we have an accident or something happens."

As soon as the words were out of John's mouth, he regretted saying them. What an idiot. He was telling her something was going to happen, and she may never see her daughter again.

Frances was furious. The very sight of John had enraged her so much that his words did not register with her. She was too livid with rage.

Beth was still holding her father's hand firmly. She looked from Frances to her father and mumbled, "Frances and I don't hug much."

John's heart broke. Beth did not even refer to Frances as mother. He said gently to his daughter, "You and I hug. Go and give your mother a big hug."

Obediently, Beth went to her mother, who was still standing on the landing, and gave her a quick hug. Frances did not respond. It was as if she were totally unaware of her daughter hugging her.

Beth quickly returned to her father. John took Beth's luggage from the butler, and turned for one last look at his ex.

"Thanks, Frances," he said sincerely, from the bottom of his heart. John and Beth held hands and skipped to the car.

On the way to Winter Park, John began to tell Beth a little about what was happening. He did not share with her anything about the horrors occurring in the world each day. He was sure Beth saw enough about that on the television news.

They stopped for a fast food lunch. John told his daughter they were going to see one of his classmates from college, and he and Beth would stay with them for a couple of days.

Beth and John arrived at the Walkers about 2 p.m.

"What a cool address, 1001 Memory Lane. I love it," Beth said.

The Walker family had attended early church that morning so they could have a picnic on the beach. They were on the beach before 10 a.m.

While there, Sarah reminded her family they could not stay all afternoon because John was bringing his daughter, Beth, and the McDonalds were bringing Jennifer, their granddaughter. The Walkers needed to be home before anyone came. This brought some grumbles from Robert.

Ann, Douglass, and Robert were unloading the last of the picnic supplies when John and Beth arrived. Sarah and Scott heard the children talking, and they came out to welcome Beth. Sarah hugged Beth warmly.

After all of the introductions, Robert looked at Beth and went over to his mother and whispered, "I'm glad we came home from the beach early."

His mother smiled.

Beth eyed Robert and murmured to her father, "I think he's cute. I like him."

John breathed a sigh of relief. At that moment he knew Beth was going to adjust to the circumstances with no problem.

"Harry called last night after he got home and told me it would be best if he brought his granddaughter, Jennifer later this afternoon," Sarah said. "They should be here shortly."

Ann, Douglass, Robert, and Beth were busy trying to draw sides and get up a volleyball game when Harry McDonald arrived with Jennifer.

Sarah welcomed her with a warm hug like she had given Beth. After the introductions were completed, Sarah called Scott's attention to how Douglass kept eyeing Jennifer. Sarah was pleased Douglass and Jennifer seemed smitten with each other at first sight.

Briefly, Sarah wondered why Martha did not accompany her husband and Jennifer. Maybe it was because Jennifer was so close to her grandfather, or because her grandmother could not accept what was happening.

Sarah encouraged the children to get involved in playing games. The five did not need further prompting. The adults went inside to discuss their plans more.

At dusk, Sarah called the children to come in and wash for supper. Everyone was seated at the table. Robert sat beside Beth and Douglass sat beside Jennifer.

Scott asked everyone to hold hands while he prayed, "Our Father, we pray the venture we are undertaking is your will and not our will. Give us the understanding, knowledge, strength, determination and faith to carry out your will.

"We feel unworthy of the trust you have bestowed upon us. We will, to the best of our abilities, do everything we can to live up to that trust. Bless this food to the nourishment of our bodies that we might be strengthened mentally and physically to carry out your will. Now let us pray together the prayer that Jesus taught us to pray saying,

'Our Father which art in heaven,
Hallowed be thy name.
Thy kingdom come, Thy will be done
In earth, as it is in heaven.
Give us this day our daily bread.
And forgive us our debts, as we
Forgive our debtors.
And lead us not into temptation,
But deliver us from evil; for thine
Is the kingdom, and the power, and
The glory, forever.' Amen."

In unison, everyone at the table repeated, "Amen" before they released hands.

Robert broke the reverent spell by saying, "I'm hungry. Please pass the biscuits."

After the meal, Scott said, "It's time for us to hold a meeting so everyone will understand fully what is happening. Each person needs to know what is expected of him or her."

Scott asked John to speak first, and Beth moved closer to her father. When John finished sharing with the children what he had learned from his contacts, Scott told the children everything that had happened to him when they were in Highlands and after they had returned home.

Ann, Douglass, and Robert listened with respect and awe. They looked at their father as if he were a stranger.

"Why haven't you told us before?" Ann asked. Douglass and Robert nodded in agreement.

"I don't know," Scott replied. "I guess I didn't believe it was important. At first I thought it was just a dream, but I've had the same dream too many times for it to be just a coincidence.

"After I heard what John has told you and what Harry is going to tell you, I knew something supernatural was happening. Now listen to what Harry has to add."

Harry shared his experiences with the group. Jennifer moved closer to her grandfather and held his arm. Harry told about his dream of trying to get Scott to open the door of the shuttle, Constitution, so Jennifer could get on board.

Jennifer squeezed Harry's arm tightly, and he kissed her on the forehead. Douglass touched Jennifer's hand to assure her Scott would let her aboard, and everything would work out fine.

"John, Scott and I want you young people to understand fully what we are planning," said Harry. "The Friday flight is on schedule. The only thing that's going to change is that you five will be on the shuttle with Sarah, Scott and a co-pilot.

"Don't worry. I will take care of everything, that's my job. Because of all the acts of terrorism going on around the world, especially in this country, there is a good possibility the flight could be cancelled. I will not let that happen!

"Replacing the original crew with all of you will be no problem, and the flight will take off as planned. Constitution will take the eight of you to the International Space Station to stay as long as necessary."

It was getting late. Scott summed up the meeting by instructing the children not to mention this to anyone. He assured them this was God's way of protecting them, just as God had protected Noah and his family by instructing Noah to build an ark.

The children's eyes sparkled with excitement about the prospect of being the first youth in space. Flying on Constitution to the ISS was above and beyond their wildest imagination.

Restraining their excitement was impossible, and all five jumped up and down with joy. They hugged each other and danced in circles until Robert announced, "God is saying the shuttle is something like a modern day Noah's Ark. In that case, it should now be called Scott's Ark."

Ann, Douglass, Jennifer and Beth shouted in unison, "We vote for that!"

18

ANN, DOUGLASS, Jennifer, Robert and Beth could not control their excitement. They were making so much noise Sarah finally asked them to go outside and work off some steam.

They went to the backyard, and soon all five were involved in a heated basketball game. Sarah hoped some physical activity would quiet them enough to allow them to go to sleep later.

Sarah insisted John and Harry stay the night with them. Harry declined because it was only an hour's drive to his home, and Martha would be concerned if he did not return tonight. After thanking Sarah for the supper, he shook hands with Scott and left.

John accepted Sarah's invitation, and she told him he could stay in Douglass and Robert's room. Sarah asked Scott to call the basketball players to come in and get ready for bed. When Scott went outside, he saw their teams were uneven.

"Two against three isn't fair. Let me play," Scott said. "Whose team can I be on?"

"Be on my team," said Robert. "Then it will be three on three."

"That isn't fair, you're too big," said Jennifer, "and besides, Robert and Douglass are winning already."

The brouhaha really got started then. They argued louder and louder until Sarah came out of the house to see what the trouble was. Scott asked her and John to come join them, so there would be eight players and the teams could be evenly divided.

After much bickering, the teams were divided into Robert, Beth, Ann, and Scott and Sarah, Douglass, Jennifer, and John. Finally they were able to begin playing, and things became quieter in the Walkers' backyard because each person was concentrating on the game and wanted to win.

Everyone was so caught up in the excitement of the game they lost all concept of time. It was almost midnight when Sarah proclaimed she was exhausted and needed to stop. Because the other players were so tired, no one objected.

Scott pointed out it was the perfect stopping time because, according to his score keeping, the teams were tied. No one could boast about winning.

When they went into the house, Ann fixed beverages for everyone while they discussed the game. Jennifer and Beth were very athletically coordinated and very aggressive players. They were proud to be complimented on their play.

Ann said she would like Beth and Jennifer to stay in her room. She had a trundle bed under her double bed, so Jennifer and Beth could sleep in the double bed and Ann would take the trundle.

Sarah agreed that would be fine. She told Douglass and Robert to fix a pallet on the floor in the playroom because John would be staying in their room.

As Sarah and Scott showered and were getting ready to go to bed, they continued to discuss how well the young people had gotten along.

"Did you notice how protective Robert was of Beth?" Sarah asked. "I couldn't believe he passed the ball to her several times, so she could take the shot instead of him.

"When he did it the first time, I had to restrain myself from going over and giving him a big hug, right in the middle of the game. I am so proud of him, and I think Beth fit right in with everyone."

"I thought Douglass played up to Jennifer just as much," Scott said. "Did you see the high five he gave her each time she scored? She's an awesome athlete, probably the high scorer on your team. Both girls fit in like lifelong members of our family."

Sarah checked to make sure everyone else had finished their baths and retired for the night. Douglass and Robert were already asleep on their pallets in the playroom.

She returned to find Scott already in bed. She slipped in next to him, snuggling closely in his arms to drift into a peaceful night's sleep.

THE FOLLOWING MORNING, John awakened to the desire for a fresh cup of coffee. He relied on that first cup of coffee to wake him fully and get his motor going. Usually having a cup of coffee was the first thing he did, but this morning his cell phone beeped before he left the room, indicating he had voice mail.

Much to his surprise, the message was from his boss, Neil Anderson. Interestingly, it was the first message he had ever received from his boss personally. Messages had always been delivered through Anderson's secretary.

Anderson's stern voice made the hairs on the back

of John's neck bristle. The harsh message commanded him to be in Anderson's office ASAP, no later than Thursday. No need for coffee to wake him up now. The sound of his boss's voice had jolted him fully.

He went to the kitchen where Sarah and Scott were having their morning breakfast. "Morning. Is Beth up?" John asked as he joined them.

"No," Sarah said she prepared a cup of coffee for John. "I told the girls last night to try and sleep in this morning. I'll call her if you'd like."

John shook his head. "Not yet. I will need to speak with her though before I leave. I just received a message on my cell phone calling for my return to the office ASAP."

John took a sip of the coffee. It was just the way he liked it, strong and black, no sugar. After a moment he said, "I may not be able to return before the lift-off."

Scott and Sarah said in unison, "Don't talk that way."

John looked at them seriously, "Even if I am able to return before the lift-off, there is no room for me on the shuttle."

"We'll work out something," Scott said.

"Scott, you know better than I do the shuttle can accommodate only eight. If we are to have any chance of survival and success, eight is all that can be on board."

He held up a hand to keep either of them from protesting more. "Let's not say anything else. Don't even think about waiting for me — that's an order, not a request.

"I can't speak for Harry, but even if I am able to get back before the lift-off, I will not get on Scott's Ark. That's final. I know I'll probably never see Beth again. That's why I must speak with her before I leave. I owe her that much, to say goodbye. Promise me you'll always take care of her."

"Beth will always be treated as if she is our own flesh and blood," Sarah said quietly, placing her hand over his. "Don't worry."

Scott nodded affirmatively. John smiled with relief. He knew he could rely on whatever Sarah and Scott said.

A moment later, Douglass and Robert came to breakfast and Sarah went to awaken the girls. The brothers had finished eating before Ann, Beth, and Jennifer made it to the kitchen.

The girls were fully dressed. Beth went to her father and gave him a big hug, which John lovingly returned. After the girls had finished breakfast, John asked Beth to come with him to the backyard where they could talk.

John took his daughter's hand as they stepped outside. He turned her to face him, and hugged her firmly until she said, "What's wrong, Daddy?"

He continued to embrace her lovingly. He could not let her see the tears forming in his eyes. He released his hold on her and held her at arm's length.

"What's wrong, Daddy?" Beth repeated.

"No matter what happens," John said. "I want you to remember your daddy loves you very much, and I will always love you."

"Daddy, please don't talk that way. Something's wrong. What is it?"

"Something is wrong. I have been ordered to return to my office in D.C. immediately. It's a long drive, and the highways are crowded. Getting there and back may take longer than I expect."

"Can't you fly?"

"No. It's necessary that I drive," John said, stroking a hand down her hair. "I might not be able to return before lift-off. Regardless, I want you to remember how much I love you. Remember also that your mother, in her own way, loves you."

John had never said anything to Beth that was critical of her mother.

"But, Daddy…"

John interrupted her before she could finish. "Sarah and Scott will take care of you, and Robert will be a good friend to you. Think about how many times he passed the ball to you so you could score last night. I think he really likes you. Give me a kiss and a big hug. I have to leave now."

Tears were flowing uncontrollably down Beth's cheeks. She pleaded with her father to let her go with him. She held him with all her strength and would not turn him loose.

Finally John pushed her away and kissed her on her forehead and cheek. He whispered, "See you when you return from ISS. I will always love you."

"Harry is here and says it's time for the children to be measured for the suits," Sarah called from the porch then she saw that Beth was crying.

She went to her and wrapped her arms around the sobbing girl. "Your father needs you to be brave and strong. He needs to see a smile before he goes."

Beth wiped away her tears, turned and smiled at her father. "I love you, Daddy. Drive carefully, hurry back before the lift-off if you can. If you can't, I'll see you as soon as we get back from the space station."

John waved back and turned quickly so Beth would not see the tears flowing down his face.

19

SARAH TOOK BETH to the house and helped her wash her face. When they were done, Sarah took her by the hand and headed for Ann's room. "Let's see if we can find what the others are doing."

When they entered the room, Ann and Jennifer were huddled over the dresser.

"What's going on?" Sarah asked.

"We're packing," Ann said.

Sarah looked at her seriously, "You know there will be no space for personal things."

"This is the cameo Grandma Kathryn gave me the last time we were in Highlands, and I want to take it. It belonged to her grandmother, and it won't take up any space," Ann said holding out the cameo in the palm of her hand.

"My grandmother gave me this locket with her picture on one side and a picture of Harry and me riding our favorite horses on the other," Jennifer chimed in. "I certainly hope I can take it."

"Besides," Ann said logically, "These won't take as much space as Robert's Monk- Monk."

Sarah cocked her head. "Robert was supposed to

have thrown that stuffed animal away a long time ago."

Ann mirrored her mother's pose. "Well, he didn't."

Sarah laughed and shook her head. "Jennifer, Monk-Monk was a curly, long tailed stuffed monkey. As soon as his small hands could grasp the monkey's tail, Robert rubbed it against his nose and upper lip. He fell asleep this way every night.

"By the time he was three, the monkey's tail was completely worn out and most of the stuffing had fallen out. He refused to sleep without it until his father and I finally convinced him first graders did not sleep with a stuffed monkey. We thought he had thrown it away."

"Nope," Ann said. "He kept it hidden. Sometimes he gets it out and just sits there looking at it. Robert and Douglass are in their room packing now."

Sarah and the three girls went to the boy's room where Robert had retrieved Monk-Monk from his hiding place. When he saw Sarah, Robert looked like he had been caught with his hand in the cookie jar.

He hugged his ragged pet. His pleading, forlorn expression spoke volumes to Sarah. She at once understood the children's need to take something on this trip that would connect them with their past.

"It's fine. We will make room," she said as she hugged Robert reassuringly.

Looking to Douglass, she asked, "What do you want to take?"

"I'd like to take this box of dry and wet fishing lures Grandpa Charles tied himself. He gave them to me when we were fishing last time we were in Highlands."

Sarah assured the five of them she would insist they be able to bring along their mementoes. She herself had a small bible she planned to take, even though the group would be in space only for a couple of weeks.

Harry and Scott were in the den talking when Sarah

and the five children came in.

"There's something I need the two of you to approve," Sarah said. "Each of us has something very meaningful we wish to take with us to the space station. I know space is limited, but these are special things we need very much to help us stay connected to who we are and where we came from. Like Monk-Monk."

"Monk-Monk!" Scott exclaimed looking at Robert. "You were supposed to bury that ragged stuffed animal a long time ago."

"I couldn't do it, Dad." Robert said, hugging the monkey as tears welled in his eyes.

Scott's heart constricted and his throat felt tight. "It's okay, Robert. Come here."

As he hugged his son tightly, he looked around at the others. "All of you can bring along one thing that's important to you, as long as it is not too large."

"I'm bringing along the bible that was given to me when I was baptized," Sarah said.

Clearing his throat to signal it was time to get back to business, Harry filled them in on the alterations shop he had found to alter the space suits quickly and confidentially.

Scott and this copilot, Gary Powell, already had their suits, and Harry had found a suit that would fit Sarah. Only the children's would need alterations.

Ann and Douglass had grown so much in the past year that a small adult space suit was not much too large for either of them. Robert and Beth's suits would require the most adjustments.

Scott drove everyone to the shop where Harry had previously taken the six space suits to be modified. While the seamstress was taking measurements, Harry and Scott walked outside to discuss the final plans for the flight to the ISS. Harry told Sarah to call out if there were any problems.

The original plans for the trip had been approved by the full NASA board over a year ago. At that time the intention was to take supplies to ISS for the longest stay ever in space. Taking recently developed new equipment to the station for testing had also been planned.

The new equipment included an air filtration device, which would ensure there was plenty of oxygen available for an exceptionally long stay in space.

Also on board would be a water recovery system to recycle liquid waste into Rocky Mountain spring fresh potable water.

Harry was increasing the amount of food the original orders had called for in case their stay at ISS had to be longer that expected. He was very excited about the improvements made recently in space food. It was now more palatable than ever.

He had tried most of the meals himself and found some almost as tasty as his wife's cooking, not that he would ever tell her. After eating, he felt comfortably full and satisfied. He was sure the children would find many of the meals to their liking.

The ease of serving the food was simplified and, according to the nutritionists who prepared the food, the meals were more wholesome than ever. The special body-building ingredients would be most beneficial to the young people.

The food preparers had been able, with some newly approved techniques, to make the food much more concentrated and lighter, thereby requiring less storage space.

An extra large supply of anti-radiation pills had also been stored for the trip. Actually, it was uncanny how well the original plans matched what was needed for this venture. Harry did not think food, oxygen, or water would be a problem for the eight people for a long, long time. If they were able to return from ISS soon, the unused supplies could be left at the station.

The most exciting pieces of new equipment were the six caddies on board to go to the ISS for testing. The caddy was a newly developed apparatus for NASA. Each was a casket-like container in which a person could be placed for an extended period of time. In the caddy, the occupant would experience the same effects of gravity as he did on earth.

First, an individual would be given an injection to put him or her in a hibernated state. The theory was that placing an individual in a hibernated state in the caddy would eliminate the problems of weightlessness that had plagued many astronauts after an extended stay in space.

All of the conditions of earth's gravity could be duplicated while one was in the cocoon-like apparatus. Later, when the caddy was opened, the occupant would be given another injection to awaken him or her from the hibernated state.

The developers believed an individual could stay in the apparatus for an indefinite period of time with only beneficial effects. They had given it the name of Dracula's Coffin or D.C. for short.

Scott was skeptical of the device working, but on paper and from what few tests had been done, the caddy was a stroke of genius. Also, in the hibernated state, the individual would require less oxygen, water, and food as well as anti-radiation capsules. Scott was excited about D.C.

By the time everyone emerged from the alteration shop, Harry and Scott had finished their discussion. Harry made arrangements for the suits to be picked up the next day.

20

ACTS OF TERRORISM were occurring with sudden frequency and severity, disrupting life in the United States. As a result, John's drive from Winter Park to Washington took much longer than he anticipated.

Traffic was extremely congested. There were numerous delays on the highways because of wrecks and damage to bridges caused by the terrorist attacks. He had to take several time consuming detours.

About 10:00 Thursday morning John finally arrived at the sentinel control panel at the gates to Equus Estate. He placed the palm of his hand on the device, but nothing happened. He placed it there again. Nothing. He shrugged thinking maybe the terrorist attacks had affected LAD.

Retrieving his plastic ID card, he swiped it through the monitor. The gates opened. He drove past his reserved space in front of the manor and instead parked behind the guesthouse.

When he realized how far he had to walk to get to the front entrance of the office, he wondered what he had been thinking.

When John entered the front door of the mansion,

everything looked normal in the foyer. The massive arrangement of fresh flowers appeared to have been placed there that morning; however, instead of the usual mix of multi-color flowers, the vase contained only white carnations. They reminded John of funerals, and struck him as an odd choice.

Walking directly through the banquet hall to the kitchen, he moved the wine rack in the pantry and placed his palm on the sentinel. The steel door did not move.

Okay, things were getting too strange. The hairs on John's neck began to bristle. Had the terrorists somehow damaged the security system?

Suddenly a man was behind him. John had not heard him approach and did not recognize him. The man placed his palm on the monitor and immediately the steel door opened.

He motioned for John to enter first. John nodded his thanks. At the elevator, the stranger again placed his palm on the panel. Again he let John step in first. Neither spoke as the elevator descended underground.

John was filled with anxious suspicion. Was he being escorted to Anderson's office by this stranger? When the elevator door opened, both men walked down the corridor toward Anderson's office.

"I need to go to the restroom," John mumbled.

"Pardon me?" the stranger asked gruffly.

John cleared his throat. "I've had a long drive. I need to go to the restroom and clean up before I report in."

"Fine. Better hurry. You know how impatient the boss is."

That alarmed John even more. How did this stranger know Anderson was waiting to see him? Before John entered the restroom, he watched the stranger continue down the hall and step into Neil Anderson's office. Instead of going directly into the restroom, John quietly tiptoed down the hall to Anderson's office.

"He's in the restroom," the stranger said. "I told you not to remove his palm print from the sentinel. Fortunately his card opened the gate. When I saw his print did not open the door in the pantry, I stepped out and escorted him down. We don't need him to become alarmed."

"I don't care if he's alarmed or not," Anderson said. "He told me his contact in the Bahamas failed to show. They did meet, and afterward the contact was assassinated.

"John lied to me. He probably gave his contact a lot of information about LAD and the CIA. He could be working as a mole for someone outside the CIA.

"John Johnston knows too much, and he needs to be eliminated immediately. That's where you come in, Brutus."

John had heard enough Stealthily he moved away from Anderson's office. Once in the restroom, he opened the spigot in the sink and left the water running. Then he flipped the lock on the inside of the door so that when the door closed behind him, the room would remain locked.

Hurrying past the kitchen, he moved down the hall to the tunnel leading to the basement of the guesthouse. As he hurried, he thanked God for guiding him to park at the guesthouse.

He rushed through the guesthouse, got in his car and drove to the entrance of Equus Estates. The gates opened automatically for anyone leaving the estate.

Inside the mansion, Anderson sent Brutus to check on John. Brutus tried the door to the restroom, but it was locked. Because he could hear water running, he casually strolled back to Anderson's office and told his boss Johnston was still washing up.

Another five minutes passed before Anderson walked to the restroom. He tapped on the door. When he heard no reply, he banged loudly. Nothing was heard except the running water.

"Brutus, break it down!"

Brutus lunged his 295 pounds of bulky muscle against the door. On the second try, the door jam splintered and he fell forward onto the tile floor. Anderson entered behind him. It didn't take long to determine the room was empty.

"You idiot!" yelled Anderson. "Why didn't you stay with him?"

Anderson dashed to his office and called security. He was informed John Johnston had just exited the gate in his car.

"Put out an APB for him immediately!" Anderson shouted, slamming down the phone.

JOHN DARED NOT drive the company car any longer than absolutely necessary. Driving to a rough neighborhood in D.C., he left the keys in the unlocked car. He hoped the car would be stripped. That would slow Anderson's tracking him.

In case Anderson had installed a tracking device in his cell phone, John discarded it through a drainage grate a block from where he abandoned the car.

He had walked less than three blocks when he heard a noise and turned to see thugs pounce on the abandoned car and begin stripping it the way vultures strip a dead animal.

He crossed the street to a bus stop and boarded an express bus to the suburbs where he found a small rental car lot. He rented a midsize, non-descript car and drove south as fast as he could. He was desperate to be sure Beth was safely aboard Scott's Ark.

THE APB BROUGHT no results. Anderson ransacked John's office, contemplating where he would go if he were John Johnston.

He knew of John's estrangement from his wife. There was no need for Anderson to look for her, even though John still had a picture of Frances on his desk.

He noticed the other picture, of John's daughter, Beth, on the desk. He recalled hearing John say something about always taking care of Beth.

"That's it," he said to Brutus. "Johnston will be where his daughter is. Find her! Wait a minute." Anderson said, smacking his forehead. "What am I thinking? I forgot about the tracking device implant."

Shortly after John Johnston had joined LAD, he mentioned he was having trouble with a sensitive tooth. Anderson suggested he see the company dentist – the best dentist in the D.C. area.

Dr. Rowe was also Anderson's personal dentist and his work never hurt. Anderson told John that whatever needed to be done would be paid for by LAD. It was an employee benefit.

John made an appointment. X-rays were taken of all of his teeth, and a dental prophylaxis was performed by the hygienist.

Dr. Rowe examined John and told him there were caries around and under a large restoration. It would be best to replace the large restoration and the additional caries with a full crown. An impression of the tooth was made and a temporary crown was put in place until the new crown could be fabricated.

One week later, John returned to Dr. Rowe for the cementing of the porcelain-fused-to-high-noble metal crown. Before cementing the crown, Dr. Rowe showed it to John. It matched the shade of John's other teeth perfectly.

John was never aware of the tracking device imbedded in the porcelain. Neil Anderson and LAD could track his every move, no matter where he went.

Anderson went to records. "Activate John Johnston's tracking device and check his movements last week."

A technician scanned through John's movements and reported, "Sunday he was in Ft. Lauderdale. He drove to Winter Park. He was at 1001 Memory Lane in Winter Park Sunday night. Monday he drove here."

"Who lives there?"

The technician cross-referenced the address. "The house is rented by Scott Walker. Right now, John Johnston is driving south on Interstate 95, but the highway is impassable in many places."

"Brutus, take the Mercedes and follow him," Anderson commanded. "We'll keep you informed where he is, but I know he is going to his daughter. When you see him, eliminate him. Get going!"

JOHN WAS in a frantic race to get near the Kennedy Space Center. Dawn was about to break on Friday morning. He had driven all night.

There were a lot of places on the highway where it was impossible to drive. He had to take a lot of detours. It was almost time for the lift-off.

He was not going to make it to the space center in time for the launch. Who could he call? Everyone should be on Scott's Ark by now. Harry McDonald. He would call him. John pulled into a gas station, saw a public phone at one side of the station, and dialed Harry McDonald's personal cell phone.

"Hello?" Harry's voice came on the line.

"It's John. Is Beth okay? Where is she?"

"She's safe. She's already on the shuttle with everyone else. Lift-off is just a few seconds away. I hope you're close enough to see it."

"I think I am. I'm at a gas station on the highway very close to the Center. I can't see the tip of the shuttle, but I can see a lot of glow from all of the lights."

"The children were very excited. The loading was extremely uneventful. Beth told me to tell you she was okay and she would see you when she returns from ISS. John, wherever you are, go outside and watch the lift-off. It's going."

John hung up the phone and walked around the corner of the gas station where he could look to the east. He was unaware of the large, black Mercedes sedan that had pulled into the station lot and parked behind his rental car. He was focused on the glow of the surrounding lights.

Suddenly the glow increased to an eye-blinding brilliance as the rockets fired. Smoke rose above the trees. The tip of the external fuel tank slowly broke free of the treetops. John could see the two attached solid rockets and then the shuttle itself.

For a moment, it seemed to pause and stand still then it streaked into the heavens. John folded his hands in a child-like prayer and whispered to God, "Thank you, thank you, thank you, God. Beth is safe now and in your hands."

He watched Scott's Ark rising to safety in the atmosphere like Noah's Ark had risen in the waters. He smiled. It was his last vision.

He never heard or felt the slug that pierced his skull and exploded in his head. He crumpled to his knees, his hands still pressed together in prayer, and fell forward, a smile on his face.

John Johnston, the voice crying in the wilderness, was dead.

Brutus had carried out his orders. He removed the silencer from his weapon. Out of habit, he blew across the nozzle of his pistol. Flipping out his cell phone, he said, "Mission completed."

21

ALL OVER THE UNITED STATES, nuclear power plants and stored weapons of mass destruction were being attacked and sabotaged by terrorists.

Many plants were unable to produce any electricity. In fact, some plants were spewing radiation into the atmosphere.

The Department of Homeland Security, trying to avoid pandemonium, denied this vehemently. The Secretary, himself, officially announced there was no cause for alarm, only the inconvenience of being without electrical power.

Harry McDonald received an order from Washington to scrub the launch of Constitution. He kept that order to himself. He let the countdown continue until the eleventh hour then he informed only the flight crew that the flight was scrubbed.

The rest of the staff involved with the lift-off continued working at their stations at Kennedy Space Center and in Houston. At first, the flight crew was disappointed, however each was anxious about the problems at their homes and nationwide.

Quietly the flight crew, except for Scott and Gary Powell, left the launch tower. Scott and Gary entered the capsule and continued their communication with the control tower and Houston. All systems were go.

Harry had Sarah and the children hidden in an area adjacent to the launch pad. As soon as the flight crew left the area, Sarah and the children, in their flight suits and gear, were ushered into Constitution.

The final countdown began. Everything proceeded on schedule like a typical sunrise lift-off from the Kennedy Space Center. With the lift-off, every minute detail of Scott Walker's dream became reality.

The space shuttle Constitution, AKA Scott's Ark, was on its way to rendezvous with the International Space Station. Everything was routine about the flight and Scott's Ark was soon approaching the ISS.

Suddenly the station exploded in front of them. A nuclear missile, fired from an unknown site on planet earth, had completely annihilated ISS. The force of the explosion threw Scott's Ark off course. There was no station and nowhere to dock.

To further complicate matters, communication between Scott's Ark and the Kennedy Space Center and Houston was disrupted.

They were speeding uncontrollably through space at plank speed, almost the speed of light, toward an unknown destination.

22

AS SCOTT'S ARK was lifting off from the Kennedy Space Center, four intercontinental nuclear ballistic missiles were launched from North Korea. Target: the west coast of North America.

Terrorists had no problem finding most of the weapons of mass destruction stockpiled in the United States. Simultaneously, coordinated suicidal terrorist attacks were launched against countless WMD sites all over the U.S.

Stored nuclear bombs were detonated. The recently developed and highly secretive 'bunker bombs' were found by terrorists and detonated in the cradle of America. This created a chain reaction, which caused the stored nuclear reactor fuel in Idaho to explode, spewing deadly radiation and cesium137 over the western half of the United States.

Nerve gas storage centers were raided. As the poisonous fumes were released into the atmosphere, the jet stream spread death across America from sea to shining sea.

Silos, which should have been demolished according to a cold war treaty with the USSR, were activated.

The nuclear missiles were reprogrammed and launched against major U.S. cities.

Biological weapons, developed and stored by the U.S., were released into major water supplies. The Department of Homeland Security was rendered powerless to stop the disastrous attacks. The complete annihilation of the North American continent seemed inevitable.

In the Middle East, Israelis and Palestinians launched every conceivable weapon they could lay their hands on against each other. Hand-to-hand fighting permeated the streets of these eternal enemies.

Elsewhere on the planet, thousands of weapons from nuclear bombs, to tanks, to chemical weapons, to biological devices, to singleshot rifles were launched by each nation against its adversary.

Libyan zealots launched their supply of poisonous gas and their lone nuclear atomic missile, obtained from ex-Soviet generals, against Europe.

The long-time feud between India and China reached the boiling point. India jumped into the fray and launched a nuclear missile against Pakistan and China. The Pakistanis immediately returned fire with Hatf-4 missiles, which delivered nuclear warheads to New Delhi. The destruction was catastrophic.

In the South Pacific, specifically in the Philippines and Indonesia, the rebel Islamic followers revolted openly against Christians with an unbelievable vengeance. Muslims invaded Australia creating havoc and destruction everywhere they went.

Long-term animosities between Japan and North Korea, as well as China, erupted into all out war. China attacked Taiwan.

In Iraq, Russian nuclear bombs that had been skillfully hidden from the UN and coalition inspectors were detonated concurrently by Saddam Hussein's fanatical followers.

Because the bombs were very deep underground, the damage done was not immediately noticeable. The massive magnitude of the explosions created internal problems. The force was transmitted through the hydrosphere and lithosphere, all the way through the mantle and even to the core of the planet.

Tectonic plates throughout the planet shifted. Subterranean earthquakes under the Mediterranean Sea caused tsunamis to race across the sea and destroy Gibraltar.

The monstrous wave forced its way into the Atlantic Ocean, increasing in size and power as it sped across the water.

By the time it reached the east coast of the United States, the wave was more than a mile high. It washed over the entire state of Florida, destroying every living creature in its path. For miles inland, the east coast of North America was inundated with water.

The shifting of incredible forces caused a split-second pause in the rotation of the planet's core. Pressure deep within the planet began to build up.

Since the beginning of time, the escape route for such pressures had been volcanoes.However, diastrophic forces closed these exit routes and the internal pressures could not be released.

The billions of gallons of oil that had been pumped from the earth for generations contributed to the shifting of tectonic plates until all volcanoes were completely blocked and inactive. Geysers in Yellowstone National Park no longer erupted.

Upwelling hot magma could no longer break through the earth's crust to reach the surface of the planet and relieve the internal pressures. Blobs of molten rock below the Pacific Ocean's Ring of Fire, one of the earth's most violent zones, could not escape.

Because the earth's core could not release the massive heat, the planet burst into a ball of fire, exploded, and vaporized into nothingness. Planet earth no longer existed.

God watched, distraught over the evil committed in this earthly conflict. Judaism, Christianity, and Islam, each in its own way, professed to be acting in God's Holy Name. Yet each had contributed to the destruction of God's creation.

Before God turned His face from earth, He lifted up Scott and all his house.

To the occupants of Scott's Ark the earth appeared to be about the size of a beach ball. As they watched in dumbfounded awe, it seemed to expand slightly, and then in one indescribable explosion the planet burst into a ball of fire and evaporated.

Seven people turned and stared at their captain. What happened to earth? Where did it go? What happened to the International Space Station? Where could they dock now? Now that planet earth and ISS no longer exist, where could they go? What was to become of them?

Scott and Gary went to the controls and ignited the Ark's thrusters, rotating the craft a complete 360 degrees, just to make sure they had not simply lost sight of earth. After completing the rotations, in all directions, Scott and the crew could see nothing except an empty void.

Planet earth was no longer visible. It had truly exploded and vaporized into less than nothing as the crew had witnessed. Scott and Gary shut down the thrusters.

Scott turned to his crew, "We've done the best we

possibly could do, and now we will have to put our faith in God."

With the earth's demise, the solar system, Mercury, Venus, Mars, Jupiter, Saturn, Uranus, Neptune, and Pluto along with all of their moons, comets, asteroids and meteors began to collapse into the sun. The entire solar system was destroyed.

Forces created by the explosion of earth caused Scott's Ark to rotate uncontrollably through space. Its speed increased dramatically until they reached the speed of light.

As it approached the outer edges of the Milky Way, the Ark was caught in the gravity of a swirling black hole. Immense forces sucked it into the vortex, swirled it through the hole's vacuum, and expelled it with tremendous, centrifugal force from the other side, into the space and time of another galaxy.

The occupants of Scott's Ark were now completely in the hands of God.

23

EVENTUALLY, THE OCCUPANTS of Scott's Ark began to recover from the shock of seeing their entire planet explode and disappear.

Scott prayed God would give him the wisdom, courage, and strength to be the leader the others now so desperately needed. Feeling a sense of peace, he knew his prayer was answered. With a positive, upbeat attitude he began assigning responsibilities to each member of their crew.

Sarah became the Chief Executive Officer. As the CEO, she was in control of the crew and all personnel matters. She controlled all schedules and everyone, with the exception of Scott, would report to her.

She saw to it all duties were equally and fairly distributed. All reports were submitted first to the CEO, for her evaluation. Only those needing the captain's attention were referred on to Scott.

Finally, she insisted each crew member maintain a neat, clean appearance, even under the extenuating circumstances.

Gary, the co-pilot, was in charge of all instruments and controls. His duties also included teaching

Douglass and Robert the mechanics and controls of the Ark.

Ann, Jennifer, and Beth were in charge of meals and housekeeping. They quickly established the rule that any complaints about the meals would result in the complainer being assigned to KP duty.

Douglass spent a lot of time relieving Ann and Beth from KP duty because he enjoyed helping Jennifer and just being around her.

At first, Douglass and Robert thought they had the easiest assignment of anyone. However, they found out differently when they became aware of how complicated Scott's Ark was. They had no idea it would involve as much study and physical work as it did.

Robert was also appointed Sergeant at Arms for all of their meetings. He proudly maintained security and order, and thought it was a prestigious position until Douglass told him he was nothing but a doorman.

Each member of the crew accepted his or her responsibility eagerly. It gave them a sense of being part of the team. Each person was made to feel important, and each person executed his duty with pride and expertise.

The Captain of Scott's Ark required regular reports from each person in "Scott's Marine Corps." Scott never let them forget he was a Marine. Strict inspections were routine. All reports were given in a very efficient, serious manner. The Captain ran a taut ship. He had to in order for the crew to survive.

Although Scott was the stern captain of Scott's Ark, he was also the loving, caring father and person any crew member could go to for comfort and understanding.

Scott established one hard and fast rule: Share and share alike the water, food, and especially the anti-radiation pills. He insisted each person take their daily dose to protect them from the deadly radiation.

There was an adequate food and oxygen supply to last the eight people some time. The new type of water recovery system assured an almost endless supply of water, and the new air filtration system provided plenty of healthy oxygen and air.

Life aboard Scott's Ark settled into a routine as the craft zoomed across the heavens. Only Scott's Marine-like orders kept life from becoming burdensome and lethargic.

Time, or rather a lack of any concept of time, became the obstacle. The elasticity of time had been stretched to the limit, until it snapped. Only the present existed. There was no sense of day or night, or week or month. Memories of the past became a vague concept. The future was too scary to even think about.

With little concept of their past and no sense of the future, hopelessness and depression overcame everyone except Scott and Sarah.

After much consultation with his CEO, Scott concluded the best solution to the problem would be for Gary and the children to be placed in a hibernated state in Dracula's Coffin for a while. The idea was discussed fully with the entire crew and received unanimous approval.

Scott and Sarah injected Gary and each youth with the medication to put them in a hibernated state. Each was then placed in D.C. where they would experience all of the conditions of gravity on earth.

In D.C., they would not need a daily dose of anti-radiation pills because radiation could not penetrate the walls of D.C.

Before each chamber was sealed, Sarah and Scott kissed each child good night. Gary's chamber was sealed last, and Sarah kissed him after Scott shook his hand. Scott told Gary that Sarah would take his place in D.C. when Gary's time in the chamber was up.

Because the Ark had passed through a strong magnetic field, none of the timers on the Ark worked any longer; however, Scott attempted to keep track of time with his wristwatch.

After what Scott estimated to be about one month, he and Sarah opened Gary's D.C. Carefully Sarah injected Gary with the drug to awaken him.

As Gary slowly regained consciousness, he felt completely rejuvenated. Scott prepared Sarah for her rotation in D.C. by giving her an injection of the drug. He whispered sweet dreams, kissed her gently on the lips and sealed her in.

Gary and Scott were in command of the Ark. They kept rotating people in and out of D.C. until each person had been in hibernation at least twice. After each person was awakened, they felt revitalized as if they had had a restful night's sleep.

Scott and Gary arranged the rotations so one of them would always be awake. Scott insisted one of them be available for control of the Ark at all times as rotations in Dracula's Coffins continued.

24

IN SPITE OF Scott and Sarah's best efforts to maintain a lively and energetic orderliness among the crew, languor gained control. Even Scott and Sarah experienced brief periods of depression, although neither of them ever let any of the crew become aware of it.

In reality, weariness had never left the Ark after the excitement of the lift-off and the shock of witnessing the destruction of planet earth wore off.

After many rotations in Dracula's Coffins, everyone was back in a state of hibernation except Scott and Sarah. They had just finished eating a skimpy meal when Sarah said simply, "I think Ann and Gary have something going."

"What do you mean?" Scott said, his fatherly protectiveness kicking in to high gear. "He better not lay a hand on my little girl."

Sarah smiled at him indulgently. "Have you really looked at Ann recently? She's no longer your little girl. She's a young lady with a young lady's desires and needs.

"When they are out of D.C. and awake, I've noticed how she looks at Gary and how he gazes at her. I believe she is falling in love with him. The feeling, I think, is mutual because he has been spending more and more time talking with her and less time with the boys."

"But she is only my little girl," Scott insisted. "I'll have a profoundly serious talk with Mister Gary Powell as soon as he gets out of D.C."

"You will do no such thing," Sarah said, placing her hand over his. "I cannot believe you are supposedly so intelligent, yet you have no concept of what is going on around you. Don't you ever take time to listen? Have you never noticed what their body language is telling you? How can you be so oblivious?"

She paused for a moment before continuing, "The last time you were in hibernation, Ann and Gary were awake and the three of us spent a lot of time talking. I was trying to break the news to you gently when I said they have something going. Actually they've fallen in love and wish to be married."

Scott opened his mouth to protest. Ann was his baby girl.

Before he could utter a sound, Sarah said, "Just be quiet and listen before you say anything. None of us, not even you, has any concept of how much time has passed since we left earth. We have only your timepiece, and we don't know how accurate it is. When I look at the children, all of them have changed so much. I'm sure a lot of time has elapsed.

"Look at your sons. Both have become very muscular young men. They're no longer little boys. All of the body-building ingredients in the food has surely benefited Douglass and Robert.

"Douglass has a beard and even your baby Robert needs to start shaving. Have you noticed how deep Robert's voice has become? Well it's time you wake up and begin to take notice of your crew! Even Beth and

Jennifer have grown into beautiful young ladies.

"I realize according to your Marine Corps tradition, you have to keep your distance from your troops, but at least get close enough to look at them with your mind's eye.

"Ann has developed into a mature, beautiful young lady who has fallen in love and wants to marry Gary. Gary loves Ann very much and is devoted to her. I believe if we were still on earth, Gary and Ann would have developed the same feelings for each other.

"Gary has been trying to get up the courage to ask you for permission to marry Ann. I gave them my blessing, and Ann gave me a wonderful hug.

"Scott, my deepest belief is that God would want us to carry on with our lives, and I believe that with all of my heart and soul. We must carry on with living our lives the best we possibly can under the circumstances and leave the rest to God.

"When Gary and Ann awake, I don't want you to say anything to either of them. Just listen to what they have to say, and notice how they look at each other. Take time to see what a beautiful, grown up lady Ann has become. The way Gary looks at Ann reminds me of the way you looked at me, once upon a time, a long time ago. Believe it or not, your daughter is so much like you that she has fallen in love just like you did.

"Don't you want her to find the happiness you found? I pray you still have that happiness. I do."

"Well, since you put it that way," Scott said humbly. "You're probably right. I will have to give it some thought. Even though we are in this unbelievable situation, I still have happiness and more, because I'm with you. You are the greatest thing that ever happened to me, and I love you more than ever."

Scott kissed his wife and embraced her tenderly.

WHEN IT CAME TIME to rouse two from the D.C., Sarah suggested waking everyone. It had been a very long time since they had all been together. She felt all of them being together would help them remain bonded better, and would be good for morale.

"And remember," she said to Scott, "after Ann and Gary are awake, nothing but positive, encouraging words. By all means, do not scowl at Gary. He is your co-pilot and has tremendous respect for you, but you are also the father of the girl he wants to marry. He is literally scared to ask you if he can marry Ann."

"See," Scott pointed out. "You just referred to Ann as a girl, but you fussed at me for calling her my little girl."

Sarah shook her head ruefully. "You know what I meant. She is my daughter and she will always be my girl, no matter how old she gets. Quit being difficult."

"Okay, I promise I won't say a word. After Gary asks me for Ann's hand in marriage, if he does, I will congratulate him and we can start planning the wedding. How's that for being positive?"

Sarah wrapped her arms around his neck and gave him a long, loving kiss.

Releasing him, she looked into his eyes. "I love you now more than ever. At each stage of our life together, I thought it would be impossible for me to love you more than I did at that time. However, as we reach another plateau in our lives, I find my love for you has grown even more intense. Instead of being two people joined by love, we are becoming as one."

Tears welled in Sarah's eyes. To keep them from running down her cheeks, she changed the subject. "Let's wake everyone. It's time, whatever time is, for them to have some food and water, and please don't let anyone forget to take their anti-radiation pills."

Scott gave each person an injection to bring them out of their hibernated state. While he did that, Sarah prepared some of the dwindling food and water.

Food and water had been rationed from day one of the venture. She wondered if it would be possible to reduce each person's food and water ration more because she was really worried about how much longer the supplies would last.

She put out an anti-radiation pill for each person, except herself. She had told no one she had stopped taking pills. She wanted to make sure there was enough for the rest of the crew.

When Scott, Gary, and the rest of the crew came into the main compartment, she pretended to be taking her anti-radiation pill with a small sip of water.

After everyone had taken their pill and had a bite to eat, Gary said, "Captain Walker, I uh, I, I, uh..." Stopping himself he took a deep breath and blurted, "Sir, may I have Ann's hand in marriage?"

"Is her hand all you want? Why don't you want the rest of her?" Robert asked, slapping his hands together and folding over with laughter.

Ann glared at her brother.

"That's enough, Robert," Sarah said. Some things never changed.

His mother's warning let Robert know he had better shut up, and shut up he did. He even looked at his sister apologetically. However, his attempt at jest had relaxed the tension and lightened the situation.

Scott looked at Ann who was holding her breath for fear her father would object. "We're going to have a wedding!" Scott said, and he went to Gary and gave him a firm handshake and hug. "Welcome to our family."

Then Scott turned to his daughter, held her lovingly and said, "Best wishes and you have your mother's and my blessings for a long and happy married life."

Ann's tears of happiness flowed unashamedly. Douglass and Robert rushed over to congratulate Gary. Beth and Jennifer scrambled over to hug Ann. Then Beth and Jennifer turned to Sarah and asked her what they could do for the wedding.

"I would appreciate it very much if you would help Ann and I plan the ceremony," said Sarah.

When Douglass and Robert went to their sister and wished her their best, tears began to run down Sarah's cheeks. She assured everyone they were tears of joy.

"Look at how lively they look now that they have something to look forward to, something to prepare for, and something to live for," Sarah said to Scott.

Before Gary had asked for Ann's hand in marriage, everyone had been talkative and happy to be out of hibernation. Now everyone in Scott's Ark, even the Captain himself, was in a state of jubilation.

Douglass, always the one to think ahead, asked, "How can they get married? No one here is a preacher, and you have to have a preacher to marry a couple."

"On a ship at sea, the captain is empowered to marry a couple," Sarah informed him. "Although we are not at sea, we are on a ship, and Scott is the captain of this ship. He can perform the wedding ceremony."

She smiled lovingly at her husband, "And it will be especially meaningful for him to unite his daughter and Gary in holy matrimony."

Scott nodded as he returned his wife's gaze. "That's right, and I'll do it. Tradition has it that the mother of the bride, aside from the bride herself, is most honored at a wedding. Besides that, they are both responsible for most of the planning. So Sarah, you and Ann get busy."

Turning to Gary, Scott said, "You will find your role, as the groom, to be the least important in the entire wedding party. All you have to do is show up."

"But, Daddy," Ann said, stepping close to Gary, "there can't be a wedding without him," and she kissed Gary passionately, drawing a synchronized whistle from her two brothers.

Gary blushed and excused himself to evaluate the cockpit instruments.

Sarah and Ann began immediately to plan for the wedding. Sarah, in addition to being the mother of the bride, would be the wedding director. Sarah insisted each person have an equally important part to play in the ceremony.

True to tradition, Gary's only job would be to show up. He would have it the easiest of everyone, although he would probably be the most nervous. Sarah asked Ann to work with Beth and Jennifer about their roles in the wedding.

Seeking out Gary, Sarah went to the control section where he was examining the instruments. He turned when she entered and thanked her sincerely. "Is it too early for me to call you mother? There are no words to tell you how happy I am now that Ann and I have your and Scott's blessings for this marriage."

"That's why I came in here to talk with you. Scott and I want to make this wedding as special and meaningful for you and Ann as we possible can. Her wedding day is the most exciting day in any young lady's life. Because of our situation, some things can't be. For example, there is no way to get a ring."

Lightheartedly, Gary replied, "I thought I'd have a chance to pick one up at Tiffany's when we returned to earth, but now…" his smile faded and was replaced by the gravest demeanor.

Sarah laid a reassuring hand on his shoulder. "Everything is going to work out fine. God will see to it."

She removed her engagement ring and gave it to Gary. "Give this to Ann now. Maybe you have already asked her to marry you, I don't know. If you have, ask her again and give her this ring. She'll love it. Don't worry, a wedding band will be available at the ceremony."

"We have talked about it a lot, but you're right, I have not formally asked her to marry me. Thank you, Sarah... I mean mother."

Gary took the ring, gave Sarah a hug and went to find Ann. He found her talking with Beth and Jennifer about their roles in the wedding. Politely interrupting, he asked Ann to come with him into the control room where they could be alone.

He was holding a piece of paper, rolled up and very wrinkled. The ends of it paper were ragged and torn slightly. Hidden in the center of the frayed edges of the paper, Gary had placed the diamond.

"You will have to call upon your wildest, most vivid imagination,"Gary said, smiling at Ann. "Close your eyes and imagine this piece of paper is a long stem, fully opened red rose. Can you do that?"

"Yes," was Ann's quick reply, and she closed her eyes tightly.

Gary placed the stem upright in her hand. "Be careful not to let the thorns prick you fingers," he said, then taking her hands in his, asked, "Ann Walker will you marry me?"

Ann opened her eyes. In her mind's eye she saw a diamond engagement ring cradled in the velvet petals of a large, long stem red rose.

It was the most brilliant, sparkling diamond she had ever seen. She gazed at it in quiet, speechless amazement for so long Gary thought maybe she was going to turn him down. Then she looked up at him with tears of joy sparkling in her eyes. "Yes. Yes, I will marry you."

SARAH PREPARED invitations in beautiful calligraphy. She had no idea what the date was. No one did. She indicated on the invitation the date for the wedding would be June 15th, a good date for a wedding.

> *Major and Mrs. Scott Walker*
> *Request the Honor of Your Presence*
> *At the Marriage of Their Daughter*
> *Ann Griffin*
> *To*
> *Gary Powell*
> *June fifteenth at half past Six o'clock*
> *Reception in the fellowship hall*
> *immediately following the ceremony*

On the designated day, at the designated time, Douglass and Robert, acting as ushers, seated the mother of the bride in her place of honor.

Scott, the minister, followed by Gary, a very nervous groom, entered the sanctuary from the rear. Beth and Jennifer also entered together. In addition to serving as Ann's bridesmaids, they had to provide the music. They sang a beautiful duet of "There Is Love."

Jennifer then moved to Scott's right, and Gary stood on Scott's left. Beth moved in beside Gary. All four faced the mother of the bride.

From the back of the wedding chapel, Robert and Douglass cupped their hands over their mouths and emitted the trumpet fanfare from Mendelssohn's "Wedding March" in *A Midsummer Night's Dream.*

Immediately, Sarah rose to stand in honor of the bride. Jennifer and Beth sang "Here Comes the Bride" as Douglass and Robert escorted their sister down the aisle to where the preacher and a grinning groom awaited her.

Sarah had made a wedding dress for Ann out of a white bed sheet. It was draped over Ann's left shoulder and pinned in place by the ivory carved cameo her Grandmother had given her.

The gown fell in soft folds over her breasts and back exposing her right shoulder and arm. A rope gathered the tunic at an empire waistline, which draped in graceful folds and pleats to the floor forming a train.

Ann was the epitome of a noble lady at a formal function in ancient Rome. Beth and Jennifer had styled Ann's hair to fall softly and gracefully over her shoulders.

A veil had been prepared from some gauze from the first aid kit. Ann carried a bouquet of white roses and baby's breath made from white paper.

When they reached the front of the sanctuary, the mother of the bride sat down and Captain Scott Walker began the wedding ceremony. "Dearly beloved we are gathered here to unite this man and this woman in Holy Matrimony. Who gives this woman to be married to this man?"

In unison Douglass and Robert said firmly, "Her mother, her father, and we do."

Then the brothers each lifted a corner of her veil, raised it and let it fall gently over the top and back of her head. Simultaneously they kissed their sister on her cheeks. Then Douglass move to stand beside Jennifer, and Robert stood at Beth's side.

Sarah was sitting at a slight angle so she could see Ann's profile. She thought Ann looked perfectly radiant, and she could hardly believe this was the same Ann who had been such a tomboy while growing up. Today her daughter was the very essence of womanhood.

Sarah was not the only one who thought Ann was beautiful. After Douglass and Robert raised her veil,

Gary froze in awe. He had not seen Ann all day. Southern tradition did not allow a groom to see his wife-to-be the day of the wedding until she walked down the aisle to join him at the altar. Scott had to nudge Gary so he would move to stand beside Ann.

"Gary," Scott said, "do you take Ann to be your lawful wedded wife, to love and cherish her, in sickness and in health, for richer or poorer as long as you both shall live?"

"I do," he responded immediately.

Scott then asked, "Ann, do you take Gary to be your lawful wedded husband to love and cherish him in sickness and in health, for richer or poorer as long as you both shall live?"

"I do," Ann replied.

"Is there anyone present who knows any reason why Ann and Gary should not be united in Holy Matrimony? Since there is no one, Gary, do you have a token to consecrate this union?"

Gary nodded and turned to Beth, who handed him Sarah's wedding band. Ann handed her bridal bouquet to Jennifer.

.   "Gary, place the ring on the third finger of Ann's left hand and repeat after me. With this ring, I thee wed."

Gary looked into Ann's eyes with all the love of his heart and repeated the vow.

"What God has joined together let no one put asunder," Scott announced. "I pronounce you husband and wife."

Asking Gary and Ann to kneel, Scott prayed, "Our Heavenly Father, Ann and Gary have vowed before you and those present to love each other and to be faithful to each other all of the days of their lives, and they have been joined in Holy Matrimony. May your richest blessings be upon them that they may find the happiness and fulfillment wedded life has to offer. Amen. Gary, you may kiss your bride."

After the kiss, Scott announced, "I present to you Mr. and Mrs. Gary Powell."

Gary and Ann turned to face the congregation. Jennifer returned the bridal bouquet to Ann who turned to face her father, kissed him and whispered, "Thank you. I love you, Daddy."

Douglass and Robert cupped their hands over their mouths and imitated the trumpet fanfare from Wagner's "Bridal Chorus in Loehngrin" as a recessional.

When the couple reached where Sarah was seated, Ann paused, pulled a rose from her paper bouquet, gave it to her mother, and kissed her.

Beth, Douglass, Robert, and Jennifer hummed the recessional until the newlyweds had left the chapel. Then hand in hand Jennifer and Douglass exited followed by Beth and Robert, also hand in hand.

Since Douglass and Robert had seated their mother before the ceremony, both came back to escort her from the sanctuary. Scott was left standing there alone, tears running down his cheeks, but he felt a completeness, satisfaction, and happiness he had not experienced in a long time. He was proud he had a married daughter, and a new son-in-law.

In a few moments, the newlyweds and all of the wedding party gathered for a reception in the fellowship hall. Scott had found the bottle of Silver Oak wine Harry McDonald had put on board the shuttle. Pouring everyone a glass of wine, he toasted the bride and groom, as did each person in turn.

Sarah brought out some bread to serve as wedding cake. Ann and Gary cut the cake, and after feeding a piece to each other, they cut a piece for each guest.

After the cake was served, more toasts were given. Then Sarah announced it was time for the newlyweds' first dance.

The bridesmaids and ushers provided the music by humming a waltz tune. Soon the father of the bride cut in to dance with his little girl, while Gary danced with his mother-in-law. Still humming a waltz, Jennifer and Douglass danced, followed by Beth and Robert.

Everyone danced and hummed, switching partners until each person had danced with everyone there. The party continued until the wee hours of whenever.

Gary thanked his new mother-in-law and father-in-law for the beautiful wedding and most of all for having Ann. Then Mr. and Mrs. Gary Powell said goodbye and left for their honeymoon, a suite Sarah had prepared in the storage compartment.

Scott gave Douglass and Robert an emphatic warning not to disturb the newlyweds.

"I remember Grandpa Charles telling me about when he and Grandma were married," Robert said. "They didn't have enough money to go away on a honeymoon so they spent their first night together at Grandma's parent's home, and all the neighbors gave them a shivaree.

"Grandpa said the neighbors serenaded them for hours, as they danced around the house and beat tin cans together." He looked at his parents with genuine caring. "Dad, Mom, can't we give them a shivaree for just a little while? We won't serenade them too long or make too much noise."

"That's an excellent idea," Sarah said smiling. "Let's all give the newlyweds a shivaree they will never forget."

25

AFTER THE EXCITEMENT of the wedding festivities waned, everyone became lethargic again except the newlyweds. Ann and Gary continued to be in a state euphoria, touching, laughing, caressing, whispering, sharing dreams and experiencing all the nuances of two recently married lovers becoming one in spirit and body.

Scott had changed the order of rotation in D.C. so Gary and Ann would be awake together. It was still necessary for Scott or Gary to be awake at all times because one of them needed to be in the control area.

At this particular time, everyone was in D.C. except Scott and Sarah. They kept themselves as busy as possible with daily chores. Sarah spent a lot of time reading her bible, though one of her most important duties was to monitor the six D.C.'s.

Scott had to spend much of his time at the controls. They alternated sleeping times so one of them was always awake.

Scott was aware of darkness, nothing but absolute darkness. There was no sound, no motion, no sign of life, only unadulterated nothingness. Yet, in the middle of the black void, something formless slithered silently.

Movement became faster and faster until the blackness began to fade into a murky, thick grayness similar to the fog on an English moor, or the heavy smog smothering Los Angeles on a sultry, summer day.

The movement became an eye, straining to find its way through the fog. A cataract-like cloud obscured the eye's vision. It squinted closed until it passed through billowy clouds, which became as white as freshly fallen snow.

As it sailed through the puffs of clouds, the eye opened and spread graceful, white wings becoming a brilliant white dove. It glided effortlessly among the white clouds as they opened to a brightness and clarity never seen before.

A rainbow of color greeted the dove: pale blue sky above green mountain peaks, tropical forests, lush meadows, and an azure ocean. The air, fresh as after a spring rain, rushed past the dove. Gracefully the dove continued to soar above the planet below in lazy circles, drawing closer and closer.

It sailed between two tall, green mountain peaks and over a rippling mountain stream that raced toward the ocean. Forming smaller circles in the sky, the dove glided closer to the lush green meadow where a single, large tree stood.

As it sailed toward the tree, the dove extended its talons to grasp the top branch. It missed, unable to clutch the limb, and collapsed, falling back into the darkness of space.

When Scott awoke, he was very excited. He was not sure about the meaning of the dream, but the fact he had had a dream was reason enough for his elation. It was the first dream he had had since they had left earth.

He knew he must remember every detail so he could share it with Sarah, and they could ponder what message was being sent to him. He remembered everything except the ending. The last thing he recalled was the dove extending its talons to grasp the limb of the tall tree.

Scott left the control complex and went to the area where Sarah was sleeping. He sat on the floor beside the narrow cot where she lay. Gently, he shook her and whispered, "Sarah, I've had a dream. Wake up, I want to tell you about it."

Sarah barely moved. He clasped her hand and raised it to his lips to kiss. With a gasp he saw the cancerous radiation sores on the back of her hand. He was too stunned to speak. Fear griped his body as his gaze moved from her hands to her face.

Although he had seen her daily, this was the first time he had really looked at her in a long time. He was shocked to find her once beautiful face was now emaciated.

She opened her eyes, which had always sparkled and been so full of life. They were ashen and spiritless.

Scott searched them deeply as he whispered, "Why? You have not been taking your anti-radiation medications, have you?"

She did not need to answer. He saw the truth on her face. "We agreed at the beginning of this we would share and share alike, especially the pills that would protect us from excessive radiation. Sarah, dispensing the pills was your responsibility. Why have you not been taking your share? Why?"

Tears began to well in his eyes.

"Shhh," she whispered in an almost inaudible voice. She was so weak; Scott could barely hear her. His eyes continued to search for an answer, something to tell him this too was a dream, not reality. No answer came.

"Why?" he begged again.

"Shhh," she whispered again, pulling his head to her breast. "Let me tell you about your dream."

He leaned slightly over her. She placed her weakened, pale hands on his head and tenderly pressed his head to her chest.

Scott was so upset he did not resist, and he was totally oblivious to what she had just said. He was in a state of shock and denial.

Sarah began to stroke the side of his head with her wrinkled hand, her frail fingers kneading his temples. The soft tone of her voice and the soothing effect of her touch soon began to relieve the tension and anxiety that gripped him. The gentle rise and fall of her breathing calmed him.

His ear was almost directly over her heart, and he could hear the faint but regular beat. He became mesmerized by the rhythmic lub dub. Scott was no longer entombed in a space ship. Instead, he was back in the security of his mother's womb.

Sarah's heartbeat and words became the heartbeat and words of his mother. Stress, strain, and turmoil would be a thing of the future. For the time being, he was back in his mother's womb reliving the wonderful, secure, peaceful serenity he had experienced before his mother expelled him into the harsh reality of the world.

Scott's conscious mind was unaware of Sarah saying anything. However, much later her words would rise from the recesses of his subconscious.

"In the beginning of your dream, there was only darkness. Then there was motion. Something moved in the darkness. It became an eye, trying to find its way. The darkness turned into gray clouds, and the eye tried to see through the clouds. The eye became a beautiful snow-white dove gliding through the white clouds into a clear, blue sky.

"A rainbow greeted the dove and guided it over an azure ocean to green mountains. With its wings effortlessly spread, it formed lazy circles in the sky, drawing closer and closer to the planet below until it sailed between two mountain peaks to a small green meadow.

"A tall tree stood in the middle of the meadow. The dove extended its talons to grasp the top limb of the tree."

Sarah paused for a long moment, not voicing that the dove had been unable to land. She had dreamed the dove vanished back into the void of darkness.

She would not tell Scott the end of her vision. Instead, in a very soft whisper she said, "Tell the children I love them. You must always take care of them."

Her hand moved slower and slower stroking the side of his temple until finally it stopped. The lub dub of her heartbeat became fainter and fainter until Scott no longer heard it. There was no rise and fall of her breast.

Unconsciously, Scott grasped Sarah's lifeless hand and began to stroke the side of his head with her hand, hoping she would continue to do it herself. He turned her hand loose and it lay there without moving. Again he grasped her hand and stroked his temple.

"Sarah?" he whispered, straining to hear a heart beat. There was none. He raised his head from her breast and called to her again, "Sarah?"

She did not reply.

Scott's training kicked in and he reflexively felt for a carotid pulse. When he could not find a pulse or detect any sign of breathing, he automatically began CPR.

After forcing air into her lungs, he began chest compressions. He repeated the procedures, over and over, with no response.

He refused to give up. Desperately he continued to administer CPR. Finally he realized the futility of his efforts. Exhausted, he collapsed over her frail body. Sarah Douglass Walker was dead.

Tears welled in his eyes, and slowly ran down his face to fall from his chin onto Sarah's lifeless body. Although he was looking directly at her, his mind's eye saw the beautiful, young college coed he had met at a party a long time ago.

He remembered thinking she was the most beautiful, most full-of-life girl he had ever seen. It was the sparkle in her blue eyes that attracted him the most. He looked down. Her eyes were so pale now in this lifeless state.

"Why, Sarah?" he whispered, holding her. Why?"

But he knew the answer. She had not taken her share of the medication because she wanted to make sure everyone else had enough.

How could she do this to him? How could she leave him now when he needed her more than he ever had in his life? He couldn't do this by himself. And it wasn't just about him. She had deserted the children too. How could she?

"Sarah, how could you do this to us, who love and need you? I hate you for leaving the children and me!"

Instantly aware of what he had said, Scott burst into uncontrollable sobs. He embraced her lifeless body and held her tightly.

On his knees, he rocked back and forth saying, "Please forgive me. I didn't mean it. I love you. The children love you. You did it out of love for us. You were trying to take care of us. Sarah, please forgive me! For God's sake, Sarah, please forgive me! I could never hate you."

Scott continued to hold her tightly and rock, wishing somehow he could restore life to her or at least hear some response to his pleas for forgiveness.

Turning teary eyes to heaven, Scott shouted aloud,

"God! God!! You let this happen. You, God, killed Sarah! It's not her fault. God, it's your fault!"

Scott's fury was now directed toward God. He continued to kneel beside Sarah's lifeless body, and in his rage, he rent the clothes from his upper body with such violent force his fingernails sliced across his chest, cutting shallow slices of flesh from his body.

When he saw the blood ooze from his self-inflicted wounds, he gouged his fingernails in and sliced them even deeper, causing more blood to gush from the wounds. He smeared the blood over his mutilated chest.

In a vengeful wrath, he jerked at the hair on his head and beard. Anguish consumed all of his rationality, and he screamed, "Damn you, God, for killing Sarah! Why did you kill her? Why did you do this to me? I have done everything I could possibly do. I have fought and struggled to get us this far, and now you do this to me.

"It would have been just as well if we had stayed on earth and died there with everyone else. All of my efforts have been in vain. I can't go on without Sarah.

"I saw your promised land. Now you have killed Sarah in this wilderness, in this space of nothingness. How could you be so cruel to let her get this close and let her die? God, I have done everything you asked of me up to now. Why have you done this to me?"

A faint moan suddenly came from Sarah's cooling body. Air forced into her lungs during CPR was escaping. As the air left her body, the arm that had been resting on her chest fell against Scott's knee. The sound and movement caused Scott to jerk back involuntarily in awe.

He froze in fear and anticipation she might still be alive. Although he knew it was impossible, he examined again for any signs of life. There were none, but Scott resumed CPR until he again collapsed from exhaustion.

In the throes of his personal agony, Scott continued

to babble incessantly until a remnant of sanity broke through, reminding him that as captain of Scott's Ark, he alone was responsible for the crew.

His anger toward Sarah and outrage toward God subsided. He recalled Sarah's reassuring him many times of God's love. Many times she had reminded Scott that God, not Scott, had brought them this far, and that God would see them the rest of the way to where He had prepared a place for them.

Sarah had reassured Scott frequently of her faith in God and confidence in Scott, but Scott was only human, not God. Her faith in God never wavered. Sometimes she questioned her confidence in her husband but never God.

She believed God, not Scott, had kept them from being destroyed on earth. She had told Scott this several times. The thought that Sarah could be right began to sink into his consciousness.

Finally Scott realized a power greater than his was responsible for their being where they were. When he recalled how he had just cursed God, he trembled with horror, and bowed his head in shame.

He was desperate for a place where he could hide from God. Shaking all over, he crawled to a corner of the compartment. He cowered before God, curling into a fetal position and writhing until his body was completely distorted.

At first, he was unable to speak then lamentations of desperation flowed uncontrollably from his mouth. He moaned and babbled until finally he was able to whisper meekly, "Forgive me."

Still curled in the fetal position, he swayed from side to side and begged for forgiveness, forgiveness from Sarah and, if there was any way possible, forgiveness from God. Despondency consumed his being until he rose to his knees, looked heavenward and pleaded, "God! God! Please, God, forgive me!"

Another lifeless moan from Sarah's body startled Scott. Although he knew it was physically impossible for her to be alive, he moved so he could see her body. He knew it was hopeless, but he reached for her to examine for any sign of life. There was none.

He recalled how Sarah had charged him over and over to always take care of the children. Scott's hopelessness evaporated, overcome by a sense of duty and obligation to his children.

He had promised Sarah he would always take care of them to the best of his ability. He was, after all, the captain of this flight. It was his responsibility to take care of everything and everyone.

Self-pity was forgotten. Forgiven or not by Sarah or God, Scott would continue to struggle and fight for the sake of his crew, his family as long as there was breath in his body.

Although he may have committed an unforgivable sin against God, Scott prayed that somehow, in His infinite mercy, God would have compassion for Scott Walker and not hold the rest of Scott's Ark accountable for his iniquities.

Scott did not want the children to see their mother in this emaciated state. To see a parent in death is trauma enough for a child. To see their mother in this cancer-ravaged condition would be too much to endure.

Scott wanted Sarah to be remembered the way she was before they boarded the spacecraft: beautiful, happy, full of life.

Although no one would see her body, Scott smoothed the wrinkles of her slacks and blouse and fixed her collar. He brushed and combed her hair.

Hoping for a miracle of miracle, he once more

examined for any sign of life. He found none.

Finding large rolls of gauze in the storage compartment, he wrapped these around her hands and feet. He knelt over her, his face directly over her face. He gazed at the lifeless, gaunt face and the glazed eyes. Gently he closed them.

In his mind's eye, he again saw the beautiful young face with the sparkling blue eyes. He saw her like she was the first time they made love, consummating their wedding vows on their honeymoon.

This was the vision of Sarah he would store in his memory bank for the rest of his life. He leaned closer until their lips touched in a tender kiss.

"Good night princess," he whispered. "Sleep well. I'll join you soon."

Raising her head from the cot, he began to wrap the gauze around, being careful not to muss her hair. He tried diligently to disassociate himself from the task before him. But try as best he might, Scott was unable to hold back his tears. They flowed down his cheeks as his completed wrapping Sarah until she resembled a mummy.

Sitting beside her on the cot, he raised her shoulders and held her tightly in his arms for one last time. The gauze pressed against his cheek.

Tears continued to flow, and Scott wailed, "Why? Why did this have to happen?"

He hugged Sarah for a long time then moved to handle the responsibilities that needed his attention. With one final kiss, he whispered, "God speed until I join you."

Scott placed Sarah's body in a plastic body bag, folding her arms across her waist. Then he removed as much air as possible before closing the airtight bag. He placed a second plastic bag around the first, expressing all of the air before closing it with an airtight zipper. Then he placed the bags back on the cot.

Nearby he saw a small piece of palm frond, which one of the children had "smuggled" aboard before the lift-off. The vivid green of the fresh frond had faded to a subdued light tan.

Scott placed the frond over Sarah's breast and paused for a moment with his head bowed in silent meditation. Then his eye caught Sarah's Bible lying beside the cot and he placed it beside the palm frond.

Sitting on the floor beside the cot, he stared at the plastic body bag. He saw absolutely nothing, felt absolutely nothing, and thought absolutely nothing. He was barely breathing. Scott Walker was in a catatonic state of total despondency.

Eventually Sarah's order: Always take care of the children, crept into his consciousness again. The children. He must tell the children about their mother. Scott snapped out of his stupor.

He rose to go wake his family from their state of hibernation. Then he noticed the blood stains on his hands and the dried blood caked on his bare chest. He could not let the children see him in this condition.

Quickly Scott removed the remnants of his shirt from his body and cleaned the clotted blood from his chest and hands as best he could. He placed the blood stained pieces of his shirt in a waste container.

When the area was cleaned to his satisfaction, he put on a fresh shirt, took one last look at Sarah, and went to rouse everyone from their hibernated state.

26

WHEN SCOTT opened the access door to the compartment where the D.C.'s were stored, he paused. He
dreaded to wake his family and crew to the reality they
would have to face.

They were no longer babies, he reminded himself.
They were young adults now, and the sooner they faced
the devastating news about Sarah's death the sooner the
shock would be over. This reassured him and helped
him get on with the task at hand.

After opening all six of Dracula's Coffins, he paused
to absorb the tranquility of the occupants. Scott asepti-
cally prepared the six injections and donned gloves. He
disinfected Gary's arm and injected him first. He would
need Gary to help with the others.

Scott then did the same for Ann, Douglass, Robert,
Beth and Jennifer. Gary was the first one to become
fully alert. He immediately took in the foreboding look
on his father-in-law's face.

"What's wrong?"

"Sarah died," Scott said bluntly.

"Oh no!" Gary said, stunned. "What happened?"

"What did you say, Daddy?" Ann mumbled, half-conscious.

Gary kissed his wife and held her. "Let's wait until everyone is fully awake."

Soon, everyone was alert and sitting upright on their cots.

"It seems like I just went to sleep," Robert said. "Dad, did you wake me up sooner than usual? Is something wrong?"

He yawned, stretched, and stood beside his cot.

Scott knew he had to be strong for everyone's sake. He took a deep breath and let out a long sigh. "Yes, something is terribly wrong. Your mother has died."

Five dumbfounded looks met Scott's announcement. Momentarily dazed, no one moved. No eye blinked. It was almost as if time had frozen.

Suddenly, Robert jumped over his cot toward his father and screamed, "Where's my mama?"

Scott wrapped his arms tight around Robert trying to console him. As spasms of emotional pain racked his body, Robert cried, "Where's my mama? What happened to her?"

Scott hugged him more tightly. "She passed away this morning."

"What happened to her, Daddy?" Ann said through her tears. "She seemed fine when she helped you put us to sleep."

"Your mother and I took turns sleeping so one of us could always be awake in the control room. Your mother was asleep on her cot, and I was in the control room.

"Evidently I fell asleep because I had a vivid dream. I woke excited and I wanted to share the dream with your mother in case she could see some hidden meaning. I went to where she was sleeping and, for the first time, I saw the cancerous sores on her hands and arms.

"She had not been taking her anti-radiation pills.

She would not answer me when I asked her why, but I know she was afraid there would not be enough pills for everyone. She wanted to make sure all of you had enough.

"I was very upset, but she put my head on her breast and told me about my dream. She recounted every minute detail, except for the ending. I believe her heart simply gave out before she could finish, but I cannot remember how it ended either.

"The last thing she said to me was to always take care of you. I was holding your mother when she passed away. Although I had seen her every day, I had not noticed how frail she had become.

"Maybe unconsciously I was in a state of denial. Maybe my mind would not accept what my eyes were seeing. When I realized she had stopped breathing, I immediately began CPR. I tried again and again.

"If I had known she was not taking her pills, I would have insisted she take her daily dose like we all agreed to do. She made this sacrifice for all of us. Cancer had mutilated her body. I have wrapped her in gauze and placed her in sealed plastic body bags."

"We want to see her," Ann said firmly. Robert nodded in agreement. Douglass was still in a state of disbelief. He had not moved.

"Don't you think it best if you remember your mother the way she was before we left earth: beautiful, smiling, always happy, always so full of life? I think that's how she would want you to remember her, not by the way she looked when she died."

Ann looked at Robert and Douglass, then back to her father. "I think you're right. I want to remember Mother the way she was before we left earth."

Robert agreed, and Douglass finally nodded.

"We must prepare for her funeral," Scott said.

He turned and led them to the compartment where Sarah was lying. When her children saw the body bag with the dried palm frond and bible lying on her chest, they began to sob. Ann moved closer and touched the body bag tenderly. Robert sat on the floor at his mother's feet.

Douglass stood beside his sister and asked his father, "May I touch the body bag?"

"Certainly," replied his father, "Your mother would like for you to touch her."

Douglass sobbed as he gently patted the bag and muttered, "Mama, please forgive me for not telling you more often how much I love you."

"Me too," whispered Ann as she rubbed her hand lovingly over Sarah's body.

Robert, sitting at foot of his mother's cot, clasped her feet, but did not utter a sound.

Scott instructed them to think of anything they would like to say to Sarah at her funeral service. He asked Ann, Douglass, and Robert to make preparations for a wake until the casket could be made. He preferred for someone to be with Sarah's body continuously and watch over it until the funeral service.

Scott and Gary went to the storage area to see what they could use to make a casket. In the storage room, Scott and Gary found a wooden crate used for food and miscellaneous supplies. With some modification, they could reshape it. They busied themselves preparing the casket.

Before they had completed it, Ann came to Scott with the schedule for the wake she, Douglass, and Robert had prepared.

Scott and his children agreed the funeral should be as soon as possible. Scott asked Ann to take her brothers and explain the schedule for the wake to Jennifer and

Beth. After they left, Scott and Gary placed the casket on top of some wooden crates beside Sarah's cot. Neither of them wanted the others to watch them when they placed her body in the casket.

Scott removed the palm frond from Sarah's breast and placed it aside. Carefully, they placed Sarah's body in the casket, leaving the lid off so everyone could view Sarah's body. Replacing the palm frond over Sarah's breast, Scott called for Ann to start the wake. Ann was scheduled to be first.

First, she went to her and Gary's compartment where she still had the paper bridal bouquet her mother had made for the wedding. Returning, Ann placed it on her mother's body beside the frond.

When Douglass relieved Ann at the wake, Jennifer sat with him. She held his hand tightly and gave him a light kiss on the cheek to comfort him.

Before Douglass' wake time was up, Robert came to replace him. Beth came with him. As Robert sat there silently staring at the casket, Beth placed her arm around his shoulder and squeezed him reassuringly.

After the wake, Scott called for everyone to come and he began the service. He and Gary removed the frond and bridal bouquet, attached the lid on the casket, and placed the flowers on top of the casket.

"Our Heavenly Father," Scott began, "we are gathered here to say goodbye to Sarah Douglass Walker, a faithful wife, a loving mother, and a friend to all she met.

"Most important, God, she was a devout believer and follower of you. Her faith and belief in you never wavered regardless of her plight. I wish I had that same faith.

"Sarah was the strength and moral fiber of this family. And now, I believe her children would like to speak."

Ann rose and went to stand at the head of the casket, "Mother, I pray somehow you are able to hear the things I should have said to you long ago. To say I love you seems so inadequate for the feelings I have for you. You have been the best role model for me, and I will strive to live and be like you. Goodbye. I will remember you and love you forever."

Douglass knelt beside the casket and sobbing his heart out mumbled, "Please forgive me for not being a better son and telling you daily that I love you. I will remember how you always encouraged me and told me I could accomplish any task if I worked at it. I am the luckiest boy in the world to have had you for a mother. Please God, let my mother hear me say I love her."

Robert touched the casket. Tears flowed down his cheeks and fell on the casket. Sobs shook his entire body. Finally he managed to speak, "Mama, why did you have to leave us? It isn't fair. God, please take good care of my mother. Mama, I already miss you so much, and I will love you forever.

"When I was much younger, I was fishing with Grandpa Charles one day, and he told me about his father dying and going to heaven. I asked Grandpa where is heaven, and he pointed to the sky. Mama, I guess you will not have to go to heaven because you are already there."

Then Gary said he would like to speak, "I don't know why there have been so many jokes about mothers-in-law. Sarah Douglass Walker was the best mother-in-law any man could have. She gave me her own wedding rings to give to my wife. She made me feel welcome in her family, and she made me feel loved.

"Mama Sarah, my only regret is you were my mother-in-law for such a brief time. I will miss you and cherish memories of you forever."

Beth and Jennifer said they would like to sing a song for Sarah. It was an old-time, mountain hymn that Jennifer's grandfather, Harry McDonald, had taught her when she was a little girl.

"It's been a long time since my grandfather taught the song to me," Jennifer said. "I can remember only one verse, but I've taught Beth the words. The hymn may have had another name, but Grandaddy always called it "I Am Bound for the Promised Land."

The two women sang,
"When I shall reach that happy place,
I'll be forever blest, for I shall see my Father's face
and in his bosom rest.
I am bound for the promised land,
I am bound for the promised land;
O who will come and go with me?
I am bound for the promised land."

After the hymn was completed, Scott said, "Let's all join hands and pray."

The family and friends of Sarah Douglass Walker encircled her casket and joined hands as Scott prayed: "God, our Heavenly Father, into your loving hands, we commit the spirit of Sarah Douglass Walker. May Sarah find in you, God, the peace that surpasses all understanding. Amen."

27

LIFE ABOARD Scott's Ark returned to monotonous tedium. The easiest thing would have been to recommend everyone except Scott or Gary return to Dracula's Coffins. However, Scott did not think it wise to suggest his children be put back into a hibernated state this soon after their mother's death. Instead, he asked Douglass and Robert to assist Gary in inspecting all of the Ark's systems and instruments.

Gary had been teaching Douglass and Robert about the instrument and control panel of the Ark, but now Scott directed him to teach them everything he knew. Now that Douglass and Robert were much older, he wanted his sons to learn as much as possible about all of the mechanics of the Ark. In case something happened to Scott, Gary would then have two capable assistants.

Scott called for a complete inspection of all instruments, especially the air filtration system, the water recovery system, and the waste disposal system. He also asked Ann to recruit Beth and Jennifer to help her take an inventory of the food, water, and medical supplies.

In addition, he wanted an accurate inventory of the anti-radiation medication. He assigned Ann to actually watch each person swallow their anti-radiation pill. He did not want what happened to Sarah to happen to another member of the crew. Keeping everyone as busy as possible would be the best thing possible for morale.

Gary reported that the air filtration system and water recovery system were working almost as well as the day the Ark left the Kennedy Space Center. The only problem Gary found was with EVE.

"Who's EVE?" Douglass asked.

"EVE stands for Emergency Vehicular Escape," Scott replied. "Really it's just a small, self-contained capsule to be used for landing in case the Ark became disabled and could not land. It's for use only in emergencies just as the name implies."

"What's wrong with it?" Scott asked.

"It appears it will no longer function automatically, and there is no possible way it can be repaired." Gary said.

"Is this a serious problem?" Douglass asked.

"It's nothing we can't overcome," Scott assured him. "Usually EVE would separate from the Ark automatically. Now it will have to be launched or separated from the Ark manually. It's not a big problem."

Scott glanced at Gary and indicated for him not to explain any more.

Ann's report was more discouraging. While the water supply was maintaining a good level because of the water recovery system, the food supply was getting very low. She suggested Scott decide if each person's daily portion of food should be reduced more.

In addition, their supply of oxygen could become a concern in the near future. Finally, there were only three doses of the anti-radiation capsules left for each person. In other words, the group would be out of radiation protection very soon.

Scott considered putting the crew back in D.C. where they would be safe from the radiation and would not need to take the pills. After much deliberation, he decided against it and prayed something would happen before the last of the anti-radiation pills was consumed.

Scott thanked Gary and Ann for their reports, and asked everyone to be thinking about the best solutions for the survival of the group considering the seriousness of the situation.

28

And it came to pass — that Noah sent forth a dove
And it came in to him in the evening; and, lo,
In her mouth was an olive leaf ...
Genesis 8:6 – 8:11

"WE HAVE A LOT of thinking and planning to do, but I think the time is appropriate for sending out a DOVE," Scott said.

"What's a DOVE?" Robert asked.

"DOVE stands for Distant Observing Vehicular Element, an electro-magnetic device to search for a planet," Scott explained.

"How does it work?" asked Robert, his curiosity peaked.

"It's somewhat similar to radar only much more sophisticated," Scott said. "Its range is thousands of times greater than radar. I don't understand it fully, but DOVE contains instruments very sensitive to infrared wavelengths of the electro-magnetic spectrum.

"DOVE will reflect from any object, in this case hopefully a planet, and send the location back to us immediately even over a tremendous distance. To activate and operate DOVE requires a lot of energy.

"Although you reported our support systems are working well, the Ark's fuel and energy level are getting dangerously low. We may not have much fuel to spare, but we have no choice but to send out DOVE. We must launch it now."

Scott moved to the control console and readied the instruments to send out the DOVE. Gary assisted him. Both were well aware of how much energy would be required to accomplish this. Gary agreed they had no other choice.

All of the instruments indicated the DOVE had been activated and was performing correctly. For a moment, Scott thought the instruments were indicating the DOVE had found something, but the momentary blip on the monitor soon disappeared. It had been nothing.

Even though the DOVE required a lot of energy, it would be necessary to leave it activated continuously. As everyone gathered so they could discuss their situation further, Scott invited any suggestions. The mood became despondent as they watched the gauge indicating how the fuel and energy were declining.

Robert, although he was the youngest member of the crew, was keenly aware of the seriousness of their situation. He sensed the gravity of the matter in his father's body language and the tone of his voice.

"Look, our lives may be desperate, but life is never hopeless!" he declared steadfastly.

Each person turned to stare at Robert, gaping in wonder at his encouraging words. They were the just the right words at the right time.

Beth was the first to go to Robert. She hugged him, kissed him, and whispered, "I love you. Now's the time to ask your father."

"Ask me what?" asked Scott as he went to Robert

and embraced him. "Son, I am very proud of you."

Very meekly Robert said, "Nothing."

Ann clasped Robert's face between her hands. She gazed into his eyes for several moments in amazement. "Was that my baby brother speaking? Those were the words from my brother — not my baby brother, but my wise brother. I love you so much, and I am so proud you are my brother. You've really grown up."

"Tell it like it is, Robert," Douglass said, grinning as he patted Robert's shoulder. "We all needed that. Now let's get busy so that when the DOVE returns, we'll be ready to do whatever the situation calls for."

With renewed hope and energy, everyone pitched into the daily routines. Even housecleaning was high on the list. The Ark was cleaned like it was going to be inspected by the Commandant of the Marine Corps himself.

Calisthenics became a fun, daily routine, especially for Douglass and Robert who used it as a means to show off their muscular physiques in front of Jennifer and Beth. Scott accused them of acting like strutting peacocks trying to entice a hen to mate.

Encouraged by Beth and Jennifer, Douglass and Robert approached their father to ask if Douglass could marry Jennifer and Robert could marry Beth.

Much to the brothers' surprise, Scott simply said, "I see no reason why both of you could not be married, as long as the girls were willing."

Beth and Jennifer had been eavesdropping, and when they overheard Scott's approval, they squealed with joy. Both rushed to Scott and hugged him excitedly.

"Douglass and I held hands during Ann's and Gary's wedding and silently spoke the vows to each other," Jennifer said.

"Well," Scott said, "if you spoke those same vows to

each other and to God, then you're already married."

"Yes," Jennifer agreed, "but we would like to hear you say we are husband and wife. That makes it more official and more binding. No way am I going to let Douglass Walker back out now."

"Beth," Scott said turning to her, "how do you and Robert feel?"

"It would be wonderful for us to hear you say, 'Beth and Robert are united in holy matrimony.'"

"In that case, let's prepare for a double wedding."

"I'll do everything mother did for my wedding to make both of yours as meaningful and beautiful as can be," Ann said. "We'll make wedding dresses, bouquets, and have everything as nice as my wedding was.

"The only problem is I can't carry a tune, period. If there is music, you'll have to sing at your own wedding. I'll bet that's been done before. We have a lot to do, let's get busy."

The wedding of Miss Jennifer McDonald, granddaughter of Mr. and Mrs. Harry McDonald, to Mr. Douglass Walker, and the wedding of Miss Beth Johnston, daughter of Mr. John Johnston and Ms. Frances van Pelt to Mr. Robert Walker came off without a hitch.

Scott proudly pronounced them husband and wife.

29

THE GROUP had concluded at their last conference that each of them had done everything they could do. The time had come for them to put their fate completely in the hands of God.

This decision was very difficult for Scott to accept. He had always believed he was in control of his own destiny, that he alone was responsible for the outcome. To Scott, conceding their fate was in the hands of God amounted to some sort of failure on his part.

He felt Sarah had died because of something he failed to do. He should have been able to prevent her dying.

Failure was something Scott had rarely experienced in his life. Although he reluctantly agreed with the decision, he harbored the belief he had to do more than anyone else to assure the rest of the group survived.

No one was in the hibernation chamber even though supplies were getting scarce. Assuming it was night, everyone was asleep except Robert. He was slumped in the pilot's chair taking his turn standing watch.

Although he was the youngest, he took his duty very seriously, watching the instruments with intensity.

The first sound from the DOVE's gauge on the instrument panel was inaudible, because it was a frequency too high for most human ears. Then the frequency lowered and the noise became audible.

The sound startled Robert, as a bright red light began to flash on the instrument panel. He yelled for his father to come immediately, shouting so loudly everyone was awakened.

Scott rushed to the control panel, yelling to Gary, "The DOVE is responding to something. It looks like it may be something very big. Come look."

Gary was at Scott's side in an instant. He gazed in awe at the flashing panel. "I can't believe it. It's none too soon either. We've got to determine the exact position of whatever the rays are reflecting from.

"If we're lucky and have enough fuel, maybe we can position the Ark so we can see whatever it is the DOVE has found."

Scott helped Gary make the necessary adjustments on the instrument panel. The gauges indicated the object was getting closer. It was positioned directly in their path.

"Let's try to rotate the Ark to get a view of the object," Scott said. "Ignite the thrusters."

Gary did as he was commanded. Everyone felt the Ark shudder as the thrusters began to rotate the craft. Slowly the front windows revealed what the DOVE had found.

Scott was the first to see the view through the blurred window. He stood frozen in reverence and awe before shouting, "Come, everyone, come see your promised land."

Fourteen eyes turned to stare through the window at the planet before them.

Robert was the first to speak, "It looks exactly like

the pictures we saw of earth taken from the space station and the moon — the swirls in the atmosphere, the color, the blue water. It must be earth."

"It can't be earth," Douglass said. "We saw it blow up and vaporize with our own eyes."

"We're still too far away to see much detail," Gary said, "especially through the murky condition of the window, but it sure looks like heaven to me."

"Nevaeh," Robert said. "That's what we should call the planet! We found it in heaven."

"What's finding it in heaven got to do with the name Nevaeh?"

"Nevaeh is heaven spelled backward," Robert explained, pleased with himself.

He had a slight problem with dyslexia when he was small and so he easily saw words backward. He had overcome the affliction, but he would still see letters in reverse order sometimes.

"Robert, that's an excellent name," Ann said, getting teary eyed. "Let's all join hands. Daddy, please lead us in prayer and praise God for leading us to this place."

Scott knelt and everyone joined him, clasping hands.

"Forgive me and my arrogance for thinking I could bring us to the promised land," Scott prayed. "I know now I could not accomplish that feat by myself, although at one time I thought I could.

"I pray for your forgiveness God. It was you, God, who prepared this place and brought us to it. We thank you God for choosing us for the venture. We feel we are unworthy of this blessing.

"We praise you God because without you we would not be. Thank you, God, for bringing us safely this far, and I pray you will guide them to a safe landing. I pray they will be aware forever of your omnipotence and the blessings you have bestowed on them. Amen."

Everyone repeated the closing. No one seemed to notice Scott's prayer was for them, not him.

"As Captain of Scott's Ark, I proclaim Nevaeh to be the official name of your new homeland."

"Scott, we have some serious calculating to do for our descent," Gary said with real concern.

"Children continue looking at your future home. Gary and I need to go to the back and check on the thrusters. We'll be right back."

At the back of the Ark, where no one could see or hear them, Scott put his hand on Gary's shoulder.

"There is no way we can land this ship. It has been too damaged," Scott said. "Too many of the instruments are not functioning, and there is not enough fuel.

"Hopefully we can get close enough to the planet to launch the Emergency Vehicular Escape. EVE is your only chance. It should have enough fuel to slow your descent until the parachutes deploy automatically. Gary, if you see any other way, I'm open to suggestions."

Gary shook his head. "But the hydraulic system to separate EVE from the Ark is not working."

Scott held his gaze steady. "It will have to be launched manually."

"But how?" Gary asked, confusion on his face.

"I will do it. It's the only way."

"No," Gary said as realization dawned. "Let me do it."

"Think, man," Scott said, "You have a wife to care for. My life is behind me; yours is ahead of you. God's letting me see the promised land is more than I deserve and I am very grateful.

"There's a reason I'm not allowed to go. Let's just leave it at that. Now let's get back with the others and celebrate."

30

And the Lord spoke unto Moses...
because ye believed me not...
therefore ye shall not bring this
congregation unto the land which I
have given them.
Numbers 20:12

This is the land...
I will give it unto thy seed:
I have caused thee to see it
With thine eyes, but thou
Shall not go over thither.
Deuteronomy 34:4

WHEN SCOTT AND GARY entered the control area, the others were in a state of joyous jubilation. They were hugging, jumping for joy, and singing at the top of their voices. Scott and Gary joined in the celebration. Beth and Jennifer suggested they sing the hymn they sang at Sarah's funeral:

"When I shall reach that happy place,
   I'll be forever blest for I
Shall see my Father's face and in his bosom rest.
   "We are bound for the promised land,
   We are bound for the promised land;
   O who will come and go with us?
   We are bound for the promised land."

Beth and Jennifer led everyone, except Scott, in singing the verse over and over again until they were exhausted.

Ann noticed her father was not singing. When she asked him why, he made an excuse about needing to study and adjust the instruments. In her happiness, she accepted his words and did not think about it any more.

There was no time to lose in preparing for the landing. Scott ordered Gary to assist him in determining how far away Nevaeh was.

If the Ark approached the planet at too steep an angle, it would burn. There was not enough fuel in the Ark to slow its entry into the planet's atmosphere. If the angle were too flat, the Ark would ricochet off Nevaeh's atmosphere and be deflected back into space, like a thrown pebble skipping over the surface of water.

Gary made the necessary adjustments in the Ark's angle of descent, which consumed the remaining fuel in the Ark. Gary motioned to Scott that their fuel was exhausted.

Scott told Douglass and Robert to find the suits they had worn when the Ark took off from earth. They rushed to the storage area and soon were back with all of the space suits, helmets and boots, even Sarah's.

Douglass handed Gary's space suit to him, and Gary began to put it on. Ann took her mother's suit because she had outgrown her own.

Because Beth and Jennifer's space suit had been much too large for them when they left earth, they were still able to get into theirs. Douglass was unable to fit into his space suit, but Robert was able to squeeze into it.

Soon everyone was suited except Scott and Douglass. With a puzzled and worried expression, he looked at the others in their spacesuits, boots, gloves, and helmets.

Scott handed his spacesuit and helmet to Douglass and told him to put them on. Eagerly, without thinking, Douglass began to put the space suit on.

Abruptly he stopped. "But, Dad..."

Scott looked at his son with pride. Douglass had filled his father's shoes. Recovering himself he said firmly, "Don't 'But, Dad' me. Put on the suit now. That's an order."

Douglass did not move.

"But, Daddy," Ann stepped in. "You've got to have a suit. Maybe I can squeeze into mine, we'll see if Douglass can get into mother's."

The time Scott had dreaded finally had come. He had to face and explain everything to his children. They were almost grown, but to Scott they would always be children.

He motioned for them to gather round. As they huddled close, he spoke in a calm voice. "Listen carefully. Everything is going to be okay. The Ark is completely out of fuel and almost out of oxygen.

"There is no way it can land on Nevaeh. You will have to get into the Emergency Vehicular Element. It has enough fuel to slow your entrance into the Nevaeh's atmosphere."

"But Daddy, you don't have a space suit," Ann repeated.

"I don't need one," Scott said calmly. "The launching mechanism is not working. I will launch the vehicle manually."

Ann's face registered shock and dismay. "We can't go without you."

"Surely you can disconnect the two vehicles from inside EVE," Robert said, as always convinced his father could do anything.

"It's physically impossible," Scott replied emphatically. "Besides, you don't need me anymore. God is with you. God has been with us all the time, though I never acknowledged it.

"I thought Scott Walker was responsible for our getting this far. That was my ego, but I have learned my lesson.

"We have no time to spare. The Ark will be deflected back into space soon. It is time for all of you to get into EVE. The vehicle is stocked with everything you will need until you land. God will see to it the automated system in EVE guides you to a safe landing."

Ann, tears flowing down her cheeks, rushed to her father and hugged him long and hard. Douglass and Robert wrapped their arms tightly around their father and sister. Both boys cried unashamedly.

Finally Scott repeated, "Everything is going to be okay. God will be with you and protect you."

As soon as Ann, Douglass, and Robert released their grip on their father, Beth and Jennifer embraced Scott.

"Thank you," they said, "Thank you for our weddings. Thank you for everything. We love you."

Scott told Gary to double check each person's space suit. Before Ann put her helmet on, she pressed her cheek against her father's cheek for a long, last moment.

"Daddy, I want to say goodbye to Mother one last time." Douglass and Robert agreed said in unison.

Scott smiled. "That's an excellent idea. I'm sorry, in my haste to get you off safely, I forgot. Please forgive me."

Everyone went to the compartment where Sarah's casket had been placed after the funeral. They surrounded it, knelt, and held hands while each person prayed silently for Sarah and told her goodbye.

Solemnly they rose, each kissing a finger and touching it to the casket. Robert open a crumpled paper bag he had been holding behind his back and pulled out Monk-Monk.

Gently he placed the tattered stuffed monkey on the casket and said, "Mom, I am leaving Monk-Monk with you and Dad. I no longer need him."

Douglass turned to Scott. "Daddy, are you absolutely sure there's no to separate the vehicles from inside EVE?"

"Absolutely," Scott said solemnly. "Even if it were possible, and even if I were allowed to go to Nevaeh, I want to stay here with your mother."

"Gary, you're in command now," Scott said, turning to his son-in-law. "It's time for you to load your crew aboard EVE. All of you can relax. The radio should allow us to stay in contact, however, I will bang twice on the bulkhead to let you know when EVE is completely separated from the Ark. I love you. Never forget God loves you."

The six of them boarded EVE, seating themselves and fastening their safety harnesses securely. Scott manually disconnected the hydraulics, opened the bay doors and manually removed the brackets connecting EVE to the Ark.

He banged twice on EVE's bulkhead as the escape vehicle fell free from the Ark. He heard the small thrusters push EVE further away from the Ark as it began its descent to Nevaeh.

Disconsolately, Scott closed the bay doors and wandered back into the main cabin. He tried to reach Gary on the radio. There was no response. The batteries were probably dead.

The Ark began shutting down faster than he had expected and he realized the others had left just in time.

All of the fuel and energies of the Ark were exhausted. The lights dimmed until the cabin was completely dark. Scott found a flashlight. In another few minutes the oxygen would be depleted.

On his way back to the main compartment, Scott noticed things were in disarray in the area where the crew had changed into their space suits. Because of his military training, he impulsively began to pick up and organize.

He was surprised when he came across Sarah's Bible. Folded inside was the tam-o'-shanter he had been found wearing as a baby. Removing it from the Bible, he ran his fingers over the tattered cap and early-life memories began to race through his mind.

He sat down heavily and began a monologue with his biological mother, "Mama, when I was old enough to understand you had abandoned me, I childishly hated you for giving me away. I even secretly hated my foster parents for what you did to me.

"Eventually my hatred of you turned to cold indifference. I have no idea what your circumstances were before my birth, but you knitted this tam for me, so I know in my heart you must have loved me.

"Only now am I able to realize you gave away your own flesh and blood so I might have a more abundant life than you thought you could provide for me. I am aware now you suffered more than I did because I eventually met and married Sarah Douglass, who became my reason for living.

"Because of her, I have had the rewarding, fulfilled

life you wished for me when you left me on the hospital steps.

"Mama, I miss the life I could have had with you, but my life has been wonderful in spite of not knowing you. My prayer is that somehow you can hear and feel the compassion and love I have for you."

Having made peace with his mama, Scott took the Bible and his baby cap, and returned to the compartment where Sarah's casket sat. His hand-held flashlight was the only light left in the Ark.

The dried palm frond and Ann's wedding bouquet were still on top of the casket. He removed them and began to remove the boards on the top and side of the coffin, exposing Sarah's body still wrapped securely in the two heavy plastic bags.

Laying the palm and flowers on the plastic bag, he knelt beside Sarah and whispered, "I love you and pray you and God will forgive me for not having complete faith.

"I thought I could accomplish everything all by myself. I am glad I was not allowed to go to Nevaeh, because I want to remain here with you. This is where I belong, at your side."

Scott lay down beside Sarah and clasped her hand through the plastic bag then he prayed. "Our father we give you thanks for life and all you have given to Sarah and me. Most of all we thank you for loving us and our children.

"Please forgive my shortcomings. We pray you will continue to be with our children and their families. Guide them to a safe landing on Nevaeh and be with them as they adjust to the place you have provided for them. Amen."

Scott spoke softly to Sarah next. "Sarah, remember the wonderful night we had on your special ledge near

Whiteside Mountain, and I sang that silly song about my special planet? Literally, my special planet did call us after all.

"I remember you said you were floating up there beside that special star for one brief moment. I am so sorry you could not actually touch it then, and I am sorry you can't go there now.

"In my dream it was beautiful, a veritable Garden of Eden, and we almost got there. That night, little did we know what a wonderful adventure we had ahead of us. We're still together, and that's all that is important.

"I love you, Sarah Douglass Walker. There is no goodbye to say because we will be together always from now on."

Scott's Ark ricocheted off the atmosphere then, surrounding Nevaeh like a flat pebble skipping over the surface of a pond.

Inside the craft, the flashlight faded into complete darkness. Scott kissed his wife, exhaled one last breath, and joined her to sail the heavens forever in Scott's Ark.

31

NO ONE SPOKE. The craft creaked and shuddered slightly as the thrusters pushed EVE farther from the Ark.

Each person tried to get a grasp of the situation. Leaving Scott behind had left them benumbed. It was impossible to comprehend that Scott had been allowed to see the promised land, yet was not allowed to "go over thither."

It was a mystification beyond their understanding.

There was no way to estimate how many years had passed since Scott's Ark lifted off from the Kennedy Space Center, or how long they had been wandering in the wilderness of space.

The mood was very somber, and no one seemed to be able to envisage that they, at long last, were going to land on another planet, the planet Robert had christened Nevaeh.

Finally, Gary broke the silence. "If the automatic landing computers function properly, there will be no problem landing. We won't have to do anything because everything is programmed. We can sit back, try to relax, and enjoy the ride down. It shouldn't be much more than an hour until touchdown."

If anyone was reassured by Gary's words, it did not show on their face. Ann had held in her tears as long as she could, and she began to sob uncontrollably. Gary loosened the straps of his harness and grasped Ann's hand in an attempt to console her.

"Sis," Robert said, "remember Dad said he wanted to stay with Mama. At least he's happy and where he wants to be, so don't cry."

"Wonder why Daddy hasn't radioed us," Douglass said.

"His radio probably wouldn't work," Gary said. "I don't think this one is working either."

Ann stopped crying and regained her composure. She assured Gary she was going to be okay and asked him to retighten his safety harness.

No one felt EVE's speed accelerate when the craft was caught in the grasp of Nevaeh's gravitational pull. However, when the reverse thrusters automatically ignited and retro-fired to slow the vehicle's descent, they were alarmed by the sudden jolt to the vehicle.

Quickly, Gary explained what was happening and reassured them everything was okay. Each time EVE began to accelerate too fast, the reverse thrusters fired automatically to slow the craft's descent.

This cycle repeated itself six times. Robert counted each cycle. On the seventh cycle, the rockets continued to fire until the speed of the descending capsule slowed to a standstill in order for the three parachutes to deploy.

When the three large parachutes unfurled, EVE came to a screeching halt. Each person gasped when they felt the unsettling jolt. Slowly EVE descended toward Nevaeh, the capsule swinging like a pendulum as it oscillated back and forth under the canopy of parachutes.

Through the small porthole, the crew got a glimpse of Nevaeh. When EVE first separated from Scott's Ark, the planet had appeared as a perfectly round, large ball with irregular, large areas of blue and brownish green.

The top and underside were covered with a white cap. A wind-swept stratum of broken clouds encircled the middle of the ball. The surrounding sky was a pale blue.

As EVE approached Nevaeh, the brownish green areas could be recognized as land. Much of the planet appeared to be covered with dark blue water. The craft drifted through billowy, scattered clouds, and the land now appeared to be green mountains. The areas covered with water could no longer be seen.

Soon they drifted below the peaks of some of the taller, craggy mountains. It looked as if EVE was going to crash into the side of the rocky peaks when a sudden updraft caught the parachutes and lifted the craft gently over the jagged mountain tops.

The wind guided EVE down the leeward side of the barren mountains toward much shorter mountains covered with towering green trees.

The craft glided between twin peaks, swaying back and forth under the parachutes until it finally touched down. It landed with a jolting thud in a small grassy meadow surrounded by a dense forest of tropical trees.

After the touchdown, the parachutes caught in a strong gust of wind and dragged EVE roughly across the terrain until the capsule was smashed against the trunk of a massive tree. It was the only tree in the center of the meadow.

In spite of their safety harnesses, all aboard were jarred by the severe collision. Finally the wind stopped, and the parachutes collapsed. Each person in the craft let out a long sigh of relief.

Gary cautioned, "Loosen, but don't unfasten your seat harness yet. The wind may still pull the parachutes up and give us another surprise. We need to make sure the parachutes are completely collapsed.

"We still have plenty of oxygen so we don't have to be in a rush to get out. Also, we need to acclimatize ourselves to the environment of Nevaeh. Thank goodness for the gravity like conditions we had in the Dracula's Coffins. Having experienced the gravitational pressure will make it easier for us to adjust to this environment's gravity."

Robert had the best view through one of the portholes. "It looks like a beautiful tropical forest on one side and a small meadow of tall grasses on the other. There is a small river or creek running through the meadow about 50 yards away. From here, the water looks clear."

"I just knew we were going to crash into the side of that craggy mountain," Douglass said. "Thank goodness for the gust of wind that lifted us over it and guided us between the twin peaks."

"Don't you think God could have been responsible for that?" said Ann. "I do. Let's join hands to thank God for landing us safely on this place."

The six joined hands and each prayed silently, thanking and praising God for saving them from the destruction of earth, for preparing this place for them, and for landing them safely on Nevaeh.

"It looks as if it is getting dark," Gary said. "Maybe we will have day and night here, similar to earth. The parachutes have not moved, so maybe the wind has stopped for a while.

"I believe it would be safe to remove our safety harness, but I think it would be best not to open the hatch until it is light again. There is enough oxygen left for two or three more days. I don't know about the rest of you, but I could use a good night's sleep right now."

Everyone agreed readily. Removing their harnessed, they stretched and moved around as much as possible in the cramped quarters.

Robert continued to peer through the porthole until it was completely dark. The only movement he saw was a slight breeze moving the leaves on the trees. He saw no sign of animal life.

Gary extinguished the small overhead light and soon all six stressed and exhausted people were in a restful sleep. It was their first night on Nevaeh.

THE FIRST RAYS of morning light shone through the small porthole and came to rest on Robert's closed eyes. He yawned and squinted his eyes. Beth was nestled in the crook of his arm.

Robert curled his arm tighter around her waist and whispered, "Welcome to Nevaeh, Mrs. Robert Walker. Can you believe we made it?" He kissed her ardently.

"Kiss me again so I will know this is not a dream," Beth said as she snuggled closer to her husband. "I can't believe we made it."

"Rise and shine everyone," Robert called loudly. "We have a whole planet to explore."

"Not all in the first day, little brother," Ann grumbled sleepily.

Slowly the others began to yawn and stretch.

"That was the best sleep I've had in a long, long time," Ann said. "I believe we should pause again to thank God for bringing us safely to this place."

They held hands and each person knelt and bowed their head in prayer.

After several reverent moments, Douglass said,

"Gary, let's see if we can pry open the hatch. It looks like it may have been warped during that rough landing."

"From what I could see through the porthole, it looks like we hit a huge tree," Robert said.

Douglass grasped the emergency latch, but the door did not move. He flexed the latch handle again. The door was wedged tightly to the frame. He plunged his shoulder against the door. Nothing.

"Here, let me try," Gary said.

He pushed as hard as he could and pounded on the door forcefully. He even kicked it. Then he looked at Douglass and they simultaneously lunged against the door with all of their might and weight, to no avail.

"Do something," Jennifer pleaded with Douglass, "Claustrophobia is beginning to close in on me."

Robert watched their efforts aloofly before moving forward. "Step aside boys, and let a real man do the job."

Making a show of it, he stepped forward, reached under the emergency handle, flipped the safety lock, and with his little finger flipped the handle and pushed the emergency door wide open.

"Ladies first," he said, bowing at his waist.

"This is no time to act like a gentleman," Beth said as she moved away from the exit. "You go first and see if it is safe."

Robert did as his wife directed. Stepping slowly through the opened hatch, he suddenly screamed, stumbled and fell into the grass flailing his arms wildly.

Beth screamed and attempted to slam the hatch shut, until she heard Robert laughing. When she looked out, he was lying in the grass grinning. "Just teasing. It's beautiful out here. Come on out. It's safe. The fresh air is wonderful. I can't believe it."

Robert continued to roll in the grass and even kissed the earth.

Gary and Douglass went outside next, followed by Ann, Jennifer and Beth. Beth walked over to where Robert was lying in the tall grass and he grabbed her leg, pulling her down on the grass beside him.

Beth playfully slapped his arm. "You scared the daylights out of me. Don't ever do that again."

Soon everyone was rolling in the lush grass, singing "We have come to the promised land" as loudly as they could.

"This is unbelievable," Ann said breathlessly. "It looks like a veritable Garden of Eden. This must be heaven."

"Sis, it may be a Garden of Eden, but this is Nevaeh, not heaven," Robert said.

"Look at all those beautiful flowers," Beth said pointing. "Some of them look like huge orchids, but I don't think I've ever seen orchids that large. There is every color in the rainbow."

She picked a light pink blossom and started to put it in her hair over her left ear.

"No. Put it over your right ear," Robert said.

"Why?" Beth asked.

"Mama said if a lady is available, she wears a flower in her hair on her left side, but if she is taken or married, she places the flower over her right ear. And you, Beth, are taken. Let me make it official."

Carefully he placed the flower over her right ear and kissed her lightly.

"Are you making this up?" Ann asked doubtfully.

"No," Robert said firmly. "Mama told me after we got home from Highlands the last time."

Mentioning their mother brought tears to Ann's eyes. Tenderly Gary wiped the tears from her cheeks, and he held her reassuringly for a long time.

When the joviality finally subsided, Gary said, "It's

time we begin to reconnoiter Nevaeh so we can better assess our situation. Let's stay close together until we know more about this place. We should not get out of sight of each other. Although this may look like a Garden of Eden, we have no idea what it's truly like."

"So far, it looks like Utopia to Jennifer and me," Douglass said. "Look at all of the fruit, or what looks like fruit. A tropical paradise couldn't look any better."

He surveyed the meadow, picked a large red fruit from a nearby bush. "This looks like a mango, and it sure smells good. I hope it's edible. I'm starving."

"Don't eat it," Jennifer ordered. "Maybe it's forbidden fruit from the Garden of Eden. Maybe it's poisonous. If you're that hungry, try those blueberries. I just saw a macaw-like bird eating them so they're definitely safe to eat."

She picked some of the berries and tasted one. "They're deliciously sweet. Have some."

She gave Douglass some, and he dropped the red fruit he was holding and gulped the blueberries hungrily.

"Seriously, Jennifer, why did you say it may be the forbidden fruit of the Garden of Eden?" Ann asked.

"I don't know," Jennifer said with a shrug. "It just came out. I wasn't even thinking."

"It's okay," Douglass said, placing a consoling arm around her shoulders. He looked at the others. "Has anyone heard God say there was something here we shouldn't eat? I haven't. Besides, this is growing on a bush not a tree."

Douglass plucked another red fruit from the bush. He held it in his hand admiring it longingly. As he bit into it, juice ran out the corners of his mouth.

With his mouth full, he said, "It looks like a mango. It smells like a mango. It tastes like a mango. So it must be a mango. Of course to be perfectly honest, I don't remember ever eating a mango. Mango smango, it's delicious. He offered Jennifer a bite. Soon everyone was eating the large fruit.

"Let's go check out that little river," Robert said. "I'm getting thirsty, and the water looks so refreshing and cool from here."

As they approached the river's edge, they could see to their right that it cascaded like white water rapids down a narrow, rocky riverbed on the side of the distant low mountain. The riverbed widened dramatically at the foot of the mountain.

Because the meadow was so level, the rushing water from the foot of the cascade slowed quickly until the water appeared not to be moving, almost like the river was asleep.

There was not a ripple; its surface looked like glass. The trees on the opposite bank reflected clearly in the still water.

Where they approached the river, it appeared to be about 50 yards wide and curved sharply to their left. Because of the bend in the river, the water appeared to be much deeper on the far side.

Each of them removed their shoes and socks and waded in. The riverbed was covered with smooth round pebbles almost the texture of sand. As they waded toward the far bank, the water became deeper.

"I wonder how long it's been since we had a real bath. I want to bathe. I need a bath, and so do all of you," Ann said. "I'm just modest enough to not want all of us to bathe together. So I suggest we separate.

"Robert, you and Beth can remain here. Douglass, you and Jennifer go to the right toward the cascade. Gary and I will go to the left. We will not be out of sight, but we can't really see each other if you get what I mean."

"Let's leave our shoes on the bank, and all meet back here when we're done," Douglass said then turned to Jennifer. "Come on wife, let's go. We need to leave these lovers alone."

They strolled hand-in-hand in the shallow water toward the cascade. When they reached a point where they could barely see the other four, Douglass said, "I think we are far enough away to undress and skinny dip in the deeper water. I'll bathe you if you'll bathe me."

Robert and Beth strolled down stream splashing each other with the cool water. When they were almost out of sight, Ann and Gary went to the bank, stripped naked and rushed back into the deeper water.

They stood in the shoulder deep water close to the opposite bank caressing each other hungrily.

"Can you believe we are back on land?" Ann asked.

"Pinch me so I'll know this is not a dream. All the rest seems like a dream, or really a nightmare. The horrors of what we saw happen to earth are unbelievable. However, we saw it with our own eyes. I hope someday that memory will be erased from my mind."

Gary placed his finger on her lips and said, "Shh. That's all in the past. We are here now, and safe. We are very lucky."

"Luck had nothing to do with it," Ann said sternly. "I think we were chosen to be saved from the destruction of earth because my father, like Noah, was a good man. Let's just be thankful and praise God for what we have." Gary pulled her toward him and kissed her passionately.

Robert and Beth had gone a very short distance when he began to undress her. "Not yet," Beth protested. "They can still see us."

"Whether they see us or not, every thread is coming off your gorgeous body. Besides, they're too busy looking at each other to look our way."

With that, Beth began to remove Robert's clothes with the same enthusiasm he was using to undress her. They dashed into the water and fell into each other's arms, fondling and cuddling each other until they were oblivious of everything except each other.

The three couples played in the slow running water until they were spent. Eventually, each couple emerged into the soft thick grass near where they had bathed. Lying down as they were, the tall grass screened them from the others.

Each couple lay in each other's arms cherishing their life together. Here, each man knew his wife for the first time in their new home on Nevaeh.

Much later, Robert waded naked back into the water. He thought he had seen a large fish in the shallow water near the river's edge. His first impulse was to get a rod and reel the way he and Douglass had done on their last visit to their grandparents' home in Highlands, but that was in another world.

He would have to get this fish all by himself with only his bare hands. He waded further downstream and stood deathly still in the ankle-deep water waiting. Soon another salmon-shaped fish casually swam beside his feet. Quickly Robert fell on the fish grabbing it tightly with both hands.

"I got it! I got it! It's huge!" he screamed.

Beth sat up in the grass where she had fallen asleep. "What's huge?"

"A fish! I caught it barehanded. Look! I'll bet it weighs at least seven pounds."

He was oblivious to his nakedness.

Beth quickly put on her shorts. She picked up Robert's clothes and took them to him saying, "Quick. Put on your shorts at least. I hear the others coming. Wow, it is big! Don't let it get away."

Robert stepped onto the bank still keeping a tight grip on the flopping fish. He refused to let go of the fish, so Beth held his shorts for him to step into.

She got them buttoned just as she heard Gary yell, "What's happening? We're coming!"

Ann and Gary dressed and ran to where Beth and Robert were standing with the fish. Douglass and Jennifer, with their clothes only half on, were a few steps behind.

Robert held the fish up proudly by its mouth and said, "We'll feast tonight, that is if Gary and Douglass remember enough about scouting to light a fire."

They returned to the capsule where Gary and Douglass busied themselves collecting wood and building a fire. Robert found a knife in EVE's survival kit and returned to the river to clean and dress the fish. Ann, Jennifer, and Beth picked berries and several pieces of mango.

Soon the fire was blazing. They sat around the campfire eating fruit and berries until the fire had banked to a glow of the hot embers.

Robert removed a metal rod from one of the seats in EVE and pushed it through the fish's mouth until it came out near the tail. Douglass pulled two Y-shaped pieces of metal from the hatch and drove them into the ground on both sides of the embers.

Robert placed the fish over the very hot coals with the ends of the rod resting in the Y shaped supports.

Everyone watched intently as the fish cooked. Robert said grace, because he was the one who provided the fish, and they ate heartily until each person's hunger was satisfied.

Everyone was so busy eating no one noticed how dark it had become until Beth said, "Look at that tiny yellowish red dot streaking across the sky. Could that be the Ark still orbiting this planet?"

"It's possible, but we'll never know," Gary said.

Tears began to roll down Ann's cheek at the thought of her parents, so close, yet so far away. Gary placed his arm tenderly around her shoulders and let her rest on his chest. Soon the dot vanished in the darkened sky, never to be seen again.

After a lengthy pause, Douglass said, "I think we need to begin discussing what we're going to do."

"What are our options?" Robert asked.

"First, we need to evaluate our situation," Gary said. "Then we'll need suggestions from everyone."

"Where are we?" Jennifer asked. "Do we have any idea?"

"We're in this beautiful small valley surrounded by a rain forest and craggy, barren mountains," Ann said matter-of-factly. "The temperature is ideal, and it feels like we're in a tropical zone. Remember the glimpses we saw of Nevaeh as we descended? It looked exactly like earth. Nevaeh is home. We must make the best of it. We will make the best of it!"

"We have a few supplies left in EVE: food, water, a first aid kit, and some tools," Robert said. "As long as we can garner enough sustenance, I suggest we keep the food in EVE. It should be edible indefinitely.

"That's an excellent idea," Gary said. "We need more suggestions like that. It does bother me that we haven't seen any animal life other than Robert's fish."

"Do you think there could be other people here?"

"Who knows?" Douglass said. "Maybe the noise and sight of EVE landing scared any animals, including people, away.

"EVE did make a lot of noise when we landed, and those colorful parachutes are huge. We can use them for shelter, especially the nylon cords."

"When Jennifer and I went up the river to bathe, we saw a cave on the side of a barren, craggy cliff," said Douglass. "I think it could be accessible. Maybe it could be a safe haven if needed.

"The parachutes could make some nice clothes too," Beth said. "Of course since we do not have needle and thread, we will have to design wraparounds."

"Excellent. Keep the ideas coming," Gary said.

"I remember seeing several different kinds of tools in the survival kit," Douglass said. "They'll come in handy .We can use parts of EVE to make whatever we need, just as we did to grill Robert's fish."

"Let's not dismantle EVE any more than we have to," Ann said. "I think we should keep the craft as intact as possible, for a refuge and as a reminder of how we got here."

Gary nodded in agreement. "Let's use what we can from inside the capsule, but keep the outside hull intact, for shelter, if not, for a monument to our past."

"I doubt if we can find a better place than this for our base camp," Douglass said. "There's plenty of fresh water, fruit, and no telling what else to eat. Also, Robert said there appeared to be a lot more fish downstream.

"From where Jennifer and I were, upstream near the cascades, we saw a large area of tall bamboo. Maybe we should consider building a common shelter for now. Later we could build individual huts close by for each couple."

"I hope we can keep up some of our traditions so we won't forget things like birthdays, anniversaries, and Christmas," Beth said. "I remember Sarah kept a diary, which, I'm sure, had the dates recorded. I don't know what happened to it, but we failed to keep it going. I have no idea how long Robert and I have even been married."

At the thought of that, tears welled in her eyes.

"I'll make a calendar," Robert assured her, wiping away the tears. "And I decree our first anniversary will be coming up in exactly seven months and three days. I will keep the calendar notched on a tree and let you know a week ahead of time so you all can do something special for me on our anniversary."

Beth was reassured by his confidence, and she kissed him lightly.

"So we all agree we should remain close by this spot," Gary said. "After all it does appear to be a veritable Garden of Eden. And we should remain close together until we explore and know more about Nevaeh. Robert, put two notches on your calendar, one for yesterday and one for today."

"Every seventh notch, we will declare to be Sunday, a day of worshipping and praising God," Ann said. "We must take care of this place God has prepared for us. Let's not pollute it or destroy it. We must all work together. That is the only way we can persist."

"Look, it's beginning to rain," Gary said. "It feels good, but maybe we should stay inside the capsule tonight. It has been shaded by the tree all day, so the interior shouldn't be too hot."

As the rain began to fall rapidly, everyone ran into the capsule. The dying embers of the fire hissed quietly until they were completely extinguished. The soothing pitter-patter of the rain on the giant tree and the metal capsule soon lulled everyone into a peaceful sleep.

32

BEFORE DAYBREAK the following morning, Ann awoke with a start. She sensed something was wrong. Lifting her head, she turned it in different directions, trying to determine what had awakened her.

She was unable to detect any sound. All of the others were sleeping very peacefully. What had awakened her? Why all of this uneasiness?

She could not figure out what was wrong. After all, they had safely landed in what looked like a Garden of Eden. She fully believed God had brought them safely to this place and was with them now.

Nevaeh was a beautiful place; food and water appeared to be plentiful. The weather was wonderful. She snuggled closer to Gary hoping to ease her apprehension.

It helped. Gary's rhythmic breathing and the closeness and warmth of his body helped her relax. She could see through the small porthole that dawn was about to break.

Serenity eventually allayed her apprehension and she returned to a deep sleep until her entire body jerked with such violence that Gary was awakened.

"What's wrong?" he mumbled.

"Hold me. Hold me tightly," she pleaded, "Something's wrong. I don't know what, but something woke me, and I can't figure out what scared me so much.

"I thought maybe I heard something, but now I hear nothing. See if you can see anything through the porthole or maybe open the hatch slightly. Be sure to look through the porthole before you open the hatch."

Their talking had awakened Jennifer who asked, "What's wrong?"

"Nothing," Gary replied reassuringly. "Go back to sleep."

Jennifer nudged Douglass, who was sleeping soundly, and said, "Get up something is wrong."

As Gary rose and went to look out the porthole, he brushed against Robert and Beth who were sleeping near the hatch. Both awoke immediately.

"I'm sorry," Ann said. "I awoke with the eeriest feeling something was terribly wrong. I didn't hear any noise, but I know I felt something. There it is again. I feel a slight vibration under EVE."

"Sis, you must have been dreaming. I don't feel anything," Robert said.

"I feel it too," Beth said. "It feels like the slightest vibration."

"You women are all alike," Robert said. "I don't feel anything."

"Everything looks calm outside, maybe a little wet. Robert, open the hatch," Gary said as he peered through the porthole.

Robert opened the hatch and stepped outside barefooted. He stood very still. "Shh! Quiet! Be very quiet. I can feel it now, through my bare feet, a slight tremor in the ground. Could it be the beginning of an earthquake?

There's a noise in the distance. Beth, come listen."

Beth removed her shoes and joined Robert outside. "The ground does feel strange, and I hear something, but it's far away. It's like a roar from some animal. It's getting louder like it may be coming this way."

"Look, on the other side of the river!" Douglass exclaimed. "I see animals running through the forest. They look like deer."

"Maybe the parachutes and the capsule frightened them away as we landed," Gary said. "It looks like something may be chasing them back this way. I see other animals, but they are running so fast, I can't tell what they are. Maybe they're animals unlike ones we knew on earth."

The noise became so loud they no longer had to strain to hear it. The thundering sound grew louder and louder, accented by trees crashing to the ground and an occasional screeching ululation of a creature in agony.

"What could be chasing the animals?" Ann asked. "They appear to be in a frenzy."

"It must be something big to make them panic like this," Robert said.

"The animals seem to be coming from down in the valley to our left," Gary said. "Robert, you're the most agile. Climb the tree beside EVE and see if you can see further down the valley."

Robert quickly scurried to the uppermost branches of the tall tree where he was able to see a great distance down the valley to his left.

"What do you see?" Douglass asked anxiously.

For several moments, Robert did not reply. Finally he said, "The canopy is so thick I can't actually see anything on the ground.

"Further in the distance, it looks as if a huge path is being bulldozed through the jungle, but it doesn't look like a machine. Really, I can't what it is, but some monstrosity is wrecking havoc with everything in its path. That's why the animals have panicked.

"Oh my God, it looks like something has caught one of the smaller animals and is slaughtering it. Whatever it is, it's gigantic and it's coming this way fast." Robert climbed down from the tree rapidly.

"Let's not lose faith that God will protect us," Ann reminded them.

"Sis, you're right," Robert said. "God gave me faith, but He also gave me sense, and we've to get out of here right now!

"The capsule will not protect us from something that large. It will crush EVE like an aluminum can. What about the cave Douglass and Jennifer told us about further up the river? I could see it from the treetop.

"I believe we can scale the rock easily to get to it and the cliff looks steep enough to prevent even a monster from climbing it. Even if it can climb, it's too gigantically huge to reach us inside the cave.

"That will be the safest place for us. I suggest we collect what provisions we have in EVE and get to the cave as soon as possible."

Affirmative nods confirmed everyone concurred. The destructive rumbles and agonizing screeches of dying animals reverberated louder and louder throughout the valley. Hastily the pilgrims entered the capsule, and grabbed anything they thought could be useful in the future.

They took the few tools aboard EVE and any other pieces of loose metal in the craft. One of them bundled as much of the nylon parachute cords as they could carry. Another folded up the parachutes themselves.

Robert gathered the three pieces of metal that he had used to make the grill to cook the fish.

The supplies were bundled efficiently into backpacks. The women carried the lighter packs, while the heaviest provisions were divided into three equal portions and securely bound together. Gary, Douglass, and Robert assisted each other in hoisting the burden to their backs.

Before they turned to leave, they looked longingly at the almost empty Emergency Vehicular Escape. Thoughts raced through each person's head: What happened to their Garden of Eden? What was driving them from this wonderful place? Would they be able to make it to the cave? Would they ever return to EVE?

Gary brought everyone back to reality when he yelled, "We need to go now!"

The hike to the cave turned more difficult when they reached the barren, craggy slope. The incline was so steep each person had to grab the jagged rocks with their hands to pull themselves up the hill.

The sharp edges made shallow cuts on their fingers and palms. They were bleeding, and painful blisters quickly popped up. Each was thankful they had shoes.

Finally they scaled the last precipitous crags and the men helped their wives onto the narrow ledge at the mouth of the cave. Ann, Jennifer, and Beth removed their backpacks and in turn, assisted the men onto the ledge.

The heavy packs fell from the men's weary bodies and they lay down, too tired to move further.

In the distance, small herds of antelope-like animals continued to flee from the dense, tropical forest. They dashed across the river through the grass and disappeared in the thick undergrowth up the side of the nearest hill. Agonizing shrills of death reverberated throughout the valley below.

"I can see all the way to the rear of the cavern," Ann informed them. "It's empty with no sign of any past occupants.

"And we're in luck, there is also a steady trickle of clear, cool water falling from the ceiling into a dished out basin near the back of the cave."

Robert, always the optimist said, "Sounds like our new suite is equipped with running water. I could use a cool drink right now."

Beth brought him some water. Ann and Jennifer did the same for Gary and Douglass. This revived the men enough to get up and move their provisions inside the cave.

The sojourners had become cave dwellers.

From the mouth of the cave, they had a panoramic view of the meadow from which they had fled. EVE sat propped against the trunk of the huge tree, looking small and forlorn.

The trees and undergrowth from which the animals had fled were disintegrating under the awesome, unknown force. The behemoths would come clearly into view at any moment.

"As much as we want to see what we're up against, we do not want to be seen," Ann said. "Like Robert said, 'God gave us faith, but He also gave us sense.'

"For the time being, we must hide. Let's move to the back of the cave."

As the pilgrims cowered in the darkest recesses of the cave, Ann reassured them, "Remember, with God's help, we will prevail no matter what."